PARADOX:
ON THE SHARP EDGE OF THE BLADE
A Time Equation novel

E. S. MARTELL

SOMETIMES A PARADOX IN TIME CAN BE A GOOD THING

Logan Walker needs to graduate from college in four years to receive his inheritance. The problem is that he's a video game-playing slacker. His attempt to earn enough credit hours takes a nasty wrong turn, resulting in a discovery that may cause him to be expelled from school.

His life becomes even more complex and hazardous when he finds he's somehow accidentally traveled in time back to the Pleistocene. Once there, he discovers he must adapt to a fierce world that allows no replays, a world where death is permanent.

His survival hinges on the goodwill of a mysterious Clovis culture girl with problems of her own. Together the two encounter enemy tribesmen, fierce animals, and war while stumbling into an unexpected relationship.

Will they survive attacks from warriors, and animals? Will Logan win out over his modern adversaries? Will the two defeat their most powerful enemy: Time itself?

This book is dedicated to my readers.

Each time you read one of my books, I'm thankful and happy that you're finding time in your life for my stories.

Thank you!

Acknowledgements

I'd like to give thanks to Fred Alan Wolf, Ph.D. whose ideas on time-travel influenced the story. I'd also like to thank the American Museum of Natural History for stimulating my childhood interest in prehistoric fauna. Finally, I'm grateful to my wife, Sally, who has been very supportive of my writing. My special thanks to Aleksandra Klepacka for her wonderful cover art. She is talented and exceptionally good at understanding what the story demands in terms of cover art. Her cover illustration compliments the story quite nicely. Grateful thanks also to Adriana D'Apolito and 3P Editing for her many invaluable suggestions. Her careful work greatly increased the readability of the manuscript.

Contents

Chapter One

Nerds of a Feather

The whip of his round kick made the fabric of his sweaty uniform crack, but despite the speed, his opponent blocked and redirected the force upwards, leaving him off balance and vulnerable to a leg sweep. He landed on his back with a "whoof". His vision flashed with the impact, then cleared in time to see the instructor hold up his hand, awarding a point to the brown-belt with whom he was sparring.

Logan rolled over, climbed slowly to his feet, and looked at his opponent again. He felt his face flush. His opponent just had to be Mandi. She was cute, and he wanted to impress her. Falling flat on his back didn't cut it. She flashed him a mocking grin as she looked back. He thought to himself, "That really hurt. It's true, Walker, you are nothing but a loser wimp."

His instructor looked at him closely. "That's enough Walker. Go to the other end of the gym and work on your forms." Then turning to the other yellow belts, he selected another victim, pointing at a wide-eyed student as he said, "Next."

Logan slowly walked to an open space. He initially thought he liked Tae-kwon-do, but he was getting tired of being shown up by a good-looking girl who he would like to ask out if he could get up the courage. Of course, she was a couple of levels above him, but he outweighed her by at least forty pounds. The only way she'd go out with him was if she found out about how much he stood to inherit and that seemed too much like trying to buy her interest. That kind of relationship definitely wasn't what he wanted.

He'd signed up for the class and it had gone well for a time, but his lack of motivation made it easy not to practice and now that he was expected to perform at a higher level, he was losing interest. He'd told his friends that martial arts would make him better at the three-dimensional shooter video games that they played most of the time. They had laughed and made fun of him, then returned to their almost continual game playing.

Three game consoles were set up in the apartment. At least one was always on, making it difficult for any of his roommates to study. They were all college students, but their poor grades made it a recurring question if they'd be around to enroll for the next session. His roommates depended on their parents to provide living expenses, but to date, none of them had demonstrated anything near the GPA needed to get any form of scholarship.

Logan Walker didn't worry about funds; he had an adequate amount of money needed to finish his college degree. He just didn't have much time left. He'd gone through three years of schooling, and the most noticeable advancement he'd made was in his ability to reach level 41 of Alien Slayers. He'd started playing it the first month after moving into his apartment and had progressed steadily, but no one was offering him a grade or credit towards graduation for his game-playing prowess.

The money left to him by his grandfather covered his living expenses and would continue for another year. After that, if he hadn't graduated, he'd have to start working for a living. The will provided for exactly four years of expenses, and then he had to have a degree. If not, the $200 million and change would go to charity.

Either he got his college degree and inherited the money, or, if he didn't get it in the specified four years, he'd be on his own resources. He had no illusions on that score. He would have to get a job stocking shelves or working as a busboy. He had absolutely no marketable skills unless someone was to offer a job playing Alien Slayers.

He'd known about the terms of the will for several years but had never worried about it. Now that his graduating on time had become an issue, he'd decided that he needed to speak to the trustee, his grandfather's attorney, Mark Schmitzke. Maybe Schmitzke could somehow find some wiggle room for him. If he could just get another six months...

Logan desultorily worked through the form he had to know in order to test for his next belt. It had several moves requiring both strength and balance that he found difficult. He had fairly good balance, but first-person shooter games didn't involve much movement besides the use of his fingers. His cardio was poor, and it only took a couple of repetitions of the forty-move form to reduce him to a limp, sweating muffin.

After the students were dismissed, he showered and started for home. Randy, Ed, and Steve were seated in front of the TV, as usual, so deep in a game that they barely acknowledged his arrival. Eddie raised his head and said, "Hey, guys, Walker the Texas Ranger just showed. Hey, Walker, why don't you call for a pizza? I'm hungry."

Logan rather grudgingly complied. The way he figured it, the pizza would arrive just in time for him to grab a couple of slices before he had to head out to his Archaeology-303 class. He'd taken a very wide range of subjects during his first and second years of study.

First, he'd thought that he was interested in philosophy. That field had been around so long that, surely, the philosophers knew what made humans tick. It didn't take too long before he dismissed that notion. Most of the reading assignments were difficult and what he could understand of them seemed to him to be some form of advanced navel-gazing.

Then he happened upon psychology. That was a subject he thought might be interesting. The psychologists claimed to be making huge gains in understanding how the human mind works. A couple of classes were enough to convince Logan that psychologists were full of it. Most of the studies were contrived investigations that required heavy statistical manipulation in order to show any valid results. He wasn't a strong mathematician and had difficulty with the statistics that were used.

Finally, he'd settled on archaeology. It was mildly interesting, and he wasn't worried about getting a job in the field after graduating. There weren't any jobs other than teaching ones, and he wasn't enthusiastic about teaching for a career. What could be more boring than teaching a bunch of boneheads like himself day after day?

Anyway, archaeology was fairly easy for him. He had a good memory and could regurgitate a lot of material after reading it once. In between game playing, he managed to keep his grades at about a C-minus average. That would be good enough to graduate – he hoped.

Unfortunately, it looked like he might be four credits short of the minimum required to graduate by his next spring deadline. Unless he got lucky, there was no way he could take the remaining required courses, including one watered-down math class, some kind of crazy requirement for sensitivity training – the university's administration was convinced that they could advance civilization by training their male students to be more aware of their privileged status – and the remaining sixteen hours of archaeology that he needed.

He hoped to get into an advanced self-directed study seminar for the summer. That would be three hours, and then if he took a five-hour course and three courses of three credits each, he'd be there. The five-hour course was something of a problem – it always filled up rapidly during enrollment. With his last name being nearly at the end of the alphabet, his assigned enrollment period would probably mean that the class would be filled by the time he showed up.

"Well," he thought, "something will show up. After all, there's the summer session and both semesters next year before I need the degree." He spent some time fantasizing that the department would make an exception and let him graduate with one less than the minimum number of hours, but then common sense prevailed. He was certain such a lucky occurrence wouldn't happen.

The pizza delivery guy was late and gave a lame excuse blaming his phone's GPS. Logan threw a couple of twenties at the guy, opened one of the boxes and grabbed two slices, then ran out, heading for class.

A couple of minutes later, he came back in, grabbed the textbook that he'd forgotten, argued with Eddie over the last slice of pizza, then left again. He was still hungry, and now he was angry with Eddie.

"People always seem to take advantage of me," he told himself with considerable self-pity.

The first two slices hadn't been enough when he wolfed them, and Eddie had spat on the last one to keep him from taking it when he came back. He sidetracked through the student union building to grab a bag of peanuts from a vending machine.

The machine refused to give him change, causing him to spend a couple of moments shaking it and telling it what he thought of its bad character. He looked away, trying to act as if he hadn't been the one swearing when two girls walked by. Things hadn't been going well. It'd been a crummy day, all told. He waited for the girls to leave, but then he remembered his class and strode off.

There was a crowd of students exiting from the building, and it took him extra time to thread through them. The end result was he ended up late.

Professor Berensten was a bit of a martinet, and, of course, she had to force him to explain his tardiness in front of the snickering class. It took him the next fifteen minutes to quit stewing about it enough to start taking usable notes. He was still scribbling the assignment for the next class when the rest of the students had exited.

He tried to remember the topic at the first of the class, writing down what he could. When he lifted his head, Berensten was standing by his desk, frowning.

"Okay, Mr. Walker, what are you doing now?" she asked in a kindly voice. He suddenly remembered that she was the primary reason he had become interested in archaeology. She not only was a good teacher, but she had also taken enough of an interest in him that she was now his adviser. She expected him to do well, and he somehow didn't want to disappoint her.

"Uh, I'm just, uh, trying to remember what you were talking about at the beginning of class. I didn't take very good notes," he answered.

She sighed, "Logan, that's your problem. You don't take anything seriously. As your faculty adviser, I have access to your records. It so happens that I reviewed them this morning for a special reason. They aren't very impressive. You're barely getting passing grades, but it looks like you might manage to graduate in a couple more years."

Logan drew a deep breath. He might as well broach the subject of graduating next year now. She'd been helpful in planning his course schedules the last couple of times he had met with her in her office. Maybe this time, she'd have another useful suggestion.

He let out the breath and started, "Dr. Berensten, I know my grades aren't very good, but I just have to figure out a way to graduate by next spring. It's very important to me."

She shook her short, gray hair negatively. "I don't see how you're going to manage. You currently need sixteen more hours in your major field. There's really not enough time unless you get in a lot of hours this summer – " She paused, then added, "And pass them. Something that I'm pretty sure you are capable of doing, but your past performance doesn't show that you're very motivated."

He didn't want to bring up the inheritance issue with her. It wouldn't help and would probably make her less sympathetic. He stretched the truth a little in his answer. "It's for my grandfather. He'd be very disappointed if it takes me more than four years to graduate."

It was her turn to sigh, then she smiled – something that made her look younger. She lifted a sheaf of papers that she had in her left hand.

"Here. Fill these out. I don't want to be responsible for disappointing your grandfather. This is an application for you to go on a dig for the first summer session. If your work is satisfactory to the dig supervisor, you'll get five hours of credit. Then, if you apply yourself, you just might make that next spring deadline you've got," she said.

She paused, and then added, "The dig positions were all filled, and there's a long waiting list, but I think I can get you into a slot that unexpectedly opened up."

He held out his hand for the papers. "Uh, when does it start?" he asked.

She said, "The Monday after finals week."

He grimaced. He'd have no time off. His finals were next Tuesday and Friday. The dig would start on the Monday after that. Ugh! After a little thought, the desirability of her solution sank in. He'd get to be outdoors tanning. How hard could a dig be anyway? Then something occurred to him, "Uh, where is the dig going to be, Dr. Berensten?"

She had already turned and started to pick up her lecture notes, but she paused, glancing back at him. "Oh, don't worry about travel. It's right here in the state. Just over in the Tampa Bay area. A short distance from here. You do have an automobile, don't you?"

He had an old motorcycle. It wasn't very reliable, but it usually got him from the university over to Ormond Beach, where his dad lived, whenever he wanted a depressing experience. His parents had divorced and then his mom had died. His dad wasn't much help and hadn't played a major role in his life. He'd been mostly left alone to make his way through high school, and then college.

His father was a heavy drinker and had a lot of trouble holding jobs in the past. He finally settled in working as a roofer. He'd done that for the last five years and now had his own company. That choice of profession made Logan cringe when he thought about it. It was a wonder his dad hadn't rolled off a roof and been killed already. Sometimes Logan thought it would be only a matter of 'when', not 'if.'

Logan's grandfather's trust was worth millions, but only a trickle of money was released for his college expenses. The trustee had full discretion over the amount Logan was to be allowed and he forced Logan to justify every penny.

Logan's dad had never received any of the funds and that was a good thing. He'd simply go on a terminal drunken spree if he had the money. Logan's grandfather had never forgiven his father for the divorce and subsequent death of his daughter. He'd set the trust up so that Logan's dad couldn't access any of the money.

He answered Berensten's question. "I can get there, no problem. How did... Uh, I mean, what happened to open a slot if there are so many people wanting in?"

She replied, "One of the senior students got injured somehow. I understand that he won't be at school this summer, so it must have been fairly serious. There are plenty of other students who'd like the chance I'm giving you. I want you to take it seriously. If you do well, it will make your chances of graduating next year more likely. Understand?"

Logan answered, "Yes. I'll do my best."

Berensten said, "Better make it better than that. Your best so far hasn't been very good."

She waved him out of the room, with instructions to get the forms back to her by noon the next day. She also instructed him to go to student health services and get both a tetanus booster and a typhoid shot. He headed towards the clinic, his steps light. Maybe this was the break he needed.

An hour later, shoulder hurting from the injections, he arrived back at his apartment. The three guys hadn't moved from their positions on the couch other than to possibly go to the bathroom. The pizza boxes were on the floor, and a few beer cans were crumpled nearby. Steve always crushed his cans after emptying them.

They ignored him when he entered and headed for his room. When he came back, Randy asked if he would take over playing for him.

"Good thing you're back, Walker," he said. "I've got a date with Lisa. We're going for a flick and a beer, then who knows?" He had a slightly lecherous grin on his boyish face.

Of the four, he was the only one with a girlfriend. The others were socially backward. Their sole outlet was gaming. The closest any of them had ever been to intimacy with the opposite sex was when they played Grand Theft Auto. Logan thought to himself, "Somehow, virtual women don't really count."

He glanced enviously at Randy's back, thinking, "If only I could meet a girl, or even get the courage to talk to one. If Mandi – " He stopped that thought in embarrassment. Sliding into the warm spot on the beat-down sofa, he took the controller and was soon involved in an all-out virtual battle. Sometime later, they broke to go out for burgers and beer.

When they returned, the other two wanted to start the game again, but Logan had a sudden fit of conscientiousness and begged off to fill out the dig application. Once that was done, he actually opened his textbook and read a chapter or so. That led him to work on a couple of other courses that seemed to have more material than he felt he could ever get through. Before he knew it, it was late. Randy was back and there was a lot of teasing banter coming from the living room.

Randy had apparently gotten lucky, though Logan didn't really believe his bragging. Steve and Eddie had quit playing and the three were roughhousing, shoving each other around the room playfully.

The shoving ceased when Randy fell over the coffee table and tipped the TV over. It flickered and went out, alarming all of them. How would they survive through the weekend without the large video display? Game playing would be almost impossible and they might even have to go to an arcade or something equally distasteful. No one thought about suggesting studying.

Once they'd cleaned up the mess and righted the TV screen, it became obvious that it had just come unplugged from the game unit. Eddie took full credit for reconnecting it and bringing it back to life.

"Hey, without me, you guys would be reduced to trying to play on your tablets," he said and then bowed.

They clapped, mockingly.

After a little more conversation, Logan retired to his room to sleep. He'd turn in the completed dig forms the next day.

Chapter Two

To Dig or not to Dig

Logan paused in the hall just outside of Berensten's office. The door wasn't quite shut, and he could hear raised voices coming through the crack. It sounded like she was arguing with a man, but he didn't recognize the voice.

He glanced around. There were only a few late students hurrying to their classes. He slouched closer to the slightly open door, trying to hear. Then he recognized the voice as Professor Dameron.

"Ugh," he thought. He didn't like Dameron at all. He was a boring lecturer, and it had been all Logan could do to stick through his class. He'd thought about dropping it several times. He stayed, but it hadn't been worth the effort. He'd almost failed, just passing by a few points.

Dameron's voice was higher-pitched than usual as he said, "What the heck do you think I'm going to do with Walker? I need people on the dig that can be taught and are willing to work. Walker doesn't study. He's an unmotivated slacker."

Logan's heart fell. Dameron was the dig supervisor. That was awful. He knew the man didn't like him. He'd made the mistake of critically questioning the Professor about one of the books they were supposed to read, not realizing that Dameron was one of the junior authors. Dameron hadn't taken it well.

Berensten replied in a quieter voice, "I think you should give him a chance."

Dameron interrupted her, "A chance? I had him in my class, and that's all the chance he's going to get from me. Not only is he a slacker, but he's rude, too. I've got plenty of other students on the waiting list. I'm not taking him."

Berensten paused, then her voice changed slightly. It wasn't as warm as it had been. Instead, a hint of iron came through in her tone.

"Professor Dameron, I want Walker to go. You'll have to adjust your thinking about him," she said.

Dameron angrily replied, "No. That's final. I'm not taking him."

Berensten sighed, then answered. "Look, George, you're coming up for a decision on tenure. I don't think I need to mention that I'm on that committee, do I?"

Dameron made some sputtering noises and then composed himself enough to say, "No. I understand. Walker is on the dig, but I want to make it clear that it's against my better judgment. If he screws up, I reserve the right to kick him off."

Berensten said, "Thanks, I knew you'd listen to reason. Don't worry. He won't screw up. I think he understands that he needs to apply himself now."

Logan suddenly realized that Dameron was going to come out of the office. He sprinted down the hall and ducked around a corner before the door opened. He immediately turned and walked slowly back around the corner as if he were just arriving. Fortunately, Dameron had gone the other way and was now heading downstairs.

The office door was open, and Professor Berensten looked up and smiled at him, "Hi, Logan. You got your shots and the application?"

He answered, "Yes, Professor. Here's the paperwork."

She scanned it and then said, "I had a little difficulty with Dameron about your participating. He wanted to take someone else. You have to promise me that you'll do your best. Don't foul up this chance. You might not get another one."

"No, no, Professor. I'm ready to go. I need the credits, and this is a great opportunity for me. I'll work hard, you'll see," he assured her.

"Good. See that you do. Now, go and report to Professor Dameron's office. His assistant will give you a packet of information about where and when you'll report. I understand that the staff will be staying at the dig in tents. There are hotels nearby, but there isn't enough funding for this project to afford rooms. Be sure and pack comfortable clothes and plenty of sunscreen. You'll be out in the sun every day for four weeks or so," she said.

"Okay, I'll get sunscreen," he said. "Thanks for the great opportunity. I really appreciate it."

He hesitated before going into Dameron's office. There was a small room with a desk nearby that was used by Dameron's graduate assistant. Logan turned in there.

The graduate student glanced at him over her heavy glasses and asked, "Yes? What do you want?"

"Uh, hi," he said, "I'm going on Professor Dameron's dig. Are there some instructions or papers about what's expected?"

She looked down her nose at him, rummaged around in a desk drawer for a moment, and pulled out a manila envelope. She picked several sheets of paper from slots in the drawer and stuffed them in the envelope before handing it to him.

"Here it is. Read it carefully and pay special attention to the clothing and personal supplies you'll need. Driving directions are in there. The formal opening is Monday after finals, but you should be there by Sunday at the latest. The Professor doesn't like any of his help to be late."

The way she said it, it sounded like a threat.

Logan browsed through the papers as he walked back to his apartment. It looked like he had pretty much everything he'd need. He didn't have work boots, but he had some cowboy boots that he thought would be almost as good. He thought boots would probably be overkill. His sneakers would suffice just as well. As for clothes, he'd take some jeans and tee-shirts. He could probably wash them somewhere. Food would be provided, so that was good.

All of his roommates were heading home for the summer and wouldn't be around until fall. The lease was up this month, and he thought he could get them to move their stuff into storage until he had a chance to arrange a rental for the fall semester. Better yet, maybe they could locate a new apartment, saving him the work. Either way, he'd leave it up to them.

When he got home, all three of the guys were gone. They'd been kind enough to leave him a note stating that they were heading to a local bar and he could catch up if he wanted. It was tempting.

Maybe he'd skip out on the meeting he'd scheduled with the lawyer who was the trust administrator. Schmitzke was hard to see. His schedule was always full. For some reason, Logan didn't think the man really wanted to meet with him. He thought it over and finally decided he'd better head over to the law office.

He took his old motorcycle and cruised slowly through the heavy traffic, heading downtown. He parked on the street and entered the lobby of the law firm. As usual, he was forced to wait for nearly thirty minutes.

Logan was resentful. He'd been right on time. Somehow Schmitzke always managed to find something to do to show him how unimportant he was.

He settled into the conference room chair across from the lawyer, who was studying some papers. At last, the man glanced up and said, "Hello, Mr. Walker. This is the trust agreement. I've just re-familiarized myself with it. Now, what question did you have for me?"

Logan wasn't quite ready to begin. He'd been feeling antagonistic and the sudden change threw him off stride. "Uh, uh. Well, I was, um, wondering if there's some way I could get an extension on the graduating thingy. I was sick a lot last semester, and that made me unable to study, so that course I dropped? I mean the math one. I don't think it's really fair to me. I passed the other courses, but now I'm short on hours. I think I'm going to need more time. You know?"

Schmitzke made a facial expression that was somewhere between a condescending smile and a sneer, then shook his head negatively. "No, I thought that this was about something like that. No, there's no way the deadline can be extended. The language is really quite clear and precisely binding. You must graduate in four years. No exception." He sat back and pompously folded his hands, wearing a satisfied expression.

Logan's face fell. "Well, what will happen if I don't make it? Is there any provision for me then?"

Now Schmitzke smiled a toothy, shark-like grin. "Should you fail to graduate on time, the money is to be given to a charity chosen by the trust administrator, me. You may be interested to know that I've already chosen a worthy charity, one that would benefit greatly from your grandfather's money. It would help a lot of people jump-start their lives."

Logan thought about that. It seemed to him that his own life could benefit greatly from a couple of hundred million. It didn't seem fair that he would take second place to a bunch of unknowns. He'd had a great relationship with his grandfather. He'd lived with his grandparents part of the time after his mother had died. Finally, he asked, "What's the charity? Maybe I'd better apply to it for some money."

Schmitzke laughed dryly. "Ha-ha. That's a good one. No, I'm afraid that you wouldn't qualify for any assistance. The Student's Democratic Assistance Fund only helps minority students who have shown exceptional promise. You're not a minority, and, so far, you haven't shown much promise either."

He made a show of checking his watch, then said, "I'm afraid that's all of the time I can afford to spare you. I've got another appointment."

Schmitzke pushed his chair back and stood up. When Logan rose, the man walked around the table and opened the door, ushering him out.

"It was a pleasure to speak to you, Logan. Don't hesitate to call me with any other questions. Oh, and, uh, good luck with your courses," he said.

Logan slumped as he walked to the reception area. He thought he could hear Schmitzke snicker as he walked away.

The motorcycle took several tries to get started. The ride home seemed even longer than the one downtown. Logan had plenty of time to think as he rode.

It seemed like the deck was stacked against him. He'd never worried about encountering difficulty graduating. Now that he was in trouble, it almost seemed like Schmitzke had planned on him failing a class. The guy certainly didn't appear to be worried about Logan's situation.

Maybe the SDAF charity didn't offer anything for students like him, but he decided that he'd investigate it a little anyway. It would be interesting to find out where the money would go if he couldn't graduate. Schmitzke seemed to relish the chance to donate the money to them.

On the Sunday after finals, he was riding the old Honda down the highway with an overstuffed backpack flapping in the wind that curled over his shoulders. The day was sunny, and things were looking positive. He had chosen smaller roads, staying off the Interstate. He didn't like the traffic, and the mostly empty roads made for a pleasant ride.

The underpowered motorcycle wasn't very fast. It was difficult to force the old beast to roll at much over the speed limit. That restriction didn't apply to the few cars. They passed him as if he were standing still. The constant worry about obstructing traffic flow made it more attractive for him to take back roads, even if it did mean that he had to drive farther.

About four o'clock, Logan bounced down the sand road in a cloud of dust and into the campsite. The overall impression was that of a bunch of semi-organized weekend campers. All of the vehicles were parked in a makeshift parking lot. Beyond that, a group of wall-tents clustered randomly about a central cooking area.

It was obvious that this was intended to be a self-sustaining site. There were a couple of canvas flies strung up. One appeared to be the kitchen and the other, an eating area judging from the picnic tables under and around it.

As far as Logan was concerned, he'd prefer to ride a few miles to the nearest fast-food place. The others could cook for themselves. If someone told him it was permissible, he would instantly have checked into the motel that was just a few miles down the highway. At least there, he'd have air-conditioning and a soft bed.

He swung his leg off the motorcycle with a resigned sigh. No doubt Dameron would require everyone to stay at the site. That would fit his impression of the man.

He walked over to the dining area. There were a number of people sitting at some folding picnic tables, enjoying the shade and talking. Not one even glanced as he came up.

He stood there uncomfortably, finally getting a guy's attention. The guy looked familiar. He felt like he recognized him, then remembered that they'd had a class together last semester. The student acknowledged him with a raised eyebrow, and Logan took that as a cue to ask, "Who do I see to check in?"

The others stopped talking and looked at him. One of the guys nudged the girl next to him and said, "Fresh meat."

She laughed and then stared boldly at Logan with a smirk.

The student he recognized raised his arm lazily, pointing out a larger tent that was somewhat away from the main cluster. "That's Dameron's tent. Check-in there with the student supervisor."

The others resumed their desultory conversation.

Logan turned and trudged across the grassy sand to the tent. Once there, another problem arose. He didn't just want to open the flap and burst in, and there didn't seem to be any way to knock on a tent. He shuffled his feet and then said loudly, "Anyone home?"

A female voice answered, "Come in."

He lifted the tent flap and stepped inside. The tent boasted a double cot and a desk. The woman at the desk looked a little familiar, but she had her head down, studying some papers. When she looked up, his heart fell. It was Mandi!

If she were the student supervisor, he'd be confronted with his inadequacy in martial arts daily.

She recognized him, at least. Her lips curved in a cursory smile, and she asked, "Are you checking in?"

When he nodded, she added, "Now there'll be someone for me to practice sparring with. Oh, wait. I forgot. You're too easy to beat. Not too much challenge there. Maybe we won't spar after all."

He could feel his face flushing but said nothing.

After an uncomfortable moment of silence, she opened a notebook and asked, "Name?"

"Logan Walker," he answered.

She referred to the notebook, frowned, and turned a page, then another one. Then she looked up, shook her head, and said, "You're not in here. Are you sure you're supposed to be here? This dig is only open to a limited number of students. You're not one of them."

He tried to smile as he thought, Damn that Dameron. He didn't even try to put my name on the list.

She looked accusingly at Logan.

He shrugged and said, "I was a last-minute addition. I guess Professor Dameron didn't have time to put my name down."

Mandi scowled and added, "Okay. For now, you're assigned to tent seven. There are already five people in there. Pick up a cot at the supply truck over by the parking lot and get your stuff arranged. We're having an organizational meeting after supper. That'll be about six-thirty, so don't miss it. Meanwhile, I'm checking with the professor about you. You'd better hope he says you're supposed to be here."

She turned away, dismissing him.

Logan looked at her back for a moment. Too bad she was so good-looking. Her attitude was a real turn-off. He turned and pushed the tent flap aside.

He located tent number seven and poked his head inside. There were five cots and a bunch of personal gear. Clothes and shoes were scattered randomly around, along with empty food containers. It looked like his tent-mates weren't concerned about attracting insects. He sighed and slouched over to the supply truck.

Supper was minimally interesting. Logan didn't like the food, and it seemed like everyone else already knew each other. No one paid him much attention. In response, he sat at the end of a table near the edge of the dining fly and kept his head down. Trying to mix with a group of new people wasn't anything he enjoyed. He need not have worried, though. They were all busy talking with each other.

As he watched the group of almost forty students, he noticed that Mandi had an in-group of three friends that most of the rest of the students aspired to impress.

It was sickening, really, he thought. Who knew that archaeologists were such suck-ups? There were only five guys who didn't seem to be trying to get in with the social power structure.

The five were uniformly overweight and grubby in their dress. He knew the type. They were probably good enough students. One or two of them might be brilliant, but they'd given up trying to socialize long ago. He'd probably get on well with them, but so far, they'd ignored him too.

People stiffened attentively as Dameron strode up. The meeting was about to begin.

Dameron had a way about him that set Logan's teeth on edge. Whether it was justified by extreme intelligence or simply unwarranted arrogance, his presentations always made Logan want to throw things.

"I know you've all been anxiously awaiting my presence," he started. "I'm here now, and you'll find that everything is perfectly organized and under control. I'll have my student dig supervisor, Mandi, hand out work assignments. You'll be expected to begin at eight a.m. sharp. Breakfast will be served at seven a.m. If you miss it, you'll have to wait for lunch. There will be no morning breaks until lunchtime. That will be at noon. You'll have precisely thirty minutes to eat. Then I expect you to be back at work on your assigned tasks. There will be a fifteen-minute break during the afternoon. That will be at two p.m. After that, you'll work until five. Supper will be at six, so you'll have time to clean up first." He paused and looked around as if daring anyone to object.

"I will expect you to spend at least two hours every evening writing up and documenting your findings. The junior students and those who have not previously been on one of my digs will be paired with an experienced student. That way, I won't have to waste my time training you on documenting and reporting. Mandi will determine work assignments. She's got an initial set of jobs for each of you, but she is free to vary those as she sees fit. In general, though, everyone will get a chance at each and every job. If your performance at a particular job stands out after the first two weeks, you may be assigned that task for the remainder of the dig."

He turned to Mandi and said, "That's all I've got for now. Give them their assignments, answer any questions, and then report to me in my tent." He strode off without a backward glance.

Mandi took her time reading through the initial assignment list, passing out info packets as she spoke. She was a little more helpful than Dameron in that she answered questions about the various jobs.

When she was done, Logan wandered over to his assigned tent. He was wondering if he'd be better off jumping on his motorcycle and leaving. His initial assignment was to help clear off over-burden. In short, he was supposed to wake up in the morning, check out a shovel, and dig – all day.

His previous experience digging with a shovel was small, but he had a vivid imagination, and he was sure that he wouldn't enjoy using the tool.

The other thing that he found bothersome was that he hadn't been paired with a more experienced student. Mandi told him that there was an odd number of people and that Dameron had instructed her that Logan would be the odd man out. He'd said something to the effect that Logan was a last-minute, unplanned addition, and he'd just have to live with the negative aspects of that.

Logan entered the tent and found a card game in progress. His five tent mates had dragged the cots into a square and were busily engaged in an animated game of gin-rummy. Their conversation was simultaneously loud and nonsensical, perhaps stimulated by the half a case of beer they'd gulped in the five minutes since the organizational meeting had ended.

Logan slipped past and lay down on his bunk, wondering if he'd have to put up with this behavior every night. Finally, one of the players said, "Gin!" loudly. He glanced over to see who had won. The winner happened to be staring directly at him, and their eyes met.

"Hey, guy, what's your name?" the student asked. The others turned to stare curiously at Logan.

"Uh, Logan Walker," he answered. They didn't look threatening, far from it. They basically looked like his roommates: nerds. All slightly overweight and sloppily dressed. They chorused, "Hi, Walker," in unison, then turned back to their game without introducing themselves.

Logan hesitated a moment. They hadn't even asked him if he wanted to play.

He didn't, in fact. He hated cards. His taste in games was exclusively digital. The noise level rose as the next hand got underway. He sighed deeply and turned his back. There was a battery-powered lantern hanging from the ridgepole, and that provided enough light to read by.

He dragged out the packet that Mandi had given him. It seemed that some of the initial work had already been done. The site already had a series of test pits dug, and a grid was set up, laid out by twine tied to stakes. Initially, the site needed to be phased.

As he understood it, that meant it had to be reduced to a contemporaneous horizon. He thought that implied it needed to be leveled out, but he was a little vague on the actual concept. Anyway, that was where his shovel and he came in. There were at least eighteen inches of sandy soil that had to be cleared before they arrived at the level where the artifacts were supposed to be distributed.

Logan put down his book and drifted off to sleep to the background of the others arguing over their cards. His last thought was, I guess I'm lucky. I've had a lot of practice sleeping with noisy roommates.

Mandi stuck her head in the tent and shouted, "Rise and shine diggers! Breakfast time. You'll have to be ready to dig in forty-five minutes, so get moving."

Logan jumped and set up. He'd slept through the night. The others had finished playing sometime after midnight. He'd awakened briefly as they settled down but then had gone back to sleep.

The other guys were groaning and tossing about. Tim sleepily said, "I'll bet she's just like last year. A slave driver."

The others just groaned.

Logan climbed out of his bag, pulled on his worn-out jeans and a tee-shirt, then headed out to breakfast. None of the others had even sat up when he left.

Breakfast consisted of greasy scrambled eggs, grits, and fried bacon. Apparently, archaeologists didn't worry about the latest fad diets. Anyway, it suited Logan. He went back for seconds, ate quickly, and was done before any of his tent mates showed up.

He walked over to the supply truck, checked out a shovel, and then turned to look at the dig site. He'd barely glanced at it before, but now that he was ready to start work, he surveyed the area more closely. Someone had already driven stakes and strung some twine in a grid pattern over the entire area.

As he looked, a wave of something like dizziness came over him. The feeling was paired with a sense of deja vu. The barren spot didn't look right for some reason. There should be a fire over there, near where the palm-frond shelters were. Logan stopped, dumbfounded. Where did that come from? There was no way that he could know anything about the place.

He wiped his hand over his forehead. Maybe he was coming down with something, but, no, he was sweating in the sun, not feverish. He shrugged and headed to where he was supposed to start digging. Maybe I was remembering somewhere else, he thought.

The feeling returned as he walked past the spot where he'd imagined the fire. This time, it was more immediate and intense. Then it was paired with an irrevocable sense of desolation or loss. He'd never experienced anything like it. He was shaking by the time he reached his starting spot. Still shaking, he drove the shovel blade into the soft earth.

Noon found him nursing blisters on both hands. He studied his palms. The blisters had formed in minutes and then broken. Now they were raw, open, throbbing sores on the bases of his fingers and thumbs. Who knew I'd be so out of practice with a shovel, he thought. I've used one before, but that was just stripping shingles off a roof, helping my dad.

It turned out that all of his tent-mates were also assigned to the shovel crew. They showed their experience, though. Logan saw that they'd brought gloves. That was something he hadn't planned on.

He walked over, and asked them, "Hey, any of you guys got an extra pair of gloves you'd like to lend me?"

The heavy-set student, Rick, sneered, "Walker, you got to learn to take care of yourself. This ain't no picnic we're on and the answer is no. We need all of our gloves for ourselves. You'd better get permission to go into town tonight and get some for yourself, that is if you last that long." He finished with a laugh, and the others joined in.

"Yeah, old Walker here must have thought he had tough hands," said Tim.

Franz commented, "Better watch out. Ole tough hands will probably kick your butt when you aren't looking."

They laughed again.

Finally, Rick added, a little more kindly, "Seriously, man, you got to have several pairs of gloves and a box or two of bandages. You'll have blisters on your blisters before this part is done. Didn't ya read the equipment list? Gloves were on it."

Logan shrugged miserably and walked back out to where he'd left his shovel. He couldn't remember having read that he'd need gloves. He picked the implement up carefully and began to slowly fill the wheelbarrow that sat nearby. He could mostly avoid the sore spots on his fingers if he held the shovel carefully, but pushing the wheelbarrow was worse. The sandy soil caused the wheel to sink in and resist his efforts, and the weight of the load meant the handles had to be gripped firmly, aggravating his sores.

⚬

Logan didn't know how he made it through the afternoon, but it felt like he'd dug several swimming pools worth of dirt by himself. He was so tired by quitting time that he was barely able to eat.

After supper, he checked with Mandi. She cursorily glanced at his hands and gave him permission to go into town. As he headed for his motorcycle, he wondered how he'd manage to hold the handlebars.

It turned out to be less of a problem than he'd feared. The feeling of relief at getting out of the dig site, even for a moment, was enough to take his mind off the blisters. They didn't start bothering him until he had reached the drug store that was located conveniently along the highway.

It turned out that they didn't carry gloves, although he was able to take care of the blisters with an antibiotic salve that also had a numbing agent. He bandaged the worst ones, then headed for a shopping center the clerk had mentioned when he'd asked. It was a few miles up the road.

There, he went into a home improvement store where he had his choice of a wide selection of gloves. He opted for some that had reinforced leather palms.

Back on his bike, he arranged the bag so that he was sitting on it. He normally used a backpack to carry things, but he'd been in such a hurry to leave, he'd forgotten to get it. He knew it was lying under his cot, but that wasn't helping.

The motorcycle started okay but sputtered a bit as he turned out of the parking lot. Logan recognized the symptom. It was nearly out of gas. The gauge was unreliable, sometimes working correctly, but other times showing more fuel than there actually was. Fortunately, there was a convenience store that he'd passed just down the road.

He rolled into the parking lot on the last fumes. His bike hiccuped and then stopped short of the pumps. Sighing, Logan dismounted and pushed the heavy machine up the slight grade.

He went in to prepay. He could have used the pump's card reader, but he didn't want to risk having his card info stolen. There had been a lot of credit information stolen recently in the area. The criminals apparently had an unlimited supply of state-of-the-art scanners that fit into gas pump and ATM reader slots.

He paid, bought a bag of beef jerky, and was back on the road in a few minutes, happily chewing on jerky and cruising at just below the speed limit, heading for the dig-site.

***

He hadn't gone two miles before a police car pulled up close behind him. The cop followed for a couple of minutes and then turned on his lights. Logan groaned, pulled over onto the shoulder, and turned off the engine.

"License and registration," the officer said as he walked up.

Logan fumbled his wallet out of his pocket, then pulled them out. It wasn't as if there was any great amount of money in the wallet, and there was only the one credit card. The barrenness of the money side reminded him of his financial situation. He sighed again and extended the license to the patrolman.

The officer looked the license over, and said, "Wait here." He walked quickly back to his unit, climbed in, and sat for several minutes, apparently doing research on the computer. When he returned, he asked, "Where were you earlier today?"

Logan was puzzled but explained. "I was at the university archaeological dig down the road about ten miles. I'm a student and I'm participating in the dig. Will be all summer. Why?"

The officer said, "There was some problem with a motorcyclist over at Yankeetown. You weren't over there, were you?"

Logan said, "No, I was working until about an hour ago. I came into town to get some gloves and band-aids."

The cop held his flashlight directly in Logan's face and asked, "Where are they?"

Logan scooted back, and pulled the bag out from under his legs, then opened it for the man. As the officer examined the bag, Logan spread his hands, displaying the blisters and band-aids. "See," he said. "I'm not used to shoveling. I just about wore my hands out."

The light flashed on his palms, and the cop said, "It looks like you've never done an hour of honest labor in your life."

That wasn't true but Logan was trying hard to be inoffensive. "Not too much physical work recently, officer. I have to study a lot. My grandfather left me a little money for school, so I don't have to work, at least until I graduate."

The officer scoffed derisively, then handed the bag back along with the license and the registration paper. He kept the light shining in Logan's face as he said, "You'd better get on back to your homework. I know where the dig is. I'll be checking tomorrow to see if you're actually working there. You'd better be. Now, get going."

Logan replaced his papers in his wallet, turned on the ignition, and started off slowly. It was just his luck to get hassled unjustly. It seemed like he was always guilty over nothing. People just liked to pick on him.

Chapter Three

Sand, Dust, and Muck

By Sunday, Logan's hands had recovered somewhat. He'd learned that there was a knack to digging, and now he didn't wear himself out as quickly. He had, he guessed, dug enough dirt to fill the Gulf of Mexico.

During breakfast, Mandi showed up and announced that they would be making an excursion to the nearby Crystal River State Park Archaeological Site. It was their next-door neighbor, so to speak, but Logan had never visited it.

The park contained a six-mound complex that had been dated to about 250 BC. The area had apparently been occupied for over two thousand years, starting about 500 BC. Copper tools from the Ohio River area had been found there, indicating early trade. No one was sure how much earlier the site had been used.

As she was talking, a university bus pulled up. She waved at it, saying, "Professor Dameron was good enough to arrange for transportation. That way we can keep close track of all of you."

She looked over her shoulder. The professor was just coming out of his tent, stretching. He strode over to the dining area, yawned, and then looked them over, a half-sneering smile on his face.

"I see you're all up and ready to go. Good. I've arranged a treat for you. We're going over to the Crystal River Park site. I expect you to stay together with your tent mates. Each tent group will write a joint report of not less than ten pages. You will cover all of the salient aspects of the site, including any geographical features that might have disposed the Paleo-Indians to select that precise location. Make careful observations and record them. Pretend that you're the first archaeologist to discover the site and that you're evaluating it as a potential dig site."

He paused for questions. There were none, so he continued, "I've got good news. We've finally gotten our Wi-Fi set up. The network name is UFArch1. The password is Dameron. You have my permission to use the Internet for research on this paper. I expect you to email it to me by tomorrow at six p.m. It will be ten percent of your grade for this session, so do a good job. Now, finish eating, and then get on the bus. We'll be leaving in fifteen minutes."

He started to turn away, but stopped and turned back. "One thing. I'm only going to warn you once. The site Wi-Fi is only to be used for research and filing reports. Anyone caught using it for gaming, video or music streaming, or X-rated activities will receive a failing grade. No exceptions. You may, however, use it for personal email. But, no social media of any kind. Understand?"

No one said anything. He looked at them, and then turned back to his tent, motioning for Mandi to follow. He disappeared through the flaps, with her close on his heels.

⚬

The bus ride was only about five minutes long. Logan couldn't see why they couldn't have taken their own vehicles or even walked. It took longer to board the students than the actual drive took. The site had a paved parking area that could have accommodated everyone's vehicles. It wasn't over half a mile from their dig site.

The students trickled out of the bus, arranged themselves in groups with their tent mates, and filtered into the site.

Logan had no confidence in his ability to notice important features of the site, but he had even less confidence in his tent mates. The other guys seemed to think that the excursion was boring. Their conversation was mostly about various celebrities. Logan lagged behind, madly taking notes of what he hoped were important aspects of the park. The threat of not graduating had gradually increased his motivation and now he was more focused on schoolwork than he'd ever been.

The group randomly wandered over to an unprepossessing, grass-covered hill that had a stairway leading to the top. The sign by the base of the stairs labeled the hill as the Temple Mound. It stood all of twenty-eight feet high.

Logan started up, but Rick, who was heavier than the others, said, "I'm not goin' to climb that thing. There can't be anything interesting up there." He paused to mop the sweat off his brow with a red bandanna that he carried, tucked into his rear pocket.

He was seconded by Tim. "Neither am I. Hey, Walker, let us know what's on top? Will ya? You're already partway up."

Logan didn't reply but trudged up the wooden steps. There was a bit of breeze on top. The wind was coming from the nearby Crystal River. He could see the water through the pine trees and palms. The breeze was refreshing and he stood there enjoying the momentary respite from the oppressive humidity and heat that clung to the ground. The river seemed slightly familiar like something seen once in a dream.

After a moment, Logan shook off the feeling, turned, and descended.

"Well? What's up there?" Tim asked. "Worthwhile?"

Logan made a noncommittal half-grin and answered, "Nice view of the water. There's a bit of a breeze up there."

That was enough for Rick. He was now perspiring heavily. "Maybe it's worth climbing after all. I'll go up there and try to come up with something to write about. Why don't you all look around? Come back and get me when you're done. Don't forget to take notes."

He turned towards the steps, missing the smirks the others made at his transparency. They all knew that he'd probably be asleep shortly after he reached the top.

They left Rick trudging heavily up the steps and headed for a nearby roofed structure. It was a simple variant of a chikee hut: just four supporting posts, a thatched roof, and a wooden fence that protected a large, irregular piece of yellowish limestone.

The stone caught Logan's eye as they approached. There was something about it that wasn't right. He stumbled a little on the uneven ground, caught his balance, and then thought, it shouldn't be there. That stone has been moved here from the beach. I wonder who did that?

He shook his head to clear it. How would he know where the stone came from?

The group reached the fence. There was a vague set of scratches on the stone. They formed a rough human face. There was a placard on the fence showing a crude face labeled: The Face in the Stone.

Logan shook his head again. He felt that the original carving was far more elaborate and he was certain the face was that of a girl, but who? And, how could he be so sure?

He asked the others, "Can you guys tell anything about that carving?"

Tim answered, "Naw, it's just some old scratchings. Those people were terrible artists."

Shawn chimed in. "Looks like an old man to me. Maybe it's supposed to be a swamp ape."

The others laughed at the absurdity.

The face continued to fascinate Logan. He lingered behind as the others walked off towards another mound. The face held a message for him. If only he could decipher it. He sank into a dream-like state.

There was danger nearby. Enemies could be close. The stone had some meaning that was expressly for him. It was something almost sacred. Something that brought a wave of loss mixed with hope over him. The carving seemed to see into him and he dreamed that he heard the carved girl's face say his name, "Logan..." from a great distance.

Just then Mandi kicked his shin. "I said, 'wake up.' You're not supposed to go to sleep. You should be with the others, taking notes."

He jumped, then looked sheepishly at her. She was good-looking. If only she'd be interested in him... No, that wasn't likely. He looked down, then said, "I was wondering about who made that carving."

She snorted, "Read your handout, dope."

He'd forgotten the sheet of paper that he'd been handed as he exited the bus. He fumbled it out of his back pocket and unfolded it to read.

The slab was limestone and the face was believed to be female. The stele was unique in Florida for that time frame. Such carvings were normally only found in Central and South America, and the Caribbean.

Mandi had walked off to check on another group of students. He paused, studying the markings again. Something about them brought tears to his eyes. It was like he had lost something or someone dear, someone he'd never see again.

He felt momentarily dizzy. "Must be the heat," he muttered. He took a couple of staggering steps, then dropped to one knee and placed his hand on the ground. After a moment, he stood up and headed towards the bus. There was a cooler there with water. He was probably dehydrated. A bottle of water would be good.

⚬

Dameron drove up in his Chrysler convertible just as Logan opened the bottle of water. He walked directly towards Logan, and said, "Mr. Walker. Taking a break already? I sincerely hope that you've enough notes to make a good paper."

Logan answered, "Not yet, Professor. I felt like I was dehydrated, so I came for some water."

By that point, Dameron was close. He lowered his tone to a semi-whisper, scowled at Logan, and said, "I didn't want you here. I don't think you're serious about school. I won't cut you any slack, Mister. If your paper or your work at the dig falls even a little bit short, I'll flunk you."

Logan started to protest, but Dameron held up his hand. "Yes, I know all about your graduation requirement. I don't care. If you have to wait tables for the rest of your life, I think that would be appropriate. That seems to be a good match for your capabilities. Now get back with your group. And try to surprise me with your paper."

As Logan walked out along the paved path to catch up with the other guys he wondered how Dameron had heard about his inheritance problem. Maybe Professor Berensten had told him. He couldn't think of any other way the man could have known. He contented himself with the idea that even Berensten didn't know how much he stood to inherit. "Or, lose," he whispered to himself.

Then it struck him. Dameron had implied that Logan would have to work if he didn't graduate. He hadn't told Professor Berensten about the trust. What did Dameron know and how?

When he rounded a clump of palmettos, he saw the group directly ahead. Rick had come down from the hilltop and was sweating along with the rest of them as they checked the next mound.

Logan sped his strides and caught up. The group as a whole had taken only a half-page of notes. That wouldn't do. He had to do something. He cleared his throat self-consciously, and said, "Hey, guys. Why don't we at least pace off the distance between the mounds, and make a map? Maybe we could walk around them, too, to get a circumference."

Rick wiped his face then said, "Okay, maybe that's a good idea. Toby, why don't you try to figure out how high each one is. That can be part of it."

Logan continued, ignoring Rick's attempt to regain control. "We also need to know how far we are from the river. These people probably had some kind of boats or canoes. They had something in mind when they built these mounds. Let's try to figure out their basic plan."

The others groaned but began to take the assignment more seriously.

The memory of the stele continued to pick at Logan as they gathered their data. Why had he responded as he had? What possible connection did the stele and the carved face have with him? It was a complete mystery. He figured that stress had finally gotten to him. Either that, or he really was suffering from heatstroke. Either way, he couldn't seem to forget the heartsick pang that he'd felt for a moment.

He'd had a puppy for a brief time before he entered first grade. A car had struck it the day before school started. He could remember feeling the same sense of loss then.

The groups gathered by the bus at noon, boarded and were transported back to the dig site. Mandi informed them that they'd each need to pick up a new assignment for the next week as soon as they ate. Sighing, Logan sat down with his sandwich and chips. He ate slowly, trying to make sense of the morning.

When he was done, he got in line to receive his new work orders. He was surprised to see that he had graduated from general digger to having a grid square assigned to his care. It wasn't one that was likely to hold any artifacts though. It was located on the far side of the dig, closer to the river and the mounds.

Chapter Four

A Revelation

Mid-afternoon found Logan sweating but happy. He was working on his own personal grid square. He hadn't found anything of note so far, but his imagination was working overtime. He could imagine himself carefully uncovering some artifact that was amazingly rare. Even a common arrowhead would be fun. If only his blisters didn't hurt so much. He hoped they'd get better in a day or so.

He'd carefully scraped dirt and sand, sifted repeatedly, and examined all of the pieces that remained on the screen. So far: nothing. But he told himself that it was just a matter of time.

As he worked, he kept an ear tuned to the other students, all of whom were working in more productive grids. Several had already turned up artifacts. Stone tools and broken projectile points were fairly common. There was an area that had apparently been the center of activity. The grids there contained a lot of charcoal along with animal bones that showed signs of human cooking.

Logan shook his head, trying to ignore an excited outburst. Someone had found a spear point or something of the sort. He glanced up momentarily and stopped dead.

Mandi was standing at the edge of his grid watching, her hands on her hips and an expression of disapproval on her face.

When she saw that she had his attention, she said, "You're going way too fast. You've got to be more careful with your trowel. Take the time to document everything you find and examine even the smallest item. Anything could offer us a useful clue as to how this site was used."

He nodded, continuing to scrape with his trowel. Following her instructions, he proceeded more deliberately.

She watched for a moment more, then turned to leave, saying, "If you don't do better, I'm going to recommend to the professor that you go back to overburden removal. We've got plenty of more skilled people."

She strode off, heading directly towards Dameron. Logan could see the professor smile as she approached. The two stood close together, talking. Dameron glanced in Logan's direction, scowled, then headed for his tent. Mandi followed.

That was no good. He'd had enough of the shoveling to last a lifetime. Now that he finally was doing something that might result in a discovery, he didn't want to quit. He continued, gradually lowering the level of the grid as he went, and taking the time to record every possible artifact in his notebook.

During the next two hours, Logan found three broken bits of stone that might once have been spearheads, a piece of burned bone, and what might have been a fragment of a flint core, leftover from knapping points. The core stone was small and had been pretty well used up. It wasn't a really good find, but he dutifully documented everything, using a unique context number for each item and location.

Once he'd recorded and stored each piece, he returned to his stratigraphic excavation, cyclically troweling the surface, looking for new contexts and edges. It was harder than he'd thought it would be. He had started with a tendency to under-cut, which meant he often failed to fully expose the items in their precise context. That might mean that his records might not match correctly when compared to other grid elements.

After Mandi's reprimand, he proceeded with more care. He fully exposed each item that he found before recording it and its context. He suspected that he was at the extreme edge of the occupied zone. There wouldn't be much to find there. Maybe the pieces he'd found had been tossed away from the fire in disgust, or maybe someone had dropped them accidentally.

He wished that he had more direct supervision, someone to actually show him what he needed to do. It was apparent that Dameron wasn't interested in his progress or understanding. He was being left to sink or swim, and Dameron had made it clear that he'd be quite happy if Logan sank.

Quitting time came before he was quite ready. He'd troweled off the surface layer, but still had a quarter of the grid to phase, that is, he reminded himself, to reduce to a contemporaneous horizon.

If he could get the hang of bringing the ground down evenly, then it would be easier to place items he found in their proper age and context with other artifacts.

Theoretically, the entire site should be cleared in such a way that all artifacts deposited at a specific time could be related to each other and not confused with ones that were deposited either before or afterward. Logan liked the idea but didn't know if he was working accurately.

He consoled himself with the idea that Dameron had probably placed him way off to the side because it wasn't an important part of the site. He probably would not find anything very interesting out here.

<hr>

After dinner, he talked to his tent mates. Their discussion made him feel a little better. They'd returned to their tent and carefully pulled the mosquito netting. No sense exposing themselves to Zika or Eastern Equine or something.

"Looks like rain. Just what we need," Rick said, bitterly. He was perspiring more than usual. It had gotten very humid and overcast during the late afternoon.

Ralph shrugged and answered, "Maybe. Bet they won't let us have a rain day."

Logan hadn't considered that. The idea of trying to dig in the rain didn't seem appealing.

"No, they know that too much water will mess up the context. We'll probably cover the important grids with canvas flies. That way we can work under shelter," Rick replied.

Ralph shrugged again and said, "Maybe. Hey, wanna play cards?"

.The other guys met the suggestion with enthusiasm. They pulled up their cots and prepared for the nightly game.

Logan sat on his cot, watching.

Toby glanced at him. "Hey, Logan. Want to play?"

At least that was some progress, getting invited to join in, but he shook his head negatively. "No, I'm no good at cards. Besides, I'm going to study a little. I need to understand what I'm doing a little better."

Rick laughed, and then said, "At least you're doing something different. We're still supposed to be digging. I'd like to stick that shovel up Dameron's butt."

The others laughed and Toby said, "Yeah, but that Mandi would probably kick your ass. I hear she's some kind of major martial artist or something."

Rick made a fruity chuckle. "I'd like to see her try. It'd give me an excuse to get my hands on her."

The others laughed again and bantered back and forth until the conversation turned to the start of the card game.

Logan rolled over, opened his textbook, and pretended to read, while he considered. If the others were still digging, it could be that Dameron believed that he had some promise. Actually, it was more likely that Dameron was just trying to put him in a situation where he'd screw up. That would mean that he probably wouldn't pass, and that meant... He sighed. Better study for real. Maybe he could teach himself what he needed to know.

There was a terrific flash outside, followed by a roll of thunder. The storm had opened right over their heads. The next minute, the tent walls sagged as the rain roared down on them. The noise was so intense that Logan couldn't hear the continuing game. He read for a while, then gradually drifted off to sleep.

When he awoke, the tent was dark. From the snoring noises, the others had finished their game and were now trying to recharge for tomorrow's work. The rain had stopped and it was quiet outside. Logan lay there listening to the sporadic dripping noise from the nearby trees. After trying unsuccessfully to get back to sleep, he realized that he needed to relieve himself.

He pulled on his pants, stepped into his shoes, and quietly headed for the row of portable toilets. As he was exiting the toilet, he saw a movement in the darkness. It was a figure walking across the campground, heading towards Dameron's tent.

Logan paused, watching. Whoever it was didn't hesitate at the tent flap. The person opened it minimally and slid through. He shrugged to himself, probably none of his business. He started back towards his tent, but driven by curiosity, he found his path deviating towards the back of Dameron's.

If he were going to spy, he might as well do it right. He walked quietly to the back of the professor's tent, taking care not to cast any shadows on the fabric. Quietly brushing at some mosquitoes that had found him, Logan crouched down, trying to avoid being observed, and listened.

There was no noise at first, but then he heard some sounds. He'd assumed there might be speaking, but this was like something else. As he listened, it gradually dawned on him that the sounds were made by a couple having sex.

The two were quiet, but at one point the girl moaned. Then he distinctly heard Dameron say, "Oh, Mandi..." followed by some whispered words that were indistinct.

Logan jerked at that revelation, then sneaked off, circling far around the camp and coming up to his own tent from behind. He checked to make sure he wasn't observed, then entered, and got back in his cot, feeling somehow hurt and jealous.

After he considered it for a while, he told himself that it didn't matter. She'd never be interested in him anyway. That helped his hurt feelings and put the tryst into a different perspective.

Still, it was quite interesting. He knew for a fact that Dameron was married. But Mandi was really attractive. Their involvement was definitely against the school's code of conduct. It went a long way towards explaining Mandi's position and her constant hovering around the professor.

He tried to put it out of his mind, but some jealous part of him continued to refuse to let it go. How could Dameron take advantage of a student? And, how could she think an almost middle-aged man was so attractive?

He eventually concluded that he would never understand women. He might not be the best Tae-kwon-do student, but at least he was about her age. He wondered if he should tell her about his prospective inheritance. Would that make a difference? Probably not. Then his habit of reticence took over. It was always best to keep one's mouth shut about finances.

———— ◄O► ————

After breakfast, he returned to his grid square. The sand was damp, but the water had soaked in and there were only a few puddles. There was a lot of work to be done to get down to the level they were targeting. This was complicated by the fact that there were more recent artifacts scattered across the site. It had been in almost continuous use over the centuries. They couldn't simply dig down to the ten thousand year level. In so doing, they'd probably miss some of the recent stuff, and that might be important.

He decided to continue to take his grid down in sections. He'd work at the northwest section first since it was closest to the known finds. Once he'd lowered it to the target depth, he'd then start moving into the northeast part.

Logan had made some good progress by lunchtime. He'd carefully troweled and brushed his way down to almost the target depth in a small area. As he was trudging across the site towards the dining fly, there was a flurry of alarmed shouts from a distant group.

He recognized Rick's voice in the mix and turned towards the sound. The distant group was scampering away from something. Logan trotted over to see what was going on.

"Hey, Logan, don't go over there," Rick shouted. He'd stopped at a safe distance and was now looking back. "There's a coral snake under some dried leaves back there."

Logan was curious. He had never been worried about snakes. He'd seen a lot of them, although he'd never seen a coral snake. He cautiously approached the spot. There was a pile of dried leaves, and there was the tail of a brightly colored snake sticking out from under the pile. He bent over to investigate more closely.

The tail was black with yellow bands. He moved the covering leaves carefully with a small stick. The banding pattern changed as it reached the main part of the snake's body. It became yellow-red-yellow-black, then repeated. It was definitely a small coral snake. Logan stepped back and looked around. His tent mates were tightly clustered about twenty feet away, looking like a family of alert meerkats, their eyes wide and fearful.

A student that Logan didn't know came up carrying a shovel. Before Logan could say anything, the man swung the shovel at the snake, cutting it in half with a hard blow.

Logan was outraged. The poor animal hadn't posed a threat. It could be easily relocated. He'd been ready to retrieve a plastic bag for that purpose. He started to say something but shut his mouth with a snap as Dameron arrived.

The professor said, "Alright. The excitement's over. Go and eat. We'll start digging on schedule, so you don't have much time if you want to be fed."

The student scooped the snake's remains onto the shovel, took it to the edge of the dig site, and buried it in a shallow hole. Logan watched the operation without moving.

Dameron, who had started back, turned, saw Logan, and said, "Go on! I meant it, Walker. You're just a screw-up."

Logan didn't reply, instead, he strode to the dining fly, gathered up some food, and retreated to his grid square, where he settled in the sand to have his lunch.

It wasn't fair to the snake, but he guessed that was about what he could expect out of the group. Dameron wasn't fair to him either. It was disgusting, and he was of half a mind to leave. Only the promise of his inheritance kept him sitting there. He calmed down as he chewed.

He ate quickly and was back at work before the others had finished their lunch.

Chapter Five

Discovery and Trouble

The sun burned down. People from northern latitudes generally didn't understand just how strong the sun was in the south. Some of the students from other states had already gotten sunburned.

Logan was wearing a broad-brimmed hat and had sunscreen on his exposed skin, but it was still hot and humid. He was dripping with sweat. His clothes were saturated, and he was covered with muddy dirt and sand.

To top it off, there were a bunch of yellow flies in the area. The cursed things kept circling, looking for an opportunity. They'd shoot in, land on an exposed piece of skin, and bite instantly. They were so fast that it was almost impossible to swat them. Luckily, he wasn't allergic to the painful bites. A couple of the other students had huge, swollen patches where they'd been bitten.

The only good thing was that it was too hot and bright for mosquitoes during the day. The nights were a different story. Everyone was glad for the university-provided mosquito netting.

—◦—

The first summer session was nearly over, and the dig was mostly on schedule. Logan had developed a good farmer's tan. His face, neck, and arms had turned red, then gradually changed to a light walnut brown.

The main center of activity was still well away from his assignment. Dameron hadn't wanted him here, and when forced to accept his presence, had stuck him in his distant grid square.

Logan had taken to talking to himself quietly as he worked. The others were at least fifty yards away, and he was isolated. Over the days, he had worked up a level of frustration and anger that he was barely able to contain.

Just what Dameron wants, he thought disgustedly. He'd like me to get discouraged and quit, or maybe make some kind of serious mistake. Then he'd flunk me.

The only benefit of his anger was that he was now determined to stick it out and earn a passing grade.

He was finishing off the last quarter of his grid square. He'd carefully logged the few items he'd discovered that looked like they might be related to humans. There hadn't been much, no large burned bones or sticks, no interesting stone tools, no carvings, basically nothing. There had been a few chips of stone and bone that might or might not be man-made. That was all that he'd found in the days he'd been working on the area. It was pretty discouraging.

⸻⸺◆⸺⸻

He was working on the last part of the quarter grid, cutting down an uneven lump in the edge of his excavation. There were no signs of prior disturbance of the soil, no pits, no digging, nothing.

"Just this one spot to go," he whispered.

The trowel hit something with a clink. Logan carefully brushed and scraped the soil away. Maybe this was important. He worked carefully, gradually exposing the middle of the thing. It seemed to be sticking out of the grid square wall. He worked from the partly exposed middle towards both ends. The odd thing was, it was very regular and apparently made of metal.

It was old and somewhat pitted, but there was a little shine. "If I didn't know better, I'd say it was some kind of stainless steel," he muttered. He stood up and looked around to see if he was the butt of some prank. No one was nearby, and no one was even looking in his direction, so that was probably out. He continued digging, scraping the soil back to expose more of the item.

Once he'd uncovered four inches of it, he stopped, wiped his face, and tried to decide what to do. It was obviously man-made, and it shouldn't be where it was. It looked for all the world like a knife blade. Moreover, it was a steel knife blade with a tanto point.

Logan knew about this kind of knife because of his gaming. It was one of the first weapons available to new players, and he'd been so enamored of it that he'd used it in the game even when better weapons became available. He didn't actually care for real knives much, though.

He told himself, "If I dig it out, Dameron won't believe that I found it here in this undisturbed dirt. I'd like to look at it to verify that I'm right about what it is, but maybe it would be better to go and get Mandi, at least, to come over when I dig it out. Maybe Dameron should be here?"

He made a tentative swipe at the thing with his brush, intending to clean a little more dirt off. A clump of soil dropped to the bottom of the trench, exposing another object. He leaned close to inspect the second thing. It looked like the base of a Clovis spear point. The shape was right, complete to the fluting in the middle of the point. Possibly a little over half of it was exposed. Logan was excited. This was the first real artifact he'd discovered. He reached out for it, intending to remove it, but then hesitated.

The spear point was exactly the same depth as the knife blade, and it wasn't over a half-inch distant. It must have been dropped there at the same time the knife was dropped. But that was impossible. There was no such thing as steel thirteen thousand years ago. Somehow the knife must have been placed recently. If only he could figure out how.

He shook his head tiredly. It was too hot to think logically. He climbed out of the hole and stood still for a moment. He made up his mind and headed for the far side of the dig. Mandi was standing over there, apparently berating some unlucky student who'd irritated her.

He got close enough to hear her snap, "Get back to work!"

He stopped, struck by an idea. As if she had been speaking to him, he swiveled and returned to his grid square.

Lucky that I thought of this. He was not into the selfie craze or much into social media and rarely used the camera on his phone. He'd almost forgotten about it. He opened his cell phone and then crouched down to take a series of pictures of the two artifacts and the soil surrounding them. Then he headed back to tell Mandi about the discovery.

As he approached her, he saw Dameron coming from the other direction. Huh, might as well tell them both at the same time, he told himself.

Dameron arrived just before him, started to speak to Mandi, and then stopped as Logan walked up.

He looked briefly at Logan and said, "Mr. Walker, shouldn't you be over there at work?" Then he turned to Mandi critically. "You need to keep these guys working or we'll never finish this project."

She frowned at Logan, then said, "Get back to work, Walker. Break time is at least an hour away."

Logan stopped and looked from one to the other. He said, "I'm still working. I've found something that I think you should see."

Dameron cocked his head. "What is it? Something important, I hope. You should know enough about what we're looking for by now not to be wasting my time."

Logan had already turned and was heading back to the spot. He said over his shoulder, "I think it's important."

⸺◆⸺

The knife, for so it turned out to be, was heavily pitted and worn. There might once have been some kind of handle on the tang, but it had rotted away. There was an indented area on the base of the blade that looked as if it might have been a manufacturer's imprint and another indefinable set of marks on the other side that might have been stamped into the metal.

The professor had unceremoniously pulled the spear point from the dirt, glanced at it, and dropped it into his pocket. Logan tried to object that he hadn't recorded it yet, but by the time he'd formulated what he was going to say, it was too late.

Unfortunately, the net effect of his discovery was not what Logan had hoped for. Dameron was angry and threatened to flunk him.

Mandi ventured the idea that he must have planted the knife, thinking he'd get a good grade for finding something important.

Dameron looked at her to see if she was serious, then he snapped, "Even Walker isn't stupid enough to think that a Clovis site would have a stainless steel knife. Someone must have buried it here. Then again, maybe he did plant it." He looked sharply at Logan, then asked, "What do you think, Walker? Is this your idea of a joke? Messing with the site is grounds for me kicking you off the dig."

Logan vehemently denied having anything to do with the knife's placement. "Look, Professor Dameron, the soil over it wasn't disturbed. You saw that, and you also saw that it couldn't have been poked into the edge of the cut. It was definitely buried there."

Finally, Dameron grudgingly admitted that it looked like Walker was telling the truth.

By then, it was time to knock off for the day. Dameron took possession of the knife, then he and Mandi headed back to his tent. Logan went through the process of logging the find, even though he felt kind of silly doing so. It was obviously out of context where he'd found it, but still, it had been there. Nothing was said about the spear point. Logan had hoped to have a chance to brag about it before he turned it in, but that was obviously out.

⚬

The next morning was a bad one. As he came to breakfast, Mandi intercepted him, saying, "Walker, get over to Dameron's tent right now."

"Okay. What is it?" he asked.

"You'll find out when you get over there," she answered.

She strode ahead of him, turning to hold the tent flap open so he could enter.

"Mr. Walker," Dameron greeted him. "I can't allow this dig to be invalidated by one of the students playing a joke. I don't know how you got the knife into the strata where it was, and I don't really care. As of now, you're off the dig. You will not be getting a passing grade. It's too late for you to drop the credit hours, but you're not welcome back. I'm going to give you a 60% grade for the time you've put in. Consider yourself lucky."

Logan couldn't believe it. He'd been sure that they understood that the find was legitimate, no matter how it had gotten there. It wasn't something that he'd planted.

"Professor!" he said. "I didn't plant that there. You can't kick me out for something I didn't do."

"I can and I will," said Dameron. "Now, get your stuff together. You can get breakfast in town on your own time. End of discussion. GO."

<hr>

As he walked away from the tent, Logan could have sworn that he heard the two of them laughing quietly.

He got his kit out of the tent, packed everything on the back of his motorcycle, and rode slowly down the dusty track to the highway, not bothering to say anything to his tent mates.

As he turned onto the asphalt, he thought, At least I'll have a good breakfast in town. Better than the junk they've been feeding me. I've wanted to quit this crummy job since I got here. Then the realization that he now had no way to get the needed credits for graduation hit him with a crushing blow. His mood fell to a new low.

During breakfast at a fast food place, he decided that he'd better go and talk to Professor Berensten. Maybe there was something she could do. He'd be willing to work for extra credit. That could solve his problem. He started his bike, turned out onto the highway, and headed for Gainesville, cursing the heavy traffic.

Chapter Six

A Hopeless Mess

Dr. Berensten wasn't going to be in until about three, according to her secretary. Then she had a couple of appointments, and those might take her until sometime after four. The secretary didn't want to schedule anything else for her, but Logan finally convinced her to pencil him in. He had to practically beg her though, and he also had to promise not to take more than ten minutes.

He left the office and headed slowly down the stairs, lost in worry.

Well, that would probably be enough time. I can tell her what happened quickly. Maybe she'll have a possible solution. I hope so, anyway. Logan, you just gotta get this graduation thing done on time. Life with that money will be so great, and without it, especially knowing that it's going to some scholarship fund that won't even consider me, will be a complete pain. I don't see how I'll ever be able to live with the memory of that possibility.

I wish I'd been a better student, and I also wish I'd been able to see this crunch coming earlier. Maybe last summer, I would have had time to make some adjustments. It's not fair. It's not like I've been totally flunking my classes either, only that I've been carrying too light a load and just doing enough to squeak by.

She'll be able to help. I just know it!

He left the Archaeology department with an optimistic feeling and headed across campus to The Hub. He'd play a video game and get some food, then go back in time to make his appointment.

———— ◆◇◆ ————

The game didn't seem to be as interesting as he remembered from the prior times he'd played it. Instead, his thoughts kept turning to the knife he'd found. How did it get there? There hadn't been any sign of disturbed soil. If there had been, he would have been suspicious.

It would fit his view of Dameron, Mandi too, for one of them to have planted the thing in order to have an excuse to get rid of him. But, no, it hadn't been planted, despite Dameron's insistence that it had been. It had been there. Moreover, it was in soil that apparently hadn't been moved or changed for thirteen thousand years. The presence of the associated spear point proved that.

———— ◆◇◆ ————

When he arrived back at Berensten's office, she was still talking to a female student. He stood courteously in the hall outside her door, leaning against the opposite wall. He was far enough away that he couldn't make out what was being said but strategically located where Berensten could see him if she'd just look up.

The two finished their conversation on a mutually satisfactory note, and the girl stood to leave. Berensten looked up as she left and saw Logan. She apparently hadn't noticed him before. He could see the rise and fall of her shoulders as she took a deep breath, then motioned for him to come in.

"Logan, what's going on with you? I went out on a limb for you and threatened Dameron to take you, but now I hear that you've done something unethical. He's asked for an ethics committee hearing. You know that could result in you being expelled and not being allowed to enroll again. What in the name of all that's ancient did you do?"

Logan was at a loss. "Uh...I hadn't heard any of that. Did he call you or something?" he asked.

"Yes, he called. He said that you'd been disruptive and that you planted a modern artifact in the dig. He thinks that might invalidate the entire summer's work, and all for a prank. His student supervisor confirmed his statement. She said that you were resentful about your digging assignment. I don't know your side of this, but I want to hear it. This is something that I take very seriously. I've helped you as much as I could, but if you've done what they say, you're on your own," she answered.

This was too much. Logan could feel his face flushing as his temper flared. "Damn those two!" he snapped.

Berensten raised her finger in warning but didn't say anything, so he continued.

"Everything was going okay. They had me reducing the site, and I used a shovel for days. They finally gave me a grid square all to myself, but it was far over to the side where there weren't any discoveries. Nothing. I found nothing but a few bits of rock. Then when I'm almost done with the location, I found a really nice spear point, and right next to it was a stainless-steel knife. A modern knife! It hadn't been planted there as far as I could see. I thought that maybe Dameron or Mandi had shoved it in the ground so I'd look like a fool. The soil was totally undisturbed, and the only thing I can say was the knife must have been dropped there at the same time the spear point was. That was supposed to have happened thirteen thousand years ago, so it can't be right – I just don't know. The thing is: I didn't have anything to do with placing either of the objects. I don't even know enough about digs to understand what invalidating one really means," he said in a rush.

Then he continued, "Dameron doesn't like me for some reason or other. I passed his course. I don't know what else I could have done. I didn't ever do anything to him or disrespect him. Except..."

"Except what?" Berensten asked.

He slowly said, "Maybe they somehow knew I was listening outside Dameron's tent that night."

Her eyebrows went up. "What do you mean by that?"

Logan realized that he was about to take a serious step if things could get any more serious than they already were.

"I went to the portable toilet in the middle of the night early on. When I came out, I saw someone go into Dameron's tent. I sneaked over and listened. They were having sex. It was Mandi."

She held up her hand, frowning. "That's enough of that. I don't want to hear it. All that will get you is disbelief from the committee, unless, of course, you can somehow prove it beyond a shadow of a doubt. Right now, all it sounds like is a stupid attempt to get revenge. Besides, even though it's against policy, the two are adults and capable of making their own choices."

He shook his head mutely but then added, "It's still going on. It's pretty obvious."

"Dameron might not be my favorite person, but he takes his job seriously. I can't believe he would ever violate university policy in that way. Besides, he's happily married; been married since before he was hired here. You'd better just forget about making that kind of accusation, Mister," she continued.

He answered, "Well, I was just thinking that might account for him not liking me."

"Yes, if it were true, but I don't believe it could be. I'm going to try and forget what you said. My advice to you is to carefully prepare your statement for the ethics committee. It won't meet until after the second summer session. Since you've been formally accused of a serious violation, you won't be allowed to enroll until the hearing is resolved, and then, most likely, only if it's resolved in your favor."

She asked, "Do you have a job? You should at least put the next six weeks to good use."

Logan didn't want to make her any angrier, so he clamped down on his emotions about the accusation and the unfairness of it all.

"No job, and I don't even have a place to stay right now. I'd planned to be staying at the dig all summer, so I gave up my apartment. My roommates have all moved in with other people or gone home. Uh...maybe I could go to my dad's place over in Ormond Beach. I could probably stay with him for a while and maybe he'd help me find something to do."

She nodded and said, "That's a good idea. Go and do that, and stay away from Professor Dameron and the department. Prepare your statement, and then be back here on August 23rd for the hearing. It will be in the admin building. I don't know the scheduled time yet. You call me in a couple of weeks. I'll probably know then. Now I've got to go. My husband is expecting me home so we can go out to dinner."

She stood up and began to gather her things.

Logan turned and slowly walked out, his shoulders drooping. He stopped, looking back, as she shut her office door. She headed the other way without a backward glance.

⸺◆⸺

An hour later, he was well on the way to Ormond Beach. Despite the pleasure of the wind on his face, Logan was in a bad frame of mind.

No one believed him. It was just his luck to think he had a chance only to have it jerked away. He didn't really want to see his dad. They hadn't been close since his mother...his mind shied away from the circumstances of her death, but then it circled around again, and he was filled with the same old sense of remorse.

He'd been there. He'd known she was depressed. He hadn't known she had those damned pills, though. If he had, maybe he could have stolen them or something, but what could a ten-year-old really do? He always ended up trying to find solace by excusing himself for his age and inexperience at the time. It was poor comfort, though.

He swerved, narrowly missing a messily dead armadillo, crushed by some traffic just ahead. His heart raced with the adrenaline released by the sudden alarm.

Maybe I'd better just concentrate on riding, he thought.

He watched the road carefully for any other obstacles, but within a mile, his mind turned back to his parents. Why had the two divorced? He suspected their basic disagreement was over money. The two had always argued about that. His father had never been able to keep a job for long.

That was one of the reasons the trust had been formed. His grandfather didn't approve of his daughter marrying William Walker and wanted to make sure he wouldn't benefit from the estate.

Logan shook his head in denial. He could understand it. His mother had never shown a great deal of strength. She'd almost always acceded to his father's demands, except for the one time she found enough strength to leave him and his abuse behind. She'd told Logan that her father knew she would never be able to keep the money away from William.

Logan knew she was right. It had been a mess. He'd been an emotional wreck for years. Then an insight struck him. He was still a wreck. It was easy to see that his interest in gaming was some kind of escape attempt. Somehow he still felt responsible for the divorce and for her death.

The traffic slowed, and he closed in on the pickup ahead of him, trying to peer around the high four-wheeler to see what the hang-up was. He grimaced. More road-kill.

A semi had hit a large alligator that was crossing the road in a swampy area. The truck had bounced but never slowed.

The cars were now swerving around the deceased creature, with the occupants looking curiously at it.

When the pickup ahead of him drew near the carcass, it slowed and pulled onto the shoulder. The passenger, a heavy-set, bald-headed guy in overalls, jumped out and headed quickly towards the alligator, a large knife in his hand. Logan flinched before he realized the man was after the skin.

The idea of skinning something made him feel nauseated. Despite finding the buried knife and feeling something of a sense of ownership for the discovery, he really didn't like knives. They were too sharp, and his mind shied away from the idea of getting cut.

He didn't even like kitchen knives. His roommates were always leaving long, sharp ones lying around where they'd been fixing something in the kitchen. Logan had taken to wiping them with a damp rag without actually picking them up. He'd wipe one side, turn the thing over, wipe the other side, and then gingerly pick up the handle with two fingers to restore the implement to its proper place in the drawer.

He swerved as far away from the man and knife as he could. Once past, he accelerated away at the old bike's best speed.

Sometime later, he pulled into his dad's driveway. The pickup wasn't there, and it looked like his father wasn't home yet.

Logan rang the bell, but there was no answer. Turning, he sat on the front step and considered his situation.

The hearing would be in seven weeks. He was effectively banned from returning to school for the second summer session, and it was too late to enroll in any other local school, even if there was a course that would be transferable and which would count towards his degree. So, it seemed his best alternative would be to get a job, work, and save up some money that could supplement the paltry funding from the trust.

As he considered his grades, he gradually came to the conclusion that he wasn't totally academically incompetent. He wasn't stupid. After all, he'd mastered Alien Slayers rather quickly. It was just that last level that was holding him up, and as far as he could determine, the coders had cheated, making it almost impossible to beat.

He shook his head. His mind was wandering. He understood all of the class materials; he just didn't care much about it, which meant that he'd been disinclined to memorize the facts needed to test well. Perhaps if he spent his evenings reading some of his old textbooks, he could rectify that gap. He didn't know if that would help, but he decided to try.

His father still hadn't shown up, so he climbed back on his bike and motored over to a fast-food place, got a burger, fries, and a drink, then came back about thirty minutes later. His dad's roofing truck was in the driveway when he turned in.

Logan's father, William, was happy to see him when he answered the door. "Hey! Look what the cat drug in. I'm glad to see ya, boy. Are ya here for the weekend or what?" he said.

Logan grinned at his dad's enthusiasm. "I'm glad to see you too. I'm taking the next session off. I gave up my apartment to save money, my plans changed, and now I don't have anywhere to stay until the fall session starts," he answered.

His dad hugged him, and said, "Great. I'm short-handed. I can use you. I've got jobs lined up for the next three months. The rains have slowed things a lot, so I'm backed up. One of my guys quit, and I had to fire another. He kept showing up high. Idiot almost dumped a bundle of shingles on my head. I mean he dropped it off the roof and it grazed me as it came down. High on your own time is one thing. High when you're working on a roof is another."

Logan shook his head in sympathy. Being hit by a full bundle of shingles would have probably broken his father's neck. "Yeah, I can see how that would be a problem," he said.

His father seemingly forgot about the problem as he continued, "You can have the spare bedroom. Hope ya don't mind a little partying. I've got some friends that show up now and then. Drink a little beer, maybe smoke a bit. Larry will probably show up around suppertime. We're going to fire up the grill and cook some burgers."

"No, that's alright with me. I'm just happy that you've got a place for me. I can use the work, too. Just go easy on me for a couple of days until I get broke in again," Logan said. He'd worked a little with his dad before and knew what a strain it was adapting to the heat and labor.

"You haven't been doing enough at school, have you?" his dad asked.

Logan responded by showing his callouses. "Well, I actually have been working pretty hard on an archaeological dig. I've shoveled a lot of sand out in the full sun. I just haven't had to carry heavy loads up a ladder."

"Did you like digging?" his father asked.

"Not any more than I like carrying shingles or stripping a roof," he answered with a grin.

His father laughed. "Point taken. I'll go easy for a bit, but I really need your help to get caught up, so be ready to go in the morning. Truck leaves at six sharp."

———◆———

Logan got settled in the spare room. He didn't have much to unpack. By the time he'd arranged his sparse belongings and some textbooks, Larry had shown up with a couple of women in tow.

The group had opened a case of beer and gone out into the backyard to get the grill started. Their loud conversation carried through the open windows.

Logan's father had never favored air-conditioning. He worked in the direct sun and heat so much that simply having a roof over his head seemed good enough. He maintained that the cold air just made it harder for him to adapt to the heat.

Logan missed the a/c from his apartment, but he'd been living in a tent for weeks. The heat didn't bother him much as a result.

He left his room, walked through the kitchen, grabbing a beer out of the fridge as he passed. Might as well go out and see what was cooking.

"Oh. Wow! Who's this?" one of the women asked. She was reclining with Larry in a hammock strung between two cabbage palms. The other woman was clinging to his dad's arm, watching as he fiddled with the charcoal grill.

Larry glanced at him, said, "Hi, Lo! Good to see ya. Ya gonna be helping us?"

Same old Larry. His dad's best friend and long-time helper. "Yeah. I'll be up on the roof with you for a while. I'm taking the next session off, so I'll be here for six weeks or so," he answered.

"Great! That's what we need, someone we don't have to break in. I'm tired of newbies who don't know which end of a nail to hit," he said loudly, slapping his hand on his knee and laughing.

Logan took a sip of beer, grinned as he remembered a joke, then asked, "Did you hear about the siding installer who threw half his nails on the ground?"

Larry looked puzzled, so Logan continued, "He said the head was on the wrong end. The on-site supervisor told him to pick 'em up and use them on the other side of the house."

Larry threw his head back and roared with laughter. Both women looked puzzled for a moment, then the one sitting with Larry said, "Oh. I get it. If the heads were on the wrong end, they'd be on the right end on the other side..." She trailed off sheepishly, looking embarrassed.

Larry rubbed his hand on the inside of her thigh. "You don't need to worry about that kinda stuff. Just leave the nailin' to me," he smirked.

She giggled momentarily and then looked at Logan appraisingly out of the corner of her eyes.

He turned to look at the grill, pretending to be interested in the food. The way she'd looked at him was like he was on the main course, rather than the burgers. They were now starting to smell good, and he was hungry.

His dad had gone in for another beer, followed by the other woman. He could hear them carrying on inside, apparently making out while getting the beer. He glanced at the other two. Larry was finishing his beer, but the woman was still watching him. He decided to flip the burgers just to have something to do. She was probably only a few years older than him, but she looked like she'd lived them hard. Well, it wasn't any of his business.

<hr>

After the beer and burgers, Larry and Cheryl left, heading for some bar where there was a blues band that Larry liked. Logan's dad and Chelle retired to the master bedroom, leaving Logan sitting in the great room watching an old movie.

It was one that he'd seen before, but he persisted. He figured he wouldn't be able to sleep for a while due to the intermittent noises that filtered through the bedroom door. Maybe they'd quiet down eventually, and then he could slip down the hall into the far bedroom.

<hr>

The movie was long over when he awakened on the couch. The house was quiet except for the TV. He switched it off, walked down the hall, and climbed into bed.

<hr>

The next three weeks seemed to go by in a blur. There was a constant round of hard work on crazily hot roofs, followed by beer-fueled drives home. They sometimes stopped for food but often grilled in the backyard. There was never a day for a break, his dad worked seven days a week, only taking off when they were between jobs, and that didn't happen often.

The work was mind-numbing, but some good things did come from it. Logan's muscles had first complained even more than they had from shoveling, but then he'd begun to bulk up, and now he felt far stronger than he ever had while living a student's life. In addition, he was putting away some cash, and that made him feel self-sufficient. He liked the feeling.

Larry and the two women came over on Friday and Saturday nights.

Logan took to going out on his motorcycle in order to avoid Cheryl. Larry didn't seem to notice, but each time she had an opportunity, she made her interest in Logan more obvious.

The last time she'd been over, she trapped him in the hall, standing close enough so that he could feel the tips of her breasts. He sensed that she was going to try to kiss him, but then Larry called her from the kitchen, and she reluctantly pulled away. He turned and ducked into the bathroom before Larry looked around the corner and said, "Hey, Cher. What ya' doin' in here?"

She replied, "Waiting on Logan to get out of the toilet. What's it look like?"

Logan took that as a signal to walk out, saying, "Sorry. Had to go."

He squeezed past the two, stopped at the refrigerator for another long-neck, then walked out onto the front porch to stare through the palm fronds at the dim street light.

He sipped at the beer and considered. He was uncomfortable here at his dad's, but there was no going back to school yet. The best thing was the pay, and he couldn't fault the free room and food, but the weekend partying and hard grind of roofing work was becoming unpleasant.

His dad was okay. Maybe he was just kind of... Logan paused. Maybe immature was the best way to describe the old man. His father tried to act more like Logan's friend rather than his parent. The nightly drinking was starting to bother him, too. His dad drank some every night and more on weekends.

Logan had never been one for getting staggeringly drunk. It interfered with game playing for one thing. He sighed and said to himself, "Oh, well. It won't be forever. If I can get reinstated and graduate, things will be okay."

If not – well, that could wait, but he resolved that he'd get a job somewhere else, and it would be sure to be one that involved working in an air-conditioned environment.

He belatedly reminded himself that he'd didn't want to lose his newly gained muscles. "I'll work out, too," he muttered.

Chapter Seven

High and Far Away

Logan was glad that it was Saturday. They had finished a roofing job that afternoon, and they weren't due to start the next one until Monday. For the first time since he'd started helping, he'd have a day off.

His dad parked the work truck at the liquor store, entered, and came out carrying two cases of beer. He stopped on the sidewalk and yelled, "Hey boy, get out of the truck and get one of these. Make yourself useful."

Logan jumped out, took a case, and transported it to the truck bed, where he placed it carefully behind some half-empty cans of roofing tar. His dad put the other in the front seat, climbed in, and immediately ripped the cardboard to get at a can.

By the time Logan had climbed in, his father had finished the first can. He tossed that one out the window into the pickup bed, then pulled another out and popped the top. After a long drink, he glanced at Logan and said, "Help yourself. Working in the sun really makes you build up a thirst, huh, Lo?"

Logan got his own beer and sipped at it as they wound through back streets on their way home. By the time they'd arrived, Larry and the two women were already sitting on the front porch.

It was going to be another long night, Logan decided. Maybe he'd get cleaned up and head out for a ride along A1A. He could find a stretch of beach somewhere and watch the waves. At least it would be quiet.

He'd eaten some barbecued chicken. If nothing else, his dad was a good backyard cook. The first case of beer was gone. The older people had practically absorbed it.

Now he was thinking about his bike when Larry came by with something in his hand.

"Hey, Lo. Y'all been good help. I want ya to know I really am glad ya came home for a while to help us catch up."

"No problem, Lar. Glad to have the work, ya know," he answered, slipping into a more southern dialect.

Larry was feeling the beer and wasn't too steady on his feet as a result. He wavered back and forth for a moment and then extended his hand to Logan. "Here. Got ya something. I was playing poker last night, and I won this offn' some guy. He was pretty pissed, but I took it anyway. It's a knife. He said it was cold steel or something like that. Anyways, I want ya to have it. A gift from me to you for your help. Look here. I gotta alphabet die set. I tapped your initials on the blade."

Logan looked. Larry had stamped "LW" on the blade. The letters weren't quite in alignment.

Logan suddenly remembered that Larry's last name was Wilson. That took some of the sentiment away from the gift.

Looking at the blade, Logan shuddered. Larry didn't know that he didn't like knives. He considered refusing, but it seemed like the best thing to do was to take the thing.

The instant he held it in his hand, a shock of recognition struck him like a thunderbolt. It was exactly like what he'd pulled out of the dig. New... but exactly like the knife that had gotten him in trouble. He wonderingly unhooked the Velcro retaining strap and pulled the blade out of the leather sheath.

It was thick and heavy with a tanto-style point. It looked sharp, and he was afraid to touch the edge, but he ran his thumb along the spine of the blade. As he did, the backyard seemed to fade.

The grill disappeared, and there were more palm trees in his vision. Something large, like a huge, animated football, trundled slowly towards him from behind some bushes. He was unable to move, paralyzed by the vision.

Larry put his hand on Logan's shoulder, shaking him a little. "Hey, don't get all choked up over it, kid."

Logan shook his head. The vision had flicked out. He was standing in the backyard. His dad was kissing Chele. Cheryl was looking over her beer at him, an evaluating expression on her face.

He shook his head again, trying to clear it. "Thanks, Larry. You're a good friend. I'm proud to be working with you," he said. To show that he meant it, he unbuckled his belt and slid the sheath on it, placing the knife on his left side.

Larry laughed, turned to the others, and said, "See why I love this kid! He's one in a million. That knife makes him look like Tarzan."

Cheryl raised her beer in a toast. "To our Tarzan! One in a million."

The others joined in.

Logan suddenly realized that his beer had worked its way through his system. He muttered, "Thanks, Larry. I gotta go."

He walked through the kitchen. Someone had put some brownies on the counter, and he grabbed one on his way to the bathroom. He shoved it in his mouth and headed down the hall. When he was done, he went into the great room and turned on the TV.

About thirty minutes later, he realized that the TV show was extremely colorful. The colors were brighter than any he'd previously seen from the cheap screen. He watched, fascinated. The people on the screen were moving slowly. It must be some sort of comedy. They were moving so slowly. He laughed.

His laugh was echoed by a low, throaty, feminine laugh. Cheryl had entered the room. He looked at her as she sat down beside him. She was pretty good-looking, he decided.

"Where's Larry?" he asked.

She scooted over against his side. "He's mostly asleep out there in the hammock. He drinks too much and isn't good for much once he's drunk," she said quietly.

Her face seemed to get larger in his vision, and he found himself somehow kissing her. It wasn't really what he wanted to do, but he felt out of control. She slid her hand over his leg, moving it upwards slowly.

There was a long moment of quiet, then she said, "I've been wanting to get you alone for a long time. Larry is drunk. Let's – "

He interrupted her. "Why are you talking so slow? It's funny." He laughed again.

Cheryl pulled back, staring at him in surprise. Then her eyes narrowed. "Did you eat one of those brownies?"

He nodded, solemnly, and giggled. He put his hand over his mouth. He'd sounded silly and childish.

She looked alarmed and said, "You didn't eat the whole thing, did you? You're only supposed to take a bite. They're really strong."

He shrugged uncomprehendingly and said, "It was good."

She looked at the door, then said, "No matter, that doesn't change what I want to do."

She straightened, grabbing his hand, pulling him up.

"C'mon. Let's go in your bedroom." She yanked his arm. "C'mon! It'll be fun."

He started to go with her, but then a wave of revulsion and nausea washed over him. Her face suddenly looked distorted and garish, as if it'd been painted on an egg. He shook her grip off and staggered towards the screen door, wondering if he'd belatedly discovered some common sense or if he'd been poisoned. What had been in that brownie, anyway?

Logan was in the front yard. He didn't remember going there, but he was looking at the streetlight. It had entrancing colored rays.

Someone was yelling at him. It was Cheryl. He turned. She was standing on the porch. No, she was walking towards him, her arm outstretched. Her face was distorted and frightening.

He turned and ran. She shouted, "Hey! Get back here! Logan..."

The ground fell out from below his feet. He was falling into the ditch by the road. He relaxed, enjoying the floating sensation. The grass looked soft. Then he struck. There was a bright flash, and he grunted. It was harder than it looked.

Logan rolled over. The sun was shining in his eyes. Things were odd-looking, and he felt sick. He turned his head to the side and vomited. He felt a little better after some time had passed.

He looked around. The house wasn't there. In fact, nothing was there. He felt too disoriented to think. There was a palm nearby, so he crawled across the sandy ground and collapsed in the shade. The surroundings wavered, and his head felt as if it were expanding and contracting, throbbing. He shut his eyes in the shade, moving until he found a position that was more comfortable, and slept.

Logan gradually became aware that he was awake. The sun's rays were longer, slanting in through the palm fronds from the west. He'd been keeping his eyes shut, but now the light was directly shining on his eyelids. He could still tell that the source was low in the sky.

Something nearby made a loud, breathy grunt. A few seconds later, some vegetation rustled, followed by the sound of breaking branches.

Logan sat upright, looking towards the noise. His vision seemed blurry, but gradually things became clearer.

There was a thicket of palmettos between him and the source of the sound. The tough little palms stood several feet high, forming an impassable barrier. Something heaved at the far side of the thicket, making the fronds jerk and sway.

A large snake, disturbed by the commotion, squirmed out of the thicket, heading directly towards Logan's feet. He jumped up and backed away. There was no sense fooling with it. He knew a diamond-back rattler when he saw one. This one was huge, a giant of its kind, nearly ten feet in length and correspondingly heavy through its body.

As he moved, the snake became aware of him. It coiled in defense and started to rattle, its tail making a deep buzzing noise. Logan backed away diagonally. The snake probably held enough venom to kill him several times over.

His movement convinced the rattler that he was no threat. It uncoiled and continued moving towards another thicket. He watched it until its tail disappeared.

"I've never seen one so large," he said aloud. At the sound of his voice, a loud grunt came from the other side of the palmettos. Logan jerked around and saw something indefinable moving towards him.

He passed his hand over his eyes in amazement. The thing looked sort of like an armadillo on steroids, although there were some differences. He wondered if he was still under the brownie's influence.

The huge creature seemed to have poor vision. It moved towards him, then stopped short, staring nearsightedly. He stepped back a short step. The animal snorted, startled. It lowered its head and turned sideways, giving him a view of a distinctly menacing, clubbed tail. The powerful appendage swung back and forth, leaving no doubt that it was preparing to defend itself against an attack.

Logan felt like he was in some kind of amusement park. He'd gone to the Raptor Encounter at Universal Studios, and it had been lifelike, but this thing was even more realistic. He stepped forward in wonder, looking to see if there were cables or wires that powered it. It snorted again and slapped the heavy tail against its side, making a 'clunk' as it struck the armored shell of the chest-high beast.

He stopped and jumped back. If that thing hit him, it would probably break his leg. The animal was huge, maybe weighing as much as a small horse. The creature spun, presenting its posterior to him. The tail moved back and forth viciously. It backed towards him, attacking in slow motion.

At the farthest extent of its swing, the tail struck a palm trunk. The impact sounded like it was made with a sledgehammer. Logan quickly backed farther away, then turned and made a wide circle around the animal. It definitely wasn't some kind of animated machine.

He racked his mind, trying to remember. He'd seen something like this thing once, a long time ago. It had been in a museum...that was it! It was a glyptotherium, a distant relative of the armadillo. The only thing was, it was extinct and had been so for thousands of years.

He couldn't come to grips with its presence. Just to make sure, he looked around to see if anyone was watching, perhaps hiding in the palm trees, laughing at him. This had to be some sort of elaborate joke.

There was no sign of anyone.

The glyptotherium had lost interest in him as he moved away. Apparently believing that it had vanquished its enemy, it trundled towards some dense weeds and began to munch on their stems.

The smell of crushed plants wafted over Logan, followed by a far more offensive odor. He coughed. The stupid thing had suddenly passed an incredible amount of gas. It paused in its chewing, lifted its tail, and dumped a steaming load of manure in a large pile.

To Logan, it was like an offensive comment directed at him. He picked up a piece of rotten wood and hurled it at the creature. The missile bounced off its shell harmlessly. The animal didn't even stop eating.

Feeling defeated, Logan turned towards the east. The ocean couldn't be too far away. At least there wouldn't be any snakes on the beach. He started walking, then stopped.

Where were the houses? He'd been in his dad's front yard. He vaguely remembered falling into the drainage ditch. Now he was out in the woods somewhere. He didn't remember anything beyond landing on the ground in the ditch. There had been some sort of flash, hadn't there? Yes. He remembered that. Now, where was he? He didn't feel like his mind was working correctly. That brownie...

He looked around. Nothing but palms and weeds. Maybe if he found the ocean, he could decide which way to go to find help. There wasn't much undeveloped land along the shore. People had built on almost every foot. It wouldn't be hard to find someone to help him.

He put the glyptotherium out of his mind. It was too unbelievable.

An interminable time later, Logan pushed through a last fringe of scrub and reached the dunes. The sand was piled high at this point, separating the beach from the scrub-covered land. He slogged through some sea oats and up the sparsely covered slope, then stopped at the top.

The ocean glinted in the long rays of the setting sun. Waves crested several hundred yards off the beach and rolled in to fade into the wet sand. Some sanderlings dashed past, their short legs moving so rapidly they seemed like little clockwork birds.

The beach looked just as it had the last time he'd been here, except for one major difference. There were no houses anywhere, neither to the north nor the south. There was no sign that the beach had ever been occupied.

He looked far to the south. He should be able to see the Vehicle Assembly Building at Kennedy from here, but there was nothing. He came to attention as he saw a distant object. It looked like a boat for a moment, but then he decided it was just a breaking wave.

"What the hell happened to me?" he whispered. "Where is everyone?" He shook his head, rubbed the back of his neck, and then turned to face the north. There was something moving a long way down the beach. He squinted his eyes a little, trying to see more clearly. The wind was blowing hard from the east, carrying a fine mist of saltwater that almost acted like fog, when one looked at distant objects.

He walked along the top of the dunes for a hundred paces or so. The distant object became clearer. It looked like a sea turtle, heading inland. It was a little early in the evening. They generally waited until after dusk to come onshore and lay their eggs. This one was anticipating the sunset by at least an hour.

He started to go closer but suddenly stopped and dropped to the ground. A large cat, a lion or tiger, he couldn't see it well enough to tell, had appeared at the top of the dunes. It was looking down at the turtle at the moment, but he didn't want it to see him.

He wondered if it was tame or would it decide that he'd be easier prey than the turtle. At the moment, it was just watching the reptile. Either way, he felt paralyzed by fear.

The cat came to a decision and trotted down the embankment towards the turtle. The sea creature turned and began laboriously heading back to the safety offered by the water, but it was too late.

The big cat used one of its paws to flip the large reptile on its back. Then it set to work at ripping the softer undershell open while the turtle waved its flippers frantically.

Seagulls clustered above, calling out in excitement. They hovered just above the cat, waiting for a chance to snatch at the dying turtle's insides.

Logan was able to see a stripe-like pattern on its furry side, and he noticed that it had a very short tail.

It didn't really look like a tiger, but whatever it was, it was big enough to be dangerous. That was enough for him. He slid back into a lower spot, then crawled quickly towards the scrub and brush. He stopped as a horrible thought struck him. If there was one cat, or whatever it was, in the brush, there might be others. What if he walked right up to one without noticing it?

His hand unconsciously dropped to his waist, where it encountered something hard. The knife was still in its sheaf on his belt. He took hold of the grip, drawing confidence from its solidity. It was designed for heavy work. The blade was thick and long enough to do serious damage to even something like the cat he'd seen. He suddenly had a warm feeling for Larry. His aversion to knives seemed less bothersome, now that he had a need for defense.

He could see some taller trees in the near distance, inshore to the west. There were some pines mixed with some oaks. That might be the safest place. He could climb a tree. It was going to get dark soon, and there were no people about.

He still couldn't figure that out.

⎯⎯◦⎯⎯

The sun was nearly down by the time he arrived at the trees. He'd been afraid to move too quickly. It wouldn't do to make too much noise.

He'd been reduced to taking a few steps then pausing to listen. In this way, he reached the edge of the thicker brush. It was a little more open within the grove of trees. The shade seemed to keep the bushes from growing so thickly.

He walked cautiously through the trees, looking for one that was climbable but also high enough to offer some protection. He couldn't remember much about big cats, but he seemed to remember that they couldn't climb too well.

It was quiet in the woods, just a light breeze feathering through the upper branches. Logan had gradually opened his senses to what he felt was an unprecedented maximum. In so doing, he realized that he normally walked around with his eyes half-unseeing and his ears mostly closed. As for scent, he couldn't remember the last time he'd tried to detect something that way, but now his nostrils twitched to every breath of the breeze.

Living around lots of people and traffic made it necessary to screen out distractions. Here, in this place, wherever it was, he felt that it was important to his survival to become as aware as possible. It was a somewhat mind-altering experience. He felt closer to nature, more aware, and despite the sense of danger, more at ease, almost peaceful.

He gradually became aware that he was being watched. He first felt a slight unease that intensified until he looked around. A fox was watching him from the shelter of a nearby bush. When he saw it, he jumped involuntarily, and the animal disappeared. Logan looked around, feeling embarrassed. Foxes weren't dangerous as far as he knew, except maybe for rabies, but this one hadn't looked ill.

There was nothing around the trees but some gray squirrels making small 'chucks' in the foliage and a few small birds. He took his time, finally deciding on a large oak. It had one huge limb that contacted another, smaller tree. The smaller tree, possibly a swamp magnolia, had enough branches that it would be relatively easy to scale. The oak branch descended in a long arch to touch the magnolia about twenty feet up. If he climbed to that point, then worked his way across the branch to the oak's trunk, the main fork might be a safe haven.

He investigated the oak. It had a very thick trunk with no branches until the first high fork. That was at least thirty feet high. Crossing from the magnolia along the branch was the only way he could see that nearly any creature, except for a squirrel, could get up there. An active cat might climb the trunk if its claws could hold on to what was nearly a vertical surface. He hoped that the bark wouldn't support a tiger's weight and was reassured when he saw that the trunk was too large for any creature to wrap legs around it.

The only problem was that climbing across the long branch was a frightening pathway. If he fell, he'd be almost certain to injure himself seriously.

It was at that point that he heard a roar from only a few hundred yards away. The cat might have sensed him or not. It made no difference. By the time the echoes had faded, he was trying to edge off the magnolia onto the oak branch.

The long branch first flexed downwards, then reached a point of equilibrium with his weight. Gingerly, he straddled the limb and started scooting along it towards the big tree. He was about halfway there when he became aware that he was being watched from below.

He stopped moving, frozen in shock, his mind locked on the huge striped cat that was staring fixedly at him. It couldn't exist.

He wondered if he was still under the influence of the brownie. The creature watching him was large, almost lion or tiger-sized, and had a short tail like the one that had killed the turtle.

That was bad enough, but the things that caused his mind to white-out in terror were the two saber-like canine teeth that hung down a good six inches on each side of the cat's muzzle.

Logan clung to the branch desperately, feeling dizzy. It was a saber-toothed tiger. Such a thing couldn't be. They'd been extinct for thousands of years, but...he searched for alternate explanations.

Maybe someone had found some viable DNA and cloned one, and it had escaped. But, he hadn't seen anything in the news about such a project. He always read the science articles, too.

His mind started working along another line of thought. There were no houses on the beach, no sign of people anywhere. He remembered falling into the ditch in the dark. The second after he landed, it was daytime. What if he'd somehow fallen through a dimensional or temporal hole into another world? That kind of thing happened in fiction. Why not to him?

It was at that moment that the saber-tooth, tired of watching, leaped upward, reaching with its claws for his dangling feet. He yelped and watched it growing closer, almost in slow motion. It stretched at the very top of its jump, reaching, but the claws fell short. The cat dropped to the ground, recovered, and snarled at him.

The oak limb proved to be much easier to traverse after that. He moved steadily towards the fork of the big tree, the tiger pacing along below. Once he reached the fork, he eased off the branch and settled into the space between three large limbs. It was almost comfortable, save for the rough bark and the air plants that grew in the crevices.

The saber-tooth hadn't given up. He was now out of jumping range, but it circled the trunk a couple of times, then decided to try and climb to where he was. It took a short running jump, leaped up ten feet, and scrabbled with its claws, gaining another eight feet before losing its grip.

It dropped with another snarl, paused for a moment to re-evaluate the situation, then tried again. It made it a few feet higher but fell off before it was within ten feet of his perch. He took a deep breath. If the oak had been shorter, he'd be supper right now.

He pulled his knife and looked speculatively at it. The blade was maybe eight inches long. It was certainly heavy and long enough to kill the tiger if the cat would only cooperate.

He had a suspicion that it wouldn't care for that idea and would be likely to work out its anger on him. No, stabbing it wasn't even a remote option. He'd just have to wait it out.

The instant he thought of that, he realized that he had no water. The very idea made him thirsty. It had been hot; he'd been drinking beer and had eaten that damned brownie with whatever it was loaded with. He was thirsty now, and his sense of want was rapidly increasing.

He broke off a chunk of bark and threw it down, striking the cat on the back of its head. It jumped and snarled but didn't try to climb the tree again. Instead, it settled down a few feet away, looking like it was going to spend the night, its eyes fixed on him.

He leaned back and closed his eyes miserably, wondering just what he'd done to deserve this.

Chapter Eight

Adaptation

The moon was high, its bright rays shining through the oak leaves. The light made strange patterns and shapes on the ground between the dark shadows cast by the trees. The blotches of darkness seemed impenetrable, making it impossible to see what lurked below.

Despite his thirst, Logan had managed to sleep. He wasn't sure how long it had been, but the moon was now nearly overhead. It hadn't risen when he had dropped off to sleep.

He carefully studied the ground. There was no sign of the big cat. Perhaps it had left, looking for other prey. Surely there was something somewhere else to attract it, something easier to catch than one scrawny human in a tree.

For a time, he considered the idea of climbing down to look for water but rejected it. Even with the moonlight, he couldn't see well enough to be sure that the cat wasn't down there, hiding, waiting for him to make a stupid move.

He was uncomfortable. The tree seemed to be intent on impressing every nuance of its rough bark on his posterior. Changing position every thirty minutes or so made the fork of the branches barely tolerable. Thirst bothered him more and more as the stars wandered towards sunrise. All in all, it was an amazingly long and restless night.

Logan had always slept late, but now he wished the sun would rise quickly. He was beginning to think that the world had stopped revolving. When that idea first popped up, he snickered. Then he considered his situation.

He was in a tree, trying to avoid some kind of big and really toothy cat thing and trying to hold out until morning so he could get a drink. He'd been in the front yard, fallen into the drainage ditch, and then this place had somehow grabbed him. He hadn't consciously wanted to come here.

He'd...Oh! He'd wanted to escape that woman. Before that, he'd eaten that brownie. Maybe something in it had given – maybe was still giving him a bad trip.

She'd said it was very strong. Still, this didn't seem like a hallucination. Everything was too real. It had that unmistakable feeling of reality, not like a dream or any kind of altered state of consciousness.

Whatever had happened to thrust him into this situation, it was beyond his understanding. It may have been related to the brownie, or it may simply have been chance. It seemed that somehow he'd fallen through a hole, ending in another world, or...another time.

The cat-creature gave one clue. He hadn't looked too closely at it, being more concerned with avoiding its jumps, but it had a tawny, sort of stripey coat and a short tail. The most obvious feature was its huge teeth. He'd thought that it reminded him of a saber-tooth tiger, but they were extinct. Only maybe not in this place. Maybe here they still prowled around looking for people to eat.

He shortly gave up trying to figure out what had happened. In a sense, it didn't matter. He was here now, and he had to learn how to survive until he could get back to where he'd come from. It really was that simple.

The idea crossed his mind that he might not be able to go back, but he shoved that concept away. That wasn't something he wanted to consider.

By this time, it was getting light. The sun was peeping over the horizon out at sea. Its light was gradually infiltrating the foliage that surrounded him. Somewhere a bird started up, singing its morning song. The song quickly changed and then changed again. It was a mockingbird; had to be. Nothing else sang so many songs at peak volume.

He heaved a sigh of relief. At least he was still on Earth. He'd feared for a moment that he might be on another planet. All he'd had to go on was the impossible cat of the saber-tooth variety. A mockingbird was at least familiar. It made the place seem very Florida-like, despite the lack of people and houses.

Logan maneuvered around and stood up, trying to stretch the cramps out of his neck and back while he waited for his left leg to regain its circulation. He'd been sitting in a way that wedged it tightly into the fork of the tree. Now it hurt and tingled.

He carefully edged over and rested his hand on one of the more vertical branches, unzipped his pants, and relieved himself. The stream spattered on the dried leaves below. There was no answering sound. He'd half expected the cat to come charging out at the noise.

Finished, he began to edge onto the connecting branch to the magnolia tree. He'd descend carefully, then see about a drink. The idea of water tormented him, and he had to mentally restrain his movements. It wouldn't be good to slip and fall. He had to be careful.

He reached the magnolia with no sign of his feline attacker. Just to make sure, he broke off a rotten stub and threw it into the bushes. It made a gratifying rustle and crunch. Then all was silent except for the mockingbird. It continued to sing somewhere, over near the edge of the stand of trees.

That was a good sign, wasn't it? Logan believed that birds might be quiet or sound some kind of alarm call if anything dangerous was nearby, but he wasn't sure that applied for mockingbirds. All his wilderness experience was his brief time at the dig site and, years ago, a week at summer camp with the Cub Scouts. He was realistic enough to recognize that he couldn't really rely on the information he'd seen on TV. Maybe mockingbirds in this place didn't act like ones he'd seen around people's houses.

"I wish I'd read more prepper stuff on the Internet," he muttered as he climbed down the smaller tree.

The last branch was about five feet up, and it decided that his weight was too much this time around. It snapped, precipitating him onto the ground in an undignified fashion. The fall knocked the wind out of him. He staggered to his feet, looking wildly around, preparing to either run or climb the tree again.

Nothing happened. The saber-tooth must have given up and gone elsewhere for its meal. Still, he felt a little nervous. He quickly moved to the cover of the underbrush. As he pushed through the bushes, something rustled on the other side. He continued forward, emerging just in time to see the tail of a fox retreating into a palmetto thicket. He wondered if it were the same animal.

The beach was over towards the sunrise. That made sense, as did the idea that there wouldn't be any freshwater over there. So, he'd have to go the other direction. He threaded his way between the bushes, trying his best not to make any noise. It was harder than he'd thought. The dry leaves crunched, as did a stick that he stepped on.

After a while, he reached an area that was full of brush. He could see that he was near the edge of the trees. The brush was the last barrier before he reached a more open space.

He wormed his way through the stuff, recognizing and avoiding a patch of poison ivy on the way. Lucky thing that he knew what that looked like.

Abruptly, the brush ended. He looked between two huge leaves and saw that he was facing a grassy area surrounded by trees. There were numerous cabbage palms scattered across the area, but not so many that he couldn't see the far side.

He decided to check thoroughly, before he stepped out, exposing himself to potentially hostile eyes. He searched the space carefully, seeing nothing. Waiting would not get him a drink. He started forward, then jerked and retreated to better cover.

There was movement on the other side of the open space. He watched intently. It was a...a woman. She was running in his direction, followed closely by a man. The man had gray hair and was having difficulty keeping up. She looked much younger and was easily out-pacing him. The old guy was limping slightly. She paused to look back, motioning impatiently for him to hurry.

Logan was paralyzed by the sight. The two were wearing clothes that looked like they were made out of animal hide, and the man was carrying what appeared to be a handful of slender spears. It was like a scene out of a movie about prehistoric times he'd once seen.

He watched, fascinated. About halfway across the space, the old man stumbled and fell. The girl, for that was what Logan now realized she was, turned, ran back, and grabbed his arm, tugging. While she tried to help him recover, there was a shout from the far side of the field. The two turned to look. The old man said something and motioned to the girl to continue running.

It was obvious that she didn't want to leave him. She said something back, and he turned to shove her. She walked a few steps, looked back, and then began to run with a smooth stride as he motioned again.

There was a sudden chorus of cries from the distance. They sounded like a pack of hounds on the trail of prey, but the noises were obviously of human origin. Logan could see a group of men burst out of the underbrush, running directly towards the old man.

The old guy had moved behind a cabbage palm, but the others knew where he was. They slowed and then spread out as they got close. They, too, were carrying spears. With a lightning-like throw, the old man let one of his missiles fly. Somehow it appeared to separate, leaving a short stick still in his hand.

The light spear flew much farther than Logan had believed it would. It was well aimed, too. It caught one of the pursuers right in the chest. The man cried out and fell on his back, disappearing in the grass. Logan could still see the end of the spear shaft pointing straight towards the sky, wobbling back and forth as the wounded man thrashed around.

The other pursuers let out yells of anger and threw their own spears back. The old man had retreated behind the cabbage palm, and the spears flew past his position to stick in the ground.

He grabbed one of the nearest ones, fitted it to the stick he held, and hurled it back. That one missed.

Logan was so fascinated that he'd forgotten about the girl. When he remembered her, she was just darting into the tree line about two hundred yards to his left.

He jerked his head back towards the fight. There had been a triumphant scream.

One of the pursuing men had struck the old man with a thrown spear. It was now sticking completely through the old guy's left thigh. That didn't stop him, however. He calmly threw another spear right back at the group, hitting another man in the stomach. That man sat down in the grass, slumped over.

Logan was beginning to realize that this was real and it was serious. Those guys weren't playing. He was watching a real-life battle, one that the older man wasn't going to win.

The group of men had spread out so that the cabbage palm no longer offered shelter. The old guy threw one more spear, but his leg prevented him from launching it with the same speed. It wobbled, missing its target.

Two spears arched in, striking the old man in the chest and abdomen. He dropped to his knees, tugging at the one in his chest. The pursuers dashed up to stand jeering at the old man.

He struggled to his feet, waving what was surely some kind of knife. One of the others thrust a spear into his back and he dropped to his hands and knees with a cry. Another man caught the long gray hair, yanked the old man's head up, and slashed his throat. Logan could see the red gout of blood.

Meanwhile, two of the others had taken off along the path that the girl had taken. The rest of the men stood in a loose group, watching the old man bleed out.

Logan suddenly realized that he was probably in a lot of danger. Those guys were killers, and their spears were lethal. He drew back farther into the heavy undergrowth, then turned and headed away from the point where the girl had entered the tree line. He wanted no part of the fight, and, besides, he didn't know her.

To give him some credit, he did think momentarily about trying to help her, but his thinking didn't get beyond the fact that he only had a knife while the pursuers had spears that they could hurl improbably far. He couldn't see how he could help. Maybe she had enough of a head start that she could escape. She was a fast runner. The only way the pursuing group had caught the two was due to the old man playing out.

———◆———

Sometime later, he crawled into a thicket to catch his breath. He couldn't hear anything from the pursuing men. They could be anywhere as far as he could tell. He didn't think they'd caught the girl. They would have set up a ruckus if they had.

The men hadn't seemed worried about any saber-tooth cats. Maybe being in a group with those spear-throwing things was enough protection. Logan didn't know and didn't care. He now had one driving purpose: to get a drink. His thirst had increased exponentially as the sun rose and as he exerted himself, fleeing the violent scene.

He had traveled maybe a couple of miles and felt fairly sure the bad guys wouldn't catch him. They were probably chasing the girl towards the coast.

He'd started thinking of the pursuers as the 'bad guys' since they had killed the old man, and were chasing the girl. She'd looked like she was about his age, and he unthinkingly took her side.

The ground was squishing a little as he walked. There was water nearby. The cabbage palms had thinned out, to be replaced by reeds. He moved through the thicket to a vantage point where he could look out over the grass-covered area again. There was a thick stand of reeds that looked like it might be a place to get a drink. He stayed low, scuttling from one bit of cover to another through the tall grass.

He arrived at a point where the ground became really mushy. He was moving through vegetation-covered muck. The reeds were thinner to the north, so he headed in that direction, coming out onto a muddy shore that fronted a small creek. The creek wound through the reeds in such a manner that there was little visibility either up or down its length.

He hesitated at the verge of the grass, wondering if there would be any disease in the water. Thirst drove him forward, leaving him no choice. He moved over the shallow mud and muck, kneeling at the water to scoop some up in his hand. It tasted heavenly. He slurped several handfuls and then bent down closer with the intent of sucking water directly from the surface.

As he bent down, he suddenly realized that there was a large shadow under the water. It hadn't been there previously. It also had two protruding eyes that were watching him. They started to move towards him, and he jumped to his feet and backed rapidly away. The alligator broke the surface with a splash, hissing in frustration at missing its prey. The thing was probably over a thousand pounds and looked like it was almost fourteen feet in length.

Logan had lived in Florida all of his life, and he knew a little about gators. This was the largest one he'd ever seen. Even larger than the biggest one at Gatorland Zoo, an Orlando tourist attraction that he'd been to a couple of times. He jumped to the side and ran as the creature lunged out of the water. It could strike very quickly but couldn't follow at top speed for a long distance.

Back in the thicket, Logan caught his breath. This was turning out to be an awful day. He considered. He'd nearly gotten eaten last night, then speared, and now nearly eaten again. At this rate, he'd be toast before more than another couple of days had passed. He'd have to be more circumspect. This place was dangerous.

A dry buzzing caught his attention. He froze, looking around. There it was: a rattlesnake. Big and mean, it was coiled under a bush a few feet away. Before it decided to move towards him, he was out of the thicket and heading back towards the taller trees.

—◆—

Nighttime found him in a tree near a small, water-filled sinkhole. There were some cattails in the water, and he'd grubbed out some of their tuber-like roots to fill the void in his stomach.

The night was hot, humid, and still. The local mosquitoes had located him, even though he was high in the branches. They hadn't found him the night before, but now he was on the menu, and it looked like they were determined to keep him awake all night despite his use of a broken, leafy branch to swish them away.

The moon rose, illuminating a quiet scene. The mosquitoes had given up about six hours after dark, and Logan was now trying to sleep while holding onto the narrow branches of his perch. He'd gotten used to the night sounds – the raucous frogs, the grunting of gators off in a hole somewhere. He sat up twice, eyes wide, listening when the distant screaming call of a large cat echoed through the trees. Sleeping in a tree wasn't his idea of an ideal situation, but at least it was relatively secure.

Chapter Nine

Discovery

The next day started with a series of roars that echoed through the trees. Logan jerked awake, clutching at the branches as he almost fell. Sleeping in trees was uncomfortable, and the repercussion for falling out of bed was likely to be serious. Still, it was better than the alternative: being waked by some predator jumping on him.

The sound wasn't repeated for several minutes. Then it came again. This time it was from much farther away. His cramped seat in the tree abruptly became unbearably painful, and he decided that he might be better off eaten than having to spend any more time off the ground.

Once down, Logan slipped through the brush until he reached a still pool that he'd located the evening before. He maneuvered through some vines and leaned out, resting his hands on a partially submerged log. He could see some small fish swimming below. They investigated some debris that his hands had knocked into the clear water.

He looked carefully around for any alligators and then lowered his head to drink. When he raised it again, he glanced across the pool. There were two eyes peering through the bushes directly at him.

A shudder of surprise shot unpleasantly up his back as his eyes met the ones across the pool. The distant eyes moved a little closer through the intervening leaves, and the surrounding face resolved to that of a young woman. Her long brown hair hung freely on either side of her perfectly proportioned face. He drew a reflexive sigh. She was beautiful.

She smiled a mysterious half-smile, then stepped backward and disappeared.

Logan started to call to her, but then caution regained control of his mind. There might be predators or, what was maybe worse, some of the spear-carrying men he'd seen. That led to another consideration. His lips moved, silently forming a question. "I wonder if she was the one I saw running from the pursuers?"

He pulled back and started around the sinkhole. Then stopped in doubt. If I go one direction and she comes the other, I'll miss her, he thought.

After a moment, he continued. The girl had looked friendly. At least she hadn't made an angry or fierce face at him. She was also beautiful. Everything about her, or at least as much as he'd seen, was attractive. Even the mud smeared on her cheek had seemed to be artfully arranged to enhance her cheekbones. It had added an air of mysterious enticement to her already intriguing look.

Logan continued working his way through the dense vegetation surrounding the deep pool. It took him some time to reach the other side, and when he did, he was disappointed. There was no sign of the girl. She had vanished.

He located the spot where she'd watched him. There was a single small footprint in a wet area. Beyond that, there was nothing. It was as if she'd never been. He was left wondering if it had actually been his imagination. He looked around, rubbing the back of his neck, but there was no clue as to her location.

There were some crows calling in the distance. It sounded like they'd found something to which they took objection. Maybe it was her. He started off, moving in the direction of their raucous calls.

When he drew close, he could see a flock of perhaps thirty of the birds clustered in the tops of several longleaf pines growing in a sandy spot. The crows were taking turns dive-bombing at a hawk that was perched on one of the higher limbs. The hawk, in turn, was doing his best to ignore the vituperation, only ducking once in a while when one of the glossy black birds zoomed too close.

The crows kept up their noise, cursing at the hapless hawk. Logan turned and strode away in disgust, trying to distance himself from the noise. He hadn't gone more than a hundred paces when he saw a panther, its eyes intent on the noisy birds. The cat was far off, partially hidden in some palmettos and scrub, and it hadn't seen him yet.

He ducked behind a convenient sand pine trunk, plotting out a retreat that wouldn't expose him to its gaze. He'd been lucky that it was fixated on the crows. There was a large thicket just a few yards away. He crawled until he was behind it, hoping that he hadn't been spotted.

Regaining his feet, he headed quickly away. It would be a good idea to have some weapon besides the knife. The knife was sharp, but the idea of hand-to-hand fighting with a panther or saber-tooth cat was not something he wanted to contemplate. Perhaps he could create some sort of spear. For that, he needed a nice, straight sapling. He began to look for a suitable shaft.

Logan had walked for several hours. The sun was now past the zenith and heading down. He'd been more concerned with thirst at first, but now hunger was setting in, and his stomach was rumbling.

The cattails had been okay, but they didn't seem to satisfy the gnawing in his middle. He hadn't wanted to try them again, but now he was more motivated. Unfortunately, he couldn't seem to locate any of the water plants.

He knew there were numerous edible plants in Florida, but some were deadly too. He was afraid to experiment; his knowledge was so spotty that he might inadvertently pick the wrong thing to eat.

As he was working his way through a thicket under oak trees, he found some scuppernong grapes on a vine that extended high into a tree. They were ripe, and he eagerly ate as many as he could reach.

Finishing the last of the grapes he'd picked, he paused and held one up to the light between his thumb and forefinger. It was definitely ripe. That was about right for August. Still, he looked at the grape suspiciously and then at the sun. Wherever he was or whenever he was, the time of year was about the same as when he'd last been at his dad's house, but that didn't really tell him anything. Where was he anyway?

His mind skittered away from the question, interrupted by a crackle of brush nearby. Something large was moving through the undergrowth. Another noise sounded from farther off. It sounded like something rumbling. He tried to place the sound. The creature in the thicket made a rumbling noise in return, echoing the first animal. It was improbably loud. Suddenly his mind clicked. It sounded like elephants.

A giant shape broke out of the bushes, moving towards the space between two oak trees. Logan caught a glimpse of the beast's side. It looked like a huge boulder covered with long, shaggy hair. On the verge of panic, he slowly lowered himself to the ground, then slithered as best he could across a few yards into some tall, coarse grass.

He could hear the beast ripping branches off the trees, intermixed with a crunching sound as it chewed on the twigs. Heart beating a tattoo and feeling short of breath, Logan tried to calm himself. He took several deep breaths, gradually slowing his pulse rate.

His mind began to work again. That thing was a mammoth! It could be nothing else. He didn't know much about prehistoric fauna, having spent most of his time studying later middle-eastern civilizations, but he definitely knew what a mammoth was supposed to look like. And this was definitely a mammoth.

As he lay in the grass, he could hear the sounds of other herd members all around him. This wasn't an optimal situation. They might not care about him, but he was pretty sure that they wouldn't view his intrusion into the middle of their herd favorably. If they discovered him, he feared they would become aggressive.

He began to slide along, trying to stay in concealment. After a bit, he neared a more open place. There was a thicket to his right and some large palms to his left. There didn't seem to be any of the huge beasts nearby, and he believed he could slip into the thicket. He was on the verge of moving over to it when he caught sight of the girl.

She was standing far back among the palm trunks, looking directly at him. When she saw that she had his attention, she motioned for him to come towards her. He pointed at the thicket, and she shook her head violently back and forth. Her flying hair seemed to make the negative even more forceful. Logan, glancing back over his shoulder, rose and trotted, stooped over, into the palms.

When he stood up, he could just see her back, receding rapidly into the trees. Forgetting about the mammoths for the moment, he gave chase. She was far more experienced at moving quietly, and his progress created considerable noise. There was an alarmed trumpet behind him, followed immediately by trumpets and rumbles from the rest of the herd.

The sound stimulated him to even greater effort, and he sprinted through the heavy stand of cabbage palms, zig-zagging between the trees in a way that would have done credit to an NFL running back. There was a crashing noise from behind him. One of the beasts was following.

The mammoth quit pursuing after fifty paces or so, evidently deciding that it had successfully seen him off. It was fortunate because Logan's breath gave out shortly after it broke off its charge.

He stopped to pant, his hands on his knees. When he recovered enough to look around, there was no sign of the girl. He'd lost her, or perhaps more to the point, she'd lost him. He didn't dare call out, so he continued on in as straight a direction as he could manage through the trees.

The palms seemed to go on forever, but he noticed that the ground was getting muckier as he progressed. He was brought up short by a stand of tall grass that proved to have saw-like edges. Even brushing it lightly left scratches on his skin that bleed as if he'd been trying to give a cat a bath. He wiped the blood from his arm and muttered, "Can't go that way. Sawgrass. Maybe to the left."

He turned and followed along the edge of the grass. After weaving back and forth for what must have been a mile or so, he saw a bare footprint in a muddy area. It was smaller than his, and he felt that it might be the girl. Moreover, she was walking in the same direction as him. Congratulating himself for his good tracking skills, he continued.

Before he knew quite what was happening, pools of water covered with lily pads surrounded him. There were some cattails in the water, scattered among the lilies, so he took a moment to dig out some of the tubers. That helped with the hunger, which had not relented even in the excitement.

After eating the crunchy white interior of several of the tubers, Logan felt like he had a little more energy. It was time to renew his pursuit. The pools weren't connected and he hoped that he could thread his way through.

Sometime later, the sun was slanting downward towards a distant stand of trees. Logan was thoroughly exhausted and depressed, not to mention completely lost. He knew the directions. The sun was setting in the west, but he was surrounded by water and clumps of saw grass without any perceptible pathway to follow. There was the grunting noise of an alligator coming from the near distance. When it stopped, another answered from farther away. Frogs croaked from the pools, adding a low note to the harmony of red wing blackbirds calling from the reeds.

He decided that he'd better find someplace to lay up for the night just as the local mosquitoes found him. It quickly became apparent that he'd need more than just a place to lie down. The blasted bloodsuckers would most likely drink him dry if given half a chance.

Waving his arms to try and keep them off his face didn't work. Finally, in desperation, he grabbed up a double handful of muck and smeared the mud all over his head. Blinking his eyes to clear them, he followed suit with his arms and neck. That helped immensely. The mosquitoes seemed baffled by the mud layer.

Not so with his clothes, though. They were able to stick their pointy mouthparts through the fabric of both his pants and teeshirt. More mud helped there also. There was a moment where he cringed about applying the muck, but he rationalized that he could always go for a swim tomorrow and wash it off, provided he could find a pool that wasn't filled with gators. As the night drew close, more and more of them seemed to be grunting all around him.

Judging by the taller trees, there looked like there might be a bit of slightly higher ground ahead. He recognized the low island as what was called a hammock. It was covered with trees. They were mostly cypress with some longleaf pines interspersed. He headed that way with as much speed as he could muster.

The higher ground of the hammock was perhaps five hundred yards away when he stopped short. Someone had just started a fire far back in the trees.

Logan didn't know what to do. It might be the girl, but he felt that she probably wouldn't advertise her presence in that way after having successfully eluded the men who'd killed her companion. It was more likely to be those men than her.

It struck Logan that people who lit a fire were probably in a group large enough to deal with unexpected threats. He wanted to go close and try to see who it was, but caution overcame that urge.

Disappointed, he turned towards a smaller hammock that was farther towards the west. About an hour later, in the dim gloaming, he found a lone oak tree that was big enough to provide a perch for the night. After a mad scramble to avoid falling, he fetched up in a moderately comfortable crotch.

It had been a long day filled with both fear and frustration. He'd been in denial about the long-toothed cat creature's identification, but recognizing the mammoths had forced him to mentally accept the fact that somehow, in some miraculous manner, he'd been transported into the distant past. With that idea in mind, he suddenly understood the weapons he'd seen the pursuing men using. They'd been using atl-atls – spear-throwers. That was why the spears seemed to separate in their hands.

He was back in prehistory at a point before the bow and arrow had been discovered. The concept was depressing in the extreme. How would he return to his own time?

His mind skittered over the events that led to his ending up here. It was too – too, maybe "spooky" was the right word. Now that he'd discovered more or less where, no, when he was, he wanted to get back to his own time more than anything else. He just didn't know how to accomplish that goal.

He tried to relax, and the thought came to him that his first priority was simply to survive. If the dangers he'd encountered so far were typical, that might not be easy. If he could survive, maybe he'd be able to eventually get back to the present.

A mosquito bit his forehead through a crack in the mud coating, and Logan slapped ineffectually at it. He had to quit thinking of when he came from as the present. He was in the present now. Only it was the wrong present, maybe twelve thousand years before he was due to be born.

Another image drifted into his mind. The intriguing girl. He hadn't seen her closely, but his impression was that she was more than moderately attractive.

No, on second thought, he was sure that she was beautiful. He drifted off to sleep with her image in his mind.

Chapter Ten

A Meeting and a Killing

Logan woke in the middle of the night. The moon was filtering through the branches above him, but that wasn't what had disturbed him. Something was moving around the tree on the ground below his perch.

From the sound of it, it was dangerous. There was a low snarl, followed by a sudden scrabble as it began to climb the tree. Totally awake now, he grasped at an overhanging limb and worked his way higher into the upper branches. Whatever it was, it wasn't having an easy time getting up the thick trunk.

In a few moments, Logan was high in the tree. The branches were thinner here, and they flexed alarmingly with his weight. Fearfully, he stared back down into the darker foliage below. There was something there. It disappeared then appeared a few seconds later on a closer limb. He suddenly saw a faintly glowing pair of eyes that were fixed on him. They moved closer. All at once, he could make out that it was a panther.

As if signaled by his recognition, the big cat screamed and lunged upwards, clawing at the branches for purchase. Logan moved farther out on the thin web of branches. They sagged under his weight, lowering him down to almost eye level with the climbing predator. It paused, evaluating the situation, then began to climb higher.

When it reached the limbs holding him, it tentatively moved outward on them. One made a cracking sound, and Logan dropped farther. He was now posed a short distance above a larger limb, one that was sufficiently thick to support his weight.

The cat moved closer, snarling as it worked its way through the intervening branches and twigs. In a rush of fear, Logan scrambled around so that both legs were clear, then dropped to the lower limb, snatched at it, slipped, then secured himself. The lightened limbs he'd left flipped up, almost dislodging the panther. It recovered and stared down at him.

The cat shifted its weight. It looked like it was considering leaping down on him. Reflexively, Logan pulled his knife, raising it towards the animal just as it sprang. By some miracle, he managed to ram the razor-sharp blade directly under the panther's gaping jaws.

The shock forced the animal's head back as it instinctively tried to strike whatever had wounded its throat. The paws slashed but missed a grip on Logan's arm. He yanked back, pulling the knife out, as the animal dropped past the limb.

The cat tried to recover, twisting in mid-air, but missed its grip on the branches. It descended through the leaves, crashing down to the ground, where it struck with a thud and a grunt. Logan came close to following it down. After a moment, he righted himself over the limb he was on. His arms were bleeding, as much from the rough bark as from the one minor scratch on his left arm the panther had made.

Shakily, he reinserted the knife into its sheathe. He thought gratefully about Larry's generosity. The man had undoubtedly saved his life with the gift.

He listened carefully. All was silent from below. It was as if the panther had never been.

As he listened, there came a series of deep howls from the far distance. Logan sighed. Wolves! What next? Dinosaurs?

After a time, he descended a little to a more secure location. Bracing his back against a thin, vertical branch, he tried to get some rest. He didn't want to go back to the original crotch where he'd planned on spending the night. It was too low. If the panther had been able to climb the thick trunk more quickly, it might have reached him before he could get to the thin branches.

———⊷———

He was awake as the birds began to sing. It was still very dim, but dawn was in the sky, and a couple of mockingbirds were engaging in a loud, vocal duel nearby. Their virtuosity was amazing. They seemed to have a precise knowledge of many different songbird calls.

Logan listened for a little while, then began to work his way lower in the tree. It was almost light enough to see the ground clearly. There was a dim lump down there, but he wasn't taking chances. It might be the panther, or it might not.

It grew lighter until he could see clearly. The panther hadn't survived its fall. It wasn't moving. He believed that it was dead.

Working his way down the craggy bark with his back to the beast was nerve-wracking. It might be shamming, just waiting for him to climb down.

Once he got his feet on the ground, he could see that it hadn't moved. He approached and gingerly poked at its leg with his toe. Nothing. Not even a twitch.

He grabbed the tail and gave a good jerk, then jumped back. The cat was dead. There was a pool of blood around the matted fur of its neck. The cat's impact hadn't killed it. The knife had done the job.

Looking all around in a somewhat ashamed fashion, Logan considered. He was practically starved. This was meat. He'd never considered eating a panther, and it seemed somehow barbarous. It was a beautiful animal, and he felt guilty about killing it. His stomach, however, had other ideas. It was so empty that even the thought of cat meat was enough to make it release a huge gush of acid.

Rubbing his belly, he bent, then grabbed one of the cat's legs and began to try to skin it with the knife, quelling his aversion to the sharp edge of the blade.

To his surprise, the skin came off easily. Once he'd slit along one side and cut around the foot and upper thigh, it hung loosely and came free with a minimum amount of work.

The leg muscle was covered with a shiny membrane. He cut into it and removed a hunk of meat. It smelled bloody. It would be one thing if he had some way to make a fire like whoever he'd seen last night on the other hammock. But, he considered, maybe it wouldn't be such a good idea to give away his position with a column of smoke. Cooking odors would carry a long way on the light morning breeze. He really needed to know more about other humans in the area. Were they friendly or automatically hostile to strangers?

Steeling himself, he cut off a bite-sized chunk, stuck it into his mouth, and chewed experimentally. It was chewy and tasted a bit like pork. He shut his eyes and gulped it down, expecting to feel queasy. Surprisingly, his stomach didn't seem to share his revulsion. Maybe he could get used to eating raw meat.

Feeling full, Logan leaned back against the tree trunk rubbing his belly. It had been his first real meal in the past, or here and now – whatever. He mentally shrugged. He'd been hungry, and the panther had solved that problem.

Now, how could he preserve the meat for later? It wouldn't last. Already flies were buzzing around the carcass.

He wondered if he could remove the skin and pack some meat in it. Skinning the entire animal seemed like it might be outside of his range of abilities, though. Even if he could get the skin off and somehow construct a pack or a bag to carry the meat in, it wouldn't last more than a few hours in the humid heat.

He compromised by carefully cutting the remaining hind leg free along with a long strip of skin. He tied the skin to the leg at both ends, forming a loop, and strung it over his shoulder, so that the leg bumped along at his waist. He could carry it for a while and maybe, if he was lucky, have lunch or even supper before the meat turned.

The next thing was to decide where to go. This swampy area seemed to hold more mosquitoes than the sandy land nearer the coast where he'd started. Maybe it would be better to go back there.

Midday found him huddled under a palm in a downpour. The rain was cold, chilling him to the bone despite the heat that the day had started with.

The shower gradually ceased as it blew off towards the swampier land to the west.

The wind had picked up with the storm, adding to his misery. It was humid, and the gusts didn't help to dry his shirt and pants. The only good thing he could find was that the mud was mostly washed off of his skin. His clothes were stained a dark brownish-black, but most of the caked soil was gone.

He squished along for a while, then stopped and addressed himself to the panther leg. It hadn't become any more attractive by his ill-treatment and by being soaked. The meat wasn't precisely high, but it definitely was less appealing. He pondered discarding it, but he needed the calories to keep moving and to stay warm.

Despite the wind, flies buzzed around his head, attracted by the meat smell, landing on his face and arms, forcing him to wave them off. They kept landing on the scratch on the back of his arm left by the panther. Maybe it smelled similar to the slightly decomposing panther meat. Logan tried not to think about it.

He choked down several mouthfuls then stopped as a wave of nausea threatened to overcome him. It passed, and he decided it was more mental than physical. Eating raw meat was something he could do, but now he knew that he wanted it to be as fresh as possible.

Logan looked dubiously at the remains of the panther leg. There was enough meat left for supper if he could stomach it. Should he discard it or continue carrying it?

Better to have it, he guessed. Sighing, he looped the hide over his shoulder and set out looking for water.

It was odd. The rain had soaked him completely, and the underbrush was wet, making it miserable to push through, but there was no standing water. It had seemingly vanished into the sandy ground. At least that was something in his favor.

After a mile or so, he came up to a small lake. Shaking his head in confusion, he wondered where this had been when he came by this way before. He believed he knew where he was, but the lake was something he hadn't seen unless he just didn't recognize it. He was so lost, that was a definite possibility.

He moved through the thinner brush, looking for an open area. At last, he pushed his way through some brush, taking care to keep away from a huge patch of thorny bushes. He came out on a small bank that sloped steeply down to the water.

There was a fallen tree that had toppled long ago from its spot on the bank. The roots were still partially entangled in the soil, but the trunk extended out into the water, gradually submerging. This seemed to offer a perfect place for him to slide out and get a drink from the clearer water away from the shore.

He worked out onto the trunk, carefully watching his steps so that he wouldn't trip, then lowered himself to his hands and knees. Then he moved forward until he could reach the water with his cupped hands. It was good, and he concentrated on quenching his thirst.

Logan reached for another palm of water and recoiled as an alligator lunged forward. The ambush predator had come along the edge of the log where he hadn't noticed it. Its snapping jaws clomped shut just shy of his hand.

He was about to become lunch himself. The alligator could easily lunge high enough to snatch him off the log. He leaped upright, slipped, almost toppled in, and started to step back.

The gator, not to be denied, lunged again, thrusting its heavy body partway out of the water, coming up and over the submerged branches, its jaws gaping open.

A head-sized piece of rock flew past Logan's side, landing directly in the open jaws. The alligator reflexively snapped down on the rough coral stone, then began to thrash around in pain, trying to rid itself of the rock which had gone deep into the back of its mouth.

Logan turned and sprinted up the log to come face to face with the girl he'd been trying to find. She jumped back with an exclamation before they collided. He tried to pull himself up from the rush but tripped on a vine and landed on his hands and knees, looking up at her.

She looked at him for a moment, her mouth partway open in shock, then a mischievous grin gradually swept over her face, making her look like a delighted pixie. She laughed quietly, then pointed at him and motioned for him to follow her.

Sheepishly, he climbed to his feet and started to resettle the panther leg. She caught at it, pulled it close, examined it, then looked appraisingly at him in a way that seemed to imply she was re-evaluating him. She felt the claws, then looked at his arms.

He held out his left arm to display the scratch the cat had left. It was a little red. She grabbed his hand, lowered her head to the scratch, and sniffed. Then she looked directly into his eyes, said something in a musical voice, and waited for his response expectantly.

Logan was entranced. She looked younger than he, but not by much. Dressed in animal hide clothing, and with her light brown hair hanging loosely, she seemed a forest spirit rather than a girl. They were standing so close that he could see beads of sweat on her face and in the fine, blond hairs on her upper lip. He was momentarily speechless.

He drew a deep breath. She was sweating, and he could smell her odor. It seemed to mesh perfectly with his olfactory receptors. He felt his blood quicken in response.

"Thanks for saving me," he said.

She jumped at his words, responding with another indecipherable burst of words in her musical tone.

Logan shook his head and said, "I don't speak your language. Sorry. You saved my life back there." He pointed back at the lake and made his hands open and close like an alligator's jaws.

Her eyes sparkled. She laughed and mimicked his motion, then pointed at the water and said something that sounded vaguely disparaging. He got the idea that she was telling the gator it was no good.

She stopped talking, abruptly turned, and started off, walking steadily towards what Logan believed was the northwest. Startled, he called, "Wait, where are you going?"

She glanced back and motioned for him to follow.

Logan looked to the east, thinking of the shore, but then started after her. There was really no choice. She knew how to survive, and he didn't. She probably knew where she was going. Hopefully, it was someplace safe. The fear that she might lead him into an ambush crossed his mind, but he couldn't entertain such perfidy in her. She was just too attractive, and she seemed friendly. He couldn't see her saving him, only to lead him to his death later. Besides, at that moment, she stopped and looked back, smiling at him over her shoulder.

—◆—

He followed her deeper into the swampy area. By late afternoon, they were far out into the St. Johns river basin. It was swampy with saw grass, cattails, and reeds. There were cypress-covered hammocks scattered across the landscape.

These higher spots of land varied in size from small ones with only a few trees to ones larger than two or three football fields, covered with a thick growth of cypress, sometimes interspersed with long-leaf pines. The sun bore down, masked at times by puffy cumulus clouds that marched westward in the onshore breeze from the Atlantic.

Their journey was made without speech. Every time he tried to communicate with her, she smiled and placed two fingers lightly on his lips, indicating that he should be silent. For her part, she never made an effort to speak.

Logan saw an Osprey hovering over an open body of water, deciding if it had a chance to stoop at a fish. A Florida Kite was flying near the closest hammock, its deeply forked tail enabling it to maneuver back and forth, wobbling along the edge of the trees in search of food. The Kite moved with an economy that left Logan feeling out of breath and stodgy. It rarely flapped its wings, instead catching the breeze and updrafts in a way that was almost effortless.

Herons and egrets clustered at water's edge, and bitterns boomed from the tall reeds. Frogs croaked incessantly. Here and there a red wing black-bird perched on a reed calling a series of liquid notes. Gators grunted in the distance.

The time seemed to pass quickly. He followed her, his eyes on the soft sway of her skin-clad hips. She carried nothing, no weapons, no food, but somehow he had the feeling that she was as at home as he might be on an afternoon excursion to the grocery store.

Eventually, they approached a smaller hammock, and it became apparent that was where she was headed. They waded for nearly a mile through shallow water. The bottom was covered with decayed vegetation and their steps stirred up swirls of darker water. Fortunately, there seemed to be firm sand under the muck, so they didn't sink in.

They finally reached a long sandy spit that was bordered by tall reeds on either side. The reeds formed a narrow pathway that wound back and forth, preventing them from seeing any great distance ahead.

Logan was looking up as he walked and was startled when he bumped into the girl. She'd halted, staring at a man with a heavily scarred face who'd just walked into sight no more than twenty feet ahead of them. The man was frozen in mid-stride, one foot partly lifted as he took in the two.

He had a small deer carcass slung over his right shoulder, and his left hand carried some slim sticks. He dropped the deer with a thud, reached for a pouch at his waist, and came up with some kind of stone knife.

With a quick spin, the girl moved behind Logan, leaving him facing Scarface. The man said something that sounded hostile but which made no sense to Logan.

Understanding that the girl expected him to protect her, he replied, "Yeah. I'm not glad to see you either, Mister Scarred Guy."

The hunter yelled at this, then charged directly at Logan, knife upraised.

Without thinking, Logan stepped into a right-leg sidekick, catching the man in the solar plexus. The knife came down, slicing through Logan's pants. A brief pain shot through his calf, but the strike mostly missed.

Logan recovered, then delivered a front kick, trying to catch the man's lowered chin. The hunter started to dodge, and the kick grazed his cheek, making him stagger to the left. Finding himself almost face-to-face with the man, Logan blocked the knife arm with his wrists crossed, then caught the wrist with one hand, pulling the man's fingers open with the other. The hapkido move worked perfectly, leaving Logan holding the knife.

He was unprepared for the counter-strike. The hunter slammed his other hand into Logan's temple. Scarface was unexpectedly strong. Stars flashed in Logan's vision, and the knife flew out of his hand. The next minute, the man had his arms around Logan and the two fell to the ground, hunter on top.

Scarface struck at Logan's head again, but Logan partly blocked, holding his arms over his face. The man raised his right fist for another strike but then suddenly arched his back, throwing his arms out to the sides, simultaneously making a cry of agony.

The girl was standing behind the man, stone knife in her hand, dripping blood. As Logan tried to understand what had happened, the hunter's mouth opened, and a gush of bright red blood vomited out, splattering Logan's face. He rolled, trying to avoid the blood, and the man fell to his side on the sand.

Logan jumped to his feet and fell into a guard position. As he did, the girl moved beside the man, grasped his long hair, and plunged the knife into his neck. More blood spurted.

Logan felt dizzy. He wasn't sure if it was the result of being punched or seeing her kill the man so adroitly. The girl spat some words at the dying hunter in a vituperative tone, then bent and removed the pouch from his possession.

She looked inside and nodded. Then she strung the strap over her shoulder and turned to Logan with a bright smile.

Her face, already pretty, transformed totally when she smiled. Logan found that he couldn't form a coherent thought. She said something quietly and placed her fingers on his lips when he tried to respond. Indicating that he should pick up the deer, she caught up the sticks the man had been carrying and disappeared into the reeds.

He shouldered the carcass. It was small, probably less than eighty pounds, so it wasn't too big a problem for his shingle-bundle hauling muscles. Momentarily at a loss, he looked in both directions. She stuck her head back through the reeds and motioned him forward.

They went deep into the reed bed and abruptly came out into an open area covered with shallow water. She paused often to listen but apparently heard nothing.

Logan was dismayed to see that she'd turned away from the small hammock and was now heading towards one that was much farther away.

He tried to get comfortable carrying the dead animal. She didn't have to tell him that the meat was valuable. He was so hungry that his stomach was thinking of climbing out his throat and starting on the deer while he walked.

He thought of roast venison, but then the vision of the bearded guy vomiting blood struck him, and he staggered with a wave of nausea. He decided that he must be in shock or something. He struggled with the idea of killing a man, but then something in his mind pulled him into a new state. The man would have cheerfully killed him. It was kill or be killed. Now all he had to concentrate on was getting the deer somewhere where they could eat in peace. Without consciously realizing it, he moved another step away from his previously civilized attitudes.

While he struggled with the killing, another part of his mind subconsciously monitored his progress, leading him to try and be as quiet as possible. The hunter might have friends nearby who would resent his death. He understood why the girl was leading him towards the distant hammock. It was only that he was getting very tired.

He staggered on behind her as the evening passed. Now, even the delightful sight of her swaying hips failed to hold his interest. He was miserable, and, with the onset of darkness, the mosquitoes were coming in. Holding the deer, he couldn't even swat at them.

He was surprised when they passed through some reeds, then tall maiden-cane, and climbed out of the water. They'd finally arrived.

She came back to him and indicated that he should put the deer down on a bare spot of sand and wait. Then she disappeared. He understood that she was scouting the new hammock. He figured that she was far more adept than he at sneaking through the underbrush. If there was anyone on the higher ground, she'd find them, and they could leave.

The thought of another long walk dismayed him. It was now nearly dark, even darker between the thick trees. He couldn't see how he could walk even another foot. Besides, his leg was hurting.

Logan rolled up his pants leg to expose a shallow knife slash. The knife had passed close to his calf, leaving a three-inch-long cut. It wasn't bleeding, but the constant soaking had made it look bad. The edges were pale and jagged.

He then looked at the scratch on his arm that the panther had made. It was red and slightly swollen. He gingerly felt it. It was a little hot. It hurt when he pressed it.

He was sure it was infected. He started to worry about antibiotics. How could he clean the wound without anything to disinfect it? What if he got blood poisoning?

About that time, the girl came back. She saw that he was inspecting the scratch as she came up. She grabbed his arm, looked at the wound, and said something quietly.

He didn't understand the words. She turned to the water's edge, grabbed some wet sand, and scrubbed the scratch with it. It hurt, but Logan kept quiet, his pride refusing to allow him to complain.

He let her work until she was satisfied. She had scrubbed the scab off the wound, and it was now bleeding freely. She inspected it, looking pleased.

Logan wasn't sure if she knew what she was doing at first, but then the idea crossed his mind that the wound was probably better off clean. The blood washed the sand away and probably most of the bacteria also.

She looked through the cattails for a moment, returning with one of last year's dried tails. She twisted it, gathering loose down in her hand, then pressed it onto the shallow wound. The fibers stopped the bleeding.

She said something in a satisfied tone, then hoisted the deer over her shoulder, motioned for him to follow, and started off.

Logan felt like it wasn't a very good job of doctoring, but since she seemed satisfied, he figured that was the best she could do. Maybe it would work.

He thought it was his job to carry the carcass, but he was so tired, he could barely get to his feet. He gathered himself, then followed, limping slightly from the cut in his leg.

They wound their way through the dark trees, finally coming out in an open area. There was a small pool of water surrounded by grass. He guessed this would be their camp for the night. The surrounding trees were so thick that they couldn't be seen from any direction.

As long as there weren't any predators around, he felt that this spot promised the most safety he'd seen since he arrived in this place. With a grateful sigh, Logan sat down and watched the girl drag some dead branches into the open area. It was obvious that she was going to make a fire. He hoped she knew that he didn't have any matches or a lighter.

Chapter Eleven

Serensaa

To Logan's surprise, the girl took next to no time to get a fire going. She collected some paper-like strips of inner bark from one of the pines, along with a pile of small sticks, in addition to the larger pieces she dragged in. Once she had what she apparently felt was enough fuel, she took a sharpened stick and two pieces of wood from Scarface's pouch, then rummaged around in it a little more, finally coming out with a twisted strip of leather.

She placed one of the pieces of wood on the ground, fitted the stick into a hole in it, stuck the other piece on the top of the stick, and held it in place by biting it. Then she wrapped the leather around the stick and, pulling alternately on either end, spun the stick back and forth until the friction created a thin plume of smoke. Then she placed the pine bark on the smoking wood, blew a little, and almost instantly had a small flame. The whole operation couldn't have taken her more than three minutes. Logan was impressed.

She carefully built the fire up and then dragged the deer over into the light. The stone knife she'd taken from the hunter seemed to be extremely sharp. She cut the deer open and shortly had a slice of liver broiling on a sharpened stick. She cut off a strip and began to eat as soon as the meat was hot.

Seeing Logan watching her, she motioned at the cooked liver with her knife hand, mumbling something with her mouth full. He scooted over, pulled the tanto knife from his belt, and cut off a chunk for himself. It was very good, he thought, or, perhaps it was just because he was hungry. Either way, he wanted more. He cut another strip off and ate it.

As he was chewing, he became aware that she'd stopped eating, her mouth partway open, with her eyes fixed on his knife. He grinned in realization and said, "You've never seen a steel knife, have you?"

She jerked her eyes up to his face, saw that he was grinning, and flushed. She looked down and resumed eating, obviously chagrined that he'd been making fun of her.

Logan decided that he'd gone long enough, calling her simply, 'The Girl". He gestured to his chest and said, "Logan."

She looked at him inquisitively.

He repeated the action.

A slow smile came over her face. She swallowed with a gulp, then pointed at his chest and accurately repeated, "Logan."

He grinned and nodded. "Yes! Logan."

She mimicked him precisely, "Yes! Logan."

He pointed at her and cocked an eyebrow.

She gestured to herself, somewhat dismissively, and said, "Serensaa."

Logan didn't quite catch the inflection, so he pointed at her again.

She looked at him as if evaluating whether he was mentally competent, then pointed at him and said, "Yeslogan," then at herself, repeating, "Serensaa."

Alarmed, he tried to correct her, "No. Not Yeslogan, Logan."

This seemed to be confusing. She frowned and said, "Yeslogan," again.

Logan realized that he'd gotten off on a path that would only become more difficult to correct the farther he went unless he carefully straightened it out immediately. He considered the problem for a moment, then pointed at her and said, "Serensaa."

She smiled and repeated, "Serensaa," pointing at herself.

He then pointed at himself and said, "Logan."

She frowned and repeated, "Logan." Then she pointed at him and said, "Yeslogan?" with an upward inflection to her voice, which he recognized as an interrogative.

He pointed at her and said, "Yes, Serensaa," Then he pointed at himself and said, "Yes, Logan." He could see her lips moving as she soundlessly repeated his words.

Then he pointed at her and said, "No. Logan," followed immediately by pointing at himself with, "No. Serensaa."

She puzzled that out for a bit, but then a gleeful look came over her face, and she laughed, a cheerful, musical sound that he found totally entrancing.

She leaned forward, shoved her finger onto his chest, and said, "No, Serensaa, yes, Logan." Then she pointed at herself, saying, "Serensaa, no Logan." Finally, to demonstrate mastery of the concept, she jumped far ahead in a way that he hadn't thought of. She pointed at him, saying, "No Yeslogan, Logan."

It was his turn for his mouth to open in amazement. She'd demonstrated that she was far cleverer than he'd believed a primitive human might be.

He wanted to keep going. He pointed at the fire and said, "Fire." She followed along. They covered deer, knife, wood, and sand in short order. Then things got a little too complex. Nevertheless, it was a great start.

The two sat watching the fire and listening to the swamp sounds. Frogs, gators, the snap of the fire, and once, far off, the sound of wolves howling. The firelight dimmed, and Logan was reminded of how tired he was. He stretched out beside the warmth.

Despite it being mid-summer, the temperature at night had fallen more than he was used to. It seemed cool, even cold. The sand was warm, though. The girl stretched out so that her head was close to his. They lay there, watching each other until Logan fell asleep.

⚬

He awoke with a start. The fire was out, and it was dark. Serensaa was nowhere to be seen. He seemed to have the memory of some kind of sound, a sound that held danger. He looked around, searching for her, then stood up. If there was something coming, he'd better climb a tree.

He moved over to the nearest pine. It wasn't very thick, and it had branches well within reach. Just as he started to climb, she appeared out of the darkness, grabbing his arm.

It startled him, and Logan gasped, placing his hand over hers.

She used her oft-repeated gesture of placing two fingers on his lips. That, more than anything else, alerted him to the fact that there was some kind of danger nearby. He nodded assent, and she removed her fingers.

Taking his hand, she led him rapidly through the trees. They moved into a reedy area, and she continued to pull at him, finally stopping where they could see out across the water to the west. Huge shapes moved along out there.

Logan stared. He couldn't quite make them out, but then their nature gradually came clear. It was a large herd of mammoths or some other elephant-like creatures. He couldn't quite tell. It was too dim. The animals faded into the distance, moving south. Logan realized he'd been holding himself tensely, worried that they might have to run for it. He let out a long sigh.

His companion turned her head to look at him. They were standing quite close, and for some reason that he preferred not to rationalize, he leaned forward a few inches and kissed her.

She froze for a moment, allowing the kiss, but then pulled back, her eyes wide, bemused by the experience. It had been far more intense than he'd intended, he leaned forward again, but she turned her head away.

He stepped back, embarrassed, but then saw that she was coyly looking at him out of the corners of her eyes.

"Serensaa, I'm sorry. I thought that...I guess I don't know what overcame me," he said, embarrassment thick in his voice.

She turned back to him as if she could understand every word. She murmured something in her musical voice. He took it to be an acceptance of his apology, but then she stepped closer and lifted her head, obviously ready for another kiss.

This time there was real fire. Logan reluctantly pulled back, breathless. What was he doing? This girl, this primitive child, couldn't know who he was. He felt like he was taking advantage of her. The thought hit him that she could never be his intellectual equal. She had no education, she had no manners, not that his were that good, but...she wasn't modern. She lived in a swamp.

She searched his face as these thoughts ran through his mind. He started to open his mouth again, and she placed her fingers on his lips and slowly turned away to lead the way back to the dead fire.

⚬

The sun was up. Not a word was said as they cooked and ate some more venison for breakfast. He tried not to look at her but couldn't help but notice that she was watching him out of the corners of her eyes again. It was somewhat disconcerting. He didn't know whether she resented his actions or liked them and wanted more.

His dismay at his realization of their differences had faded as he watched her restart the fire and cook. She was perfectly able and well adjusted, given her milieu. She was a Paleolithic human, and there was no comparison with a modern girl, but he also realized that he, a modern man, was barely able to survive in her world. In fact, if he hadn't met her, he'd probably have been killed or starved by now.

He inspected his calf. The knife slash had sealed itself and showed no signs of infection. Then he looked at the panther slash. Serensaa's rough treatment had worked. The cattail fluff and clotted blood had worn off, leaving a reddish healing scratch.

He looked up. She was watching him with a slight smile.

He grinned back at her, pointed to himself, and said, "No, Logan."

Her eyebrows arched, then she smiled broadly, saying, "Yes. Logan. Yes, Serensaa."

Logan wondered what she meant, but his wondering was interrupted by a cracking noise from somewhere back in the trees. Both humans jumped to their feet, looking through the dimly lit trees. Nothing was visible, but the cracking sound came again. Then it was silent.

Logan looked at Serensaa. She glanced at him and moved her head slightly to the side in a half shrug. It was obvious that she didn't know the source of the sound.

Wordlessly, the two slipped into the trees, Logan close behind the girl. Her small, moccasin-shod feet moved carefully between brush and leaves, creating almost no sound. In contrast, Logan felt like he was making enough noise for a herd of cattle. His sneakers, now somewhat the worse for wear, crunched leaves and sticks that he could not seem to avoid.

At a certain point, she turned to him and held out her palm. He understood and held his position while she moved forward. He looked around, wondering what he'd do if she didn't return. In a few minutes, she appeared in view beside a distant tree, motioning for him to come.

He walked forward as quietly as he could. When he caught up to her, he noticed that she was far more relaxed than she'd been previously. Whatever it was must not be dangerous.

There was another breaking sound mixed with the rustling of branches just ahead. They slowed, and Serensaa pointed. Logan could see something moving through the intervening trees. It was large but didn't seem to be moving quickly.

They cautiously walked the remaining yards, and Logan finally saw the creator of the noise. It was quite a large creature. He wasn't immediately sure what it was until it stood on its hind feet to reach an overhanging branch. Huge claws hooked the branch, pulling it down to the animal's mouth. A long tongue came out and stripped the foliage from the branch.

The creature moved slowly and deliberately, and it was that style of motion that cued Logan. He suddenly realized that it was a giant sloth. Not aggressive, surely, but still well able to defend itself. The very size of its claws was intimidating, and its forearms were thick and powerful.

The two watched the animal feed for a short time, then turned and retreated to the fire. On the way back, Logan noticed for the first time that the girl had carried one of the slim sticks that had belonged to the enemy hunter. He'd been too nervous to pay much attention before.

Chapter Twelve

Pursuit

The two were almost back at their camp when Serensaa jerked to a halt, then moved sideways into some bushes. Taken by surprise, Logan stood there, looking at the bushes for a moment. She peeked back at him and angrily waved him to follow.

He suddenly heard the sound of voices. Belatedly realizing what had alarmed her, he slipped into the undergrowth. She immediately moved away, and he was hard put to keep up.

Serensaa set a fast pace, leaving no doubt in Logan's mind that the voices belonged to the men who'd killed her previous companion. After they'd gone several hundred yards, making a minimum of sound, she sped up, trotting steadily along towards the southern edge of the hammock.

They came out of the trees and moved into another cattail bed. She searched for a pathway through it, finding a beaten-down trail that the two followed. It occurred to Logan that gators probably made the trail. After that idea crossed his mind, he kept a nervous watch to the sides.

The trail gradually submerged until they were wading along hip deep. This didn't help with Logan's apprehension. He lagged behind, trying to watch everywhere at once, until she stopped and hissed at him, making an exasperated motion of her arm to indicate he should keep up. When they reached the edge of the cattails, the water was chest-deep and covered with torpedo grass interspersed with taller maiden cane.

Serensaa turned back to the west and headed along a course that would skirt the hammock. Logan believed that was probably a good idea. No sense continuing in the same direction they'd been following. It would be too easy to track. This would get them out of sight a little faster and might throw off pursuit. There was a heavy growth of reeds between their path and the trees, providing cover. They would have to be very unlucky to be seen from the shore.

A distant screaming cry came from far back in the trees on the hammock. Serensaa looked around, startled, then sped up, practically leaving a wake in the water. Logan realized that the men, whoever they were, had found their trail and were now following.

The two moved from reed bed to reed bed, always trying to keep a screen of vegetation between them and their pursuers. The morning sun beat down. Its heat ameliorated only slightly by the puffy clouds that marched westward overhead. Despite walking in water, sweat poured down Logan's face, getting in his eyes and making it hard to see. He kept wiping his arm across his eyes, attempting to clear the burning sweat away, but it didn't help much.

The only thing that made their slog through the swamp slightly bearable was that the mosquitoes didn't bother them. Most of the bloodsuckers weren't active during the day and those that were often provided a quick snack for the innumerable dragonflies that filled the air.

The dragonflies took turns perching on the extreme tip of reeds, a look-out position from which they launched themselves like small, colorful, metallic-hued rockets towards any unfortunate insect that came by. Logan never tired of watching their activity. It gave him something to do besides slog along, following Serensaa.

For her part, the girl seemed to have no doubts about where she was going. They'd passed two hammocks that provided some visual screening from potential pursuers. She had set a westward course that only deviated enough to keep the intervening clumps of trees between them and the hammock where the pursuers had discovered their camp.

Logan periodically looked over his shoulder, anticipating a group of spear-carrying warriors hot on their trail, but nothing came in view. He wondered if the voices they'd heard belonged to the men he'd seen kill her companion or perhaps some totally unrelated group.

Maybe it had been some other group of men, men who wanted nothing to do with them and who were now fleeing in the opposite direction. He didn't know. All that he knew was that Serensaa wasn't stopping and that he was both tired and hungry.

In the middle of the afternoon, she finally halted for a brief rest in the water off the west edge of a large hammock. Looking coyly at him out of the corner of her eyes, she indicated that he was to remain where he was while she moved into a reed bed. The water was shallow here, and they were mostly walking on sand with a shallow covering of decayed vegetation.

Logan waited, shifting his weight back and forth in the hot sun. After a bit, he heard the sound of water trickling faintly and realized that she was relieving herself.

She came out shortly after that and started onward. Logan, now in a rush to empty his own bladder, said, "Wait!"

She looked at him inquisitively. For some reason, he found her attention embarrassing. He realized he was blushing as he pointed at the passage into the reeds that she'd used. She grinned companionably as he walked through the opening, increasing his discomfort.

There was a small open area that she'd apparently used. He took care of his needs there.

As he came back through the screening reeds, there was a splash, followed by a crunching noise as something forced its way through the tall vegetation towards them. Serensaa whirled, grabbed a flint-tipped stick from her pouch, and stuck it into the end of the slim shaft she had been carrying.

Logan suddenly realized that the shaft had become a spear. She was holding the spear, pointing it directly at whatever was coming.

There was a rustle in the reeds, then a crunch, as a pony-sized, striped animal popped its head out and stared in shock at them. It obviously hadn't detected them in its flight from whatever had startled it.

The girl lunged forward, driving the flint spearhead directly into the beast's lower chest under its upraised head and long, rubbery nose. It squealed loudly, jumped, then staggered. A gush of blood rushed out of the wound, and the animal slumped to its knees, then slowly toppled over on its side.

Logan was astounded. Serensaa had killed it as effectively as if she'd shot it with a rifle. She squatted and removed the short fore-shaft with its attached point from the wound. It had come out of the spear socket when the animal jumped.

Turning towards him, she motioned for him to help her drag the creature into the open. As they pulled on its forelegs, there was a grunting roar from deep in the reeds. He recognized it as an alligator. From the sound, it was a large one.

Serensaa jumped at the noise. She quickly used the spear-point to cut off a rear quarter. As she finished, the gator appeared, its toothy head coming through the reeds. It stopped for a moment, sizing up the situation, and then it lunged forward. Its jaws snapped shut on the animal's foreleg, and it backed up, dragging the creature with it.

The two humans looked at each other mutely. Serensaa grinned and said something that sounded as if she were amused. Logan wished that he could understand her. She might be a primitive from his past, but she also fitted nicely into all of his criteria for 'desirable.'

The two started out again, Logan lugging the haunch of meat in his arms. It was cumbersome, and he finally settled for carrying it over his shoulder. That worked better, but the blood leaking out attracted flies, so he swished his free hand back and forth to shoo them away from his face.

As he walked, Logan wondered if killing the creature, he thought it might have been a tapir, had been a mistake. Would their pursuers stumble on their trail and realize that humans had killed something there.

He decided that the alligator might have provided cover for them. It was a messy feeder, and its attack could have spilled the blood that was scattered around the area. Serensaa didn't seem too worried about it, even though she was setting a fast pace.

— ◇ —

The sun was slanting down through the cypress trees to the west when Serensaa slowed. For the first time, she seemed to be unsure as to her direction. Logan shifted the tapir haunch to his other shoulder, watching her expectantly. She'd been acting as if she knew exactly where they should go, but now she looked back and forth indecisively.

He cleared his throat, hoping to get her attention. She frowned at him for a moment and then abruptly seemed to make up her mind. They made a sharp right turn and headed for what looked like a distant hammock.

It was nearly dark by the time they approached the tall trees. Logan had noticed that the cypress trees were backed by sand pines and hoped that indicated they'd reach some higher ground. They waded through a deep area filled with water lilies, then through some torpedo grass, his feet tripping on the tough stems. They finally exited the stand of cypress by climbing onto a muddy bank covered partially with coarse grass.

The cypress trees gave way to sand pines and swamp magnolias. The sandy ground was littered with pine needles. They passed between large clumps of palmettos. As they walked farther into the dark woods, oak trees began to appear.

Serensaa finally stopped by an ancient oak, if size were any indication of age, and plopped down on the leaf-covered ground. He sat next to her, shifting the haunch of meat to an area covered with dry leaves.

He could see her white teeth in the fading light as she smiled at him. She made some noises as she dug in her pouch, coming out with the flint spearpoint. It must have been quite sharp. She made a couple of passes with it and pulled off a strip of meat from the haunch. Noticing Logan watching her, she hesitated and then held it out to him. When he took it, she immediately cut off another piece and crammed it into her mouth.

Logan hesitated, but his hunger overruled his squeamishness. The meat tasted warm and raw, then something in him reached out, bypassing his rapidly thinning veneer of civilization. It was food. He found himself eating rapidly.

He used his knife to cut off another strip. The girl watched closely as he did, then held out her hand. He placed the strip in her fingers. She shook her head, then held out her other hand. Logan realized that she wanted to inspect his knife. He hesitated. She'd been interested when he'd first used it but had apparently forgotten about it.

Now she was all but insisting that he let her examine it. She said something in a demanding tone. Logan was sure that if he could understand her, she had just told him: "Give that to me!"

He looked at her face. She was frowning slightly, perhaps with impatience.

He held it out to her, waited until she reached, then jerked it back. She snorted, making a frustrated sound, then looked at him. He grinned at her, and her face slowly changed from incipient anger to amusement. Her smile was breathtaking.

Logan drew in a deep breath and placed the knife, hilt first, into her hand. Serensaa didn't look down at it. She kept her eyes on his face, and smiling, said something. He thought it sounded more like a thank you than anything else.

He smiled back. Figuring that she couldn't understand him anyway, said, "You're beautiful. I shouldn't let you have that, but I can't resist your smile."

His tone of voice or mannerism must have communicated more than he intended. She lowered her eyes, blushing.

As if she were seeking to cover her confusion, she carefully examined the weapon, feeling the rubberized grip, the smooth blade, and cautiously testing the edge with her finger. He straightened as she gasped. A tiny drop of blood welled out where she'd pressed a bit too hard.

She carefully handed the blade back, haft first, exactly the way he'd given it to her. He took the knife with one hand and simultaneously caught her hand with his other. Laying the weapon aside, he lifted her hand to check the cut. It wasn't deep. The tanto was so sharp that he had worried she'd opened a serious cut.

Holding her hand, he looked up at her face. Her eyes were wide, and her lips were parted. Something took him at that moment, and he bent over her hand and kissed her palm. He could hear her gasp deeply as his lips contacted the slightly calloused skin.

Before he'd finished kissing her palm, her other hand brushed slowly over his cheek. He raised his eyes to hers. She was still flushing, but her gaze held his for a moment, then she lowered her eyes again.

Logan found that his heart was pounding. He felt as if his skin had suddenly become ever so much more sensitive. The night breeze seemed colder than it had been, and he shivered a little.

Serensaa moved towards him a little, and he moved so that they were close to each other. Her arms came up around his neck, and he suddenly found himself kissing her deeply. It was as if he'd never kissed any woman before. He could barely breathe, and all of his senses were focused on the taste of her lips, the slightly smokey smell of her hair, and the warm feel of her skin against his.

They broke apart, and his tongue passed over his lips, tasting a little blood from the raw meat that she'd been eating. She was panting in turn.

She said something in a soft tone. Logan didn't understand the words, but the tone and her expression said more than the words could have. He wrapped his arms around her and pulled her close for another kiss.

He had believed that she was shapely, in a slender fashion, but holding her that closely, with her breasts pressed against his chest, made him realize that her deerskin shirt had concealed more than he'd thought. His breath came fast. She responded by opening her lips against his. The tip of her tongue slid between his lips, and he responded in kind.

Both of them were shaking with passion. Logan wasn't sure what would come next, but he was certain that it would be amazing. He pulled back to look into her eyes. He didn't need to speak her language; what they were saying to each other was universal. There was no need for words. They'd ignited a mutual fire. She had definitely found his kiss as exciting as he'd found hers. He started to pull her close again.

A distant sound echoed through the trees. Serensaa leaped up, now all business. Logan stood up, still shaking with passion. She whispered something, then placed her fingers on his lips when he started to answer.

He looked towards the direction that the noise had come from. More sound filtered through the nearly dark woods. Somewhere over there, a fair distance away, men were talking. He looked at Serensaa in alarm.

She was sniffing the air carefully. She pointed towards the sounds, and following her finger, he could see the faint flickering of a fire reflected on the undersides of the tree branches. Their pursuers were close and were setting up camp for the night.

He caught up the tapir haunch, settled it over his shoulder before Serensaa grabbed his free hand to lead him away into the dark woods. They walked quietly, carefully avoiding underbrush and feeling out each step.

They moved silently for a while, but then she stopped so abruptly that he collided with her shapely posterior. Something was moving up ahead. He could hear a crackling noise in a thicket.

They were standing directly under a large live oak that spread a thick canopy. Serensaa moved to the trunk and seemed to climb it as easily as a squirrel, her fingers and toes finding small holds in the rough bark. Logan put the tapir haunch down and followed as best he could. A few days ago, he wouldn't have dreamed of attempting such a climb in the dark, but that was before he had seen some of the predators that frequented this ancient world.

They reached the first fork and continued upwards. In a couple of minutes, they were resting in the top branches of the big tree. Their ascent was barely in time. As they arranged themselves, Logan heard a snarl from below, followed by the sound of a heavy body rearing up and clawing on the tree.

The girl said something that sounded vaguely like, "Piskata." Logan didn't understand, but his imagination formed a picture of the big-toothed cat that had made a try for him when he first arrived in the past. The creature circled the tree, snarling softly as it did. When it came to the haunch, it stopped. There was the sound of chewing. In a short time, the first animal was joined by another, then yet another. There was a brief spat of low snarling as the animals struck at each other over the tapir meat.

The two humans sat quietly high in the canopy, listening. Logan was worried about the beasts down below but also quite pleased. Serensaa was sitting between his legs, leaning her back against his chest, her hair brushing his face. It would have been extremely pleasant had it not been for the danger.

The tapir meat hadn't lasted very long. The creatures continued to prowl around below, occasionally letting out a rumbling snarl. The waning moon hadn't yet risen, and it was quite dark up in the branches. Logan was wedged into a fork in such a way that he was moderately comfortable and not in danger of falling. He kept his arms wrapped around Serensaa's waist.

After a time, she shifted a little. Alarmed, he clutched at her, ending with his hand on her breast.

In Logan's experience, a girl of his time might have been offended, but Serensaa didn't respond other than to shift a little more and lean into him harder. He rather reluctantly slid his hand back down to her ribs, at which she turned her head and kissed his cheek.

The two sat silently after that. Logan found himself trying to sleep. They would need to move quickly in the morning. Pursuit was near. If the piskata, whatever they were, hadn't treed them, the two would have continued moving to get a better start on their trackers.

⸺◆⸺

Logan awoke when Serensaa moved slightly. There was a bird calling softly in a nearby tree. It wasn't quite light yet, but the left hand of dawn was definitely showing in the east.

He wondered if the predators were still below, and also if their pursuers would get an early start or possibly wait until the rising sun made it easier to trail.

Serensaa pressed her two fingers on his lips to indicate silence, then began to descend, working her way carefully down through the branches. Logan followed, trying not to miss a step in the dim light. In starts and stops, they climbed down to the first main fork.

She paused, standing on a branch, holding onto a vertical limb with one hand. He could see that she was searching the ground below. He looked but couldn't see anything.

Serensaa froze, pointing. Logan followed her finger. There was something in the bushes where she pointed. He studied the pattern of shadowed and lighter areas, then gradually made out the stripy face of one of the big-toothed cats in the dim light. It was looking directly at them, obviously hoping they'd come on down.

He took a deep breath, preparing to say something, but she jerked, straightened a little, and then pointed down their back trail. Someone was coming.

This was getting worse and worse. Logan wasn't sure what they'd do. They couldn't go down. The saber-tooth would get them for sure. If the enemies found them in a tree, he was sure that it would be an easy task for their pursuers to spear them and drag them down.

He glanced back at the saber-tooth. It had vanished, pulling back into the leaves. As he watched, three spear-carrying men came through the brush.

The first man was bending over, obviously following their trail of the night before. He stopped at the edge of the clearing, where the smaller vegetation thinned out in the oak's shadow and pointed across the more open area. The other two consulted with him quietly, then all three came ahead, directly towards the sheltering oak.

The men walked silently across the leaf mold, inspecting the ground, then they found the spot where Logan and Serensaa had climbed the tree. One of them jerked his head up and spotted the two.

He let out a blood-curdling scream and prepared to throw his spear at them. It was at that instant that the hidden saber-tooth tigers launched their ambush.

The big cats were close but so well camouflaged that Logan hadn't seen the other four. All he'd seen was the one in the bushes.

The men spun around, yelling in horror. One managed to throw his spear, striking one of the charging cats in the neck, but the other four tigers overwhelmed the three men before they could do more than scream a second time. There was a brief and bloody struggle below then the deadly animals were crouched over the hunter's still bodies.

Logan was shocked. The hunters hadn't had a chance. The ambush had been too well carried out. The only damage they'd done was the spear sticking from one cat's neck. That animal was having difficulty breathing. The shaft had struck nearly in the center of its throat and had probably penetrated the windpipe. As Logan watched, it clawed at the spear, finally pulling it out.

A gush of blood came out with the flint tip, and the tiger coughed once, gagged, and coughed again weakly. It took several staggering steps towards the bushes, then collapsed, dead or dying.

After a brief disagreement involving roaring and slapping at each other with their claws, three of the tigers caught hold of the corpses and headed off through the trees. They were so strong that they were able to grasp a hunter by the small of the back and walk off. One started out dragging its prey but shortly fell behind. It finally picked up the man's body and trotted off after its companions. The fourth tiger stood indecisively for a moment, looking at the others as they walked away. It glanced up at the two humans in the tree and snarled, but when they didn't move, it turned and followed the others.

The speared tiger moaned once, then was quiet.

Serensaa looked at him quietly. When their eyes met, she shrugged as if to say: "Too bad for them, but we've got to get going."

She faced the trunk and climbed downwards. Logan followed.

He missed his footing when he was near the ground, partially falling and making a scrabbling sound as he tried to catch himself.

He looked up from where he'd landed to see her gathering some of the deceased pursuers' spear shafts. She gathered up three of the slender shafts along with some of the fore-shafts that had tumbled out of their pouches. She also picked up two of the spear-throwers that lay on the blood-covered ground. She handed the spears to him. Then striding over to the deceased tiger. She quickly cut into its back and removed part of one of its thick backstraps.

When he approached, she stood, handed him the meat, took three of the thin spears from his bundle, and headed out in a direction that was directly away from where the men had come from and about ninety degrees away from the departing tigers' trail. Logan realized that she feared the men more than the tigers.

⸺◆⸺

The birds were singing, and the sun was bright as they walked across a wide grassy space. Near the edge of the trees where they'd come out was an extensive area of loam that had been plowed up.

Serensaa took the time to point out a clear, slotted hoof print in the wet earth. Logan initially thought it might have been made by a deer, but after a little consideration, he understood that it was made by some kind of pig. The rooted-up area was the defining clue. He didn't think it was the kind of wild hog that he knew about in his own time, but perhaps it was a peccary or something like that. A hog, most certainly.

This made him look around apprehensively. Such creatures could be very aggressive. The slim bundle of spears he was carrying didn't give him any great confidence.

He inspected them as well as he could while carrying the meat. The shafts didn't even have points. He'd seen Serensaa fit a fore-shaft with a point to one of the spears. He looked and found that each shaft had a socket that was reinforced with tight rawhide wrapped around it. The fore-shaft that carried the stone tip would fit tightly into the socket.

He grinned appreciatively. It was a well-thought-out weapon system, one that he'd neglected to study in the one class he'd had that briefly touched on the Clovis culture.

The spear points looked more or less like ones he'd seen that were called 'Clovis points,' and based on that tentative identification, and he thought that was the culture of Serensaa's people.

The spear-thrower had been called an 'atl-atl' by his professor, but Logan doubted that Serensaa would have the same name for it. The throwing stick had a hooked part that fitted against the butt of the spear shafts while the other end was held in the throwing hand. The additional leverage provided by the two-foot-long thrower allowed for a far more powerful throw.

He wanted to try the thing, but Serensaa was moving too quickly and seemed anxious to put as much distance between them and the site of the morning ambush as possible in the remaining daylight.

They re-entered the trees. The forest had a thick barrier of scrub along the edge, but it opened out a little once they'd forced their way through. The trees were a blend of long-leaf pines, various oaks, swamp magnolias, some palms, and other trees that he didn't recognize.

He carefully avoided a patch of poison ivy. There was a lot of it growing in the shady areas. He wasn't surprised to see that Serensaa avoided it also. He assumed that she would likely know about the plants in her world from past experience.

Chapter Thirteen

Mammoths

They'd walked for what seemed like a long distance. Logan was beginning to think fondly of the tiger meat he was carrying when Serensaa interrupted his thoughts of food with a quiet exclamation.

She'd discovered a heaping mound of dung. Looking at the huge pile, Logan knew it could only have been made by an elephant. Mammoth, he quickly corrected himself.

As he walked on, following the girl, he stumbled. Catching himself, he realized he'd stepped into a depression. He was suddenly aware that there were numerous such indentations in the soft ground. From that observation, it was an easy leap to the understanding that a large group of mammoths had passed through the area. He looked around and saw that they'd left ample sign in the form of dung heaps, tracks, and, now that he was looking more closely, broken branches that they'd torn off of trees while feeding.

A freshly broken stub that was fifteen feet up a tree caught his eye, emphasizing the true size of the creatures. They had to be really huge. He stumbled again, drawing a look of caution from Serensaa. She pointed ahead and to the left.

Logan couldn't see anything in that direction. He shrugged.

The girl made a wry face at him and held her hand up to her ear. She meant for him to listen, something that he hadn't really been doing. There was a low rumbling noise, almost at the bottom frequency of human hearing, coming from the direction she indicated. It must be a mammoth, or mammoths.

They veered off to the northwest. Logan understood that she was trying to avoid the creatures. He wondered again where she was heading. Since he had no real destination, nowhere to go, he didn't much care, as long as it was somewhere safe. To him, lost in the primitive wilderness, any one place was as good as any other place, better if it held food and safety.

A bothersome yellow fly made a pass at Logan's face. He brushed it off. A second later, he flinched as another one bit his lower arm. He slapped at it ineffectually. The biting insects followed them for a while but then gave up as the two humans passed through a more open area.

Logan rubbed his arm. The bite was a little painful but unlikely to be a problem for him. He knew that some people were violently allergic to the fly bites, but they'd never bothered him in the past, and...he almost laughed out loud at the bitter thought. For him, this truly was the past.

He bumped into Serensaa. She'd stopped short and was now looking around. She suddenly, and without warning, broke into a run. He panicked and ran too, following her.

There was a crashing in the trees to their left, followed by an incredibly loud trumpeting noise. A mammoth had sighted them. Logan leaped at the noise and redoubled his speed. Both of them were running full out towards a thicker part of the forest.

There was nowhere they could run that a sufficiently determined mammoth couldn't follow. It could easily push through underbrush that a human could barely navigate. Climbing a small tree would be useless. There weren't any large boulders or rocks due to the geology of the area. They needed to find a large oak, one they could climb, but one that was too thick for a mammoth to uproot.

The sounds from behind were louder. The mammoth was apparently angry at their intrusion into what it must consider its territory. Logan glanced back, speeding up as he saw not one but a whole herd of the large beasts chasing them.

The two humans had momentarily gained a little, weaving through the trees, but the edge was wearing off their endurance, and they were slowing. At least he was. Serensaa was gradually starting to draw ahead of him.

She swerved sharply to the left, dashed past a clump of trees, and disappeared. Logan, following, panted past the trees blindly, then yelped in surprise as the ground disappeared from beneath him. He fell, seeming to hang in mid-air for an instant, then plunged into deep water.

When his head broke the surface, he choked, coughed, and then wiped his eyes. Serensaa was close by, clinging to a mass of vines that hung down the rock face they'd fallen down. She was looking at him in glee, laughing.

Logan wiped his eyes again. Yes. She was laughing. She'd found their close escape funny in some fashion. He paddled around so that he could inspect the surrounding rock walls.

They'd jumped, fallen in his case, into a sinkhole. It must have formed relatively recently. The walls were steep, not eroded or crumbling, and there was no possible way the mammoths could reach them.

A large shadow loomed overhead, and Logan looked up to see their pursuers. First one, then several mammoths appeared, extending their trunks downward, trying to reach the humans. One of the frustrated beasts trumpeted, and the sound bounced around between the rocky walls making a racket that sounded so loud, it even startled the mammoths.

Logan slowly stroked over to the girl. She reached out a hand as he drew near, catching his wrist and pulling him close.

He was still feeling hurt because he suspected that she'd been laughing at him, but the feel of her slim body against his drove that thought instantly out of his mind. He smiled at her. She smiled back and pulled him closer until their lips met. The mammoths faded into obscurity as they kissed.

The fear that he'd been feeling from the chase somehow morphed into arousal. When they broke apart, he was panting almost as hard as he had been while running. Her lips were slightly parted, and her cheeks were flushed. Her eyes sought his, and he felt that he could see the depths of her soul in her deep gaze.

He grasped the vines with one hand, then belatedly looked around, wondering if there might be an alligator in the pool. There didn't seem to be anything to worry about. He moved closer to her again, looking into her eyes. Before they touched, some subconscious part of his mind noted the silence from above, and he glanced up.

The mammoths had disappeared. He pointed, and Serensaa looked. She shook her head negatively. He wasn't sure if she meant that the animals had given up or were hanging around to ambush them when they climbed out.

In either case, she didn't seem to be in any rush to get out of the sinkhole. Her free arm curved around his neck, pulling him close again. This time, he wondered if the water might turn to steam around his flushed body. He pulled her close, pressing his hips against hers.

The girl pressed back and made a soft noise. They kissed again and again.

Logan's mind had seemingly split into two parts. One part wanted nothing so much as to get her out of the water onto firm ground, so as to pursue their current activity with more efficiency. The other part, a part that was sitting back dispassionately, watching their aroused bodies press together, was critical.

His thoughts traveled over the same ground they had previously. The girl was a primitive. He didn't know anything about her. She seemed to be at least his age, but she might only be in her early teens as far as he actually knew. She wasn't educated and couldn't possibly be his intellectual equal. She certainly wasn't going to be able to help him return to his own time.

For a moment, he felt ashamed. Taking advantage of her in this way seemed like exploitation, but then she kissed him and slid the tip of her tongue into his mouth. All thoughts of this not being a mutually enjoyable activity melted away like frost touched by a blowtorch. Passion drove the last bit of discord from his mind, and he pulled her closer, regretting that he had to hold onto the vines with one hand.

Her legs wrapped around his thighs, and her hips rubbed against his. Logan felt as if he were about to blackout. His breath was so short. He was considering whether he could wrap his arm around a vine so as to be able to hold her with both hands when a large rock splashed into the water beside them.

The two jerked apart and looked upwards. One of the mammoths was back. It had been trying to find a spot where it could step down, and the rock had given way. The huge creature was poised right above the two, just on the verge of toppling over the edge. A large mass of vine had somehow been knocked loose and was sliding slowly down the rock face below the struggling mammoth.

As Logan watched, horrified, the twelve thousand pound animal lost its footing and tumbled forward. He had just enough time to force Serensaa against the rocks before the mammoth struck the water behind him, landing directly on its back.

There was a huge splash, and the wave slammed into the two, knocking them loose from the vines and momentarily lifting them up. Then a second wall of water drove them deep under the surface. Logan held onto Serensaa's wrist as he struggled to break free from the mass of tangled vine that had landed directly on top of them.

He pushed frantically against the clinging vegetation, desperately trying to break the surface for a breath. Finally, his head poked out, and he gasped deeply, inhaling some droplets as he did. He went into a series of convulsive coughs, dragging at Serensaa as he tried to clear his lungs.

Her head rose through the clear water and came out of the vines. Her eyes were closed, but then she opened them and grinned excitedly at him.

He wasn't surprised this time. She was just a little crazy. She seemingly felt that this was some kind of fun water park ride.

Serensaa used her other arm to work free of the vine that was wrapped around her shoulders while Logan pulled them back to the rock wall.

There was a loud snort, sounding like someone blowing spit from a brass tuba. Logan jerked around. The mammoth was swimming towards the far side of the pool, breathing through its trunk like a snorkel. It bumped the precipitous rock wall, the trunk feeling for a grip. Finding nothing, it began to swim around the edge of the pool. Its fellow herd members milled around, moving back and forth on the edge above, making a chorus of distressed noises.

Logan didn't want to be there when the swimming mammoth reached their location. He felt sorry for the beast but didn't think it would be in good humor when it arrived. He didn't know what it would do, and he was absolutely sure he didn't want to find out. Playing water polo with a mammoth was not a good idea.

Some parts of the hanging vine were still clinging to the rocks above their heads. Logan grabbed the sturdiest-looking clump and tugged. It might just be possible to climb out of the reach of the swimming mammoth. They couldn't climb to the top, though. The other herd members were still up there, and from the sounds, they were making, they were quite worked up.

Serensaa's head popped out of the water beside him. She grabbed at the vine and began to clamber up, feet braced against the wall. About ten feet above him, she paused, brushed aside a curtain of greenery, then carefully moved over onto a narrow ledge that had been hidden. She slid over, making space for him, as he followed her up.

Shortly, the two were safely dangling their feet over the ledge, watching the swimming mammoth circle the pool below them. It hadn't paused as it went past their position and likely was unaware that they were above it.

The herd was still rampaging around on the edge above them. Logan hoped that they didn't knock off any more rocks. That could spell disaster for the two.

The situation was grim. They could probably climb out, but they wouldn't survive more than a few seconds once they reached the top. The ledge was narrow and uncomfortable. Logan couldn't see the two of them sitting there until the mammoth herd had lost interest. The way they were carrying on, he figured that would take hours.

He leaned to the side to look upwards. One of the angry beasts was extending its trunk downward right over his head. Fortunately, there was still a lot of distance between them. It couldn't possibly reach him. Nevertheless, he flinched a little, thinking of what it could do.

When he turned back, he was shocked to see that Serensaa had disappeared. He quickly slid over to where she'd been. Suddenly, her hand appeared from the middle of some thick vines clinging to the rock face just beyond the end of the ledge. She'd somehow managed to reach the vines and then swung into some space behind them. Her hand waved for him to follow.

Steeling his determination, he checked the swimming beast. It was on the far side of the sinkhole again. If he slipped, he would have time to climb back out of its way.

Shakily, he worked his way to a standing position, then leaned out and grabbed for the vines. They gave sickeningly when he put his weight on them. He scrambled wildly for a moment and got his elbow over the new ledge. It was hidden in thick greenery, and the vegetation almost caused him to slip off, but he managed to worm over the edge and between the vines.

Inside the vines, the ledge opened into an area that was wide enough for the two to relax comfortably. The green plants filtered the slanting sunlight that slanted down at an angle, lighting the niche with a greenish glow. It was as if they were hidden behind an emerald waterfall.

Serensaa was seated on the sandy floor, leaning against the back wall of the overhang, her smile bright in the dim light. Logan marveled. Nothing ever seemed to disturb her for long. Hidden in the greenly lit area, she seemed so calm. It was like they hadn't just escaped from certain death. He moved over beside her on his hands and knees. The overhang was too low to stand.

The two sat companionably side-by-side for a while, listening to the ruckus from overhead. Logan was of mixed emotions. Part of him wanted to continue their exploration of each other, while another part wanted to try to communicate with her. This was inadvertently the most secure location they'd been in since they met. He didn't want to miss the chance to try to speak to her.

She was looking straight ahead at the vines. Tentatively, he asked, "Serensaa?"

She replied, "Vuss?"

He was elated. He could almost recognize that as a word. He quickly asked, "Where are we going?"

She looked puzzled, then put her hand on his cheek and said, "Logan." Then she smiled while shaking her head in a negative manner.

Logan sighed. It wasn't going to work so easily. He was a horrible linguist. He'd almost failed Spanish in high school, and he had only taken the bare minimum of German classes in college, sliding through by the skin of his teeth.

He considered what he wanted to know. Then he noticed that the floor of the overhanging area had a thin covering of sand. That might work.

He quickly sketched the outline of Florida, showing both coasts, the keys, Tampa Bay, Lake Okeechobee, Lake George, and what he believed might represent the Harris chain of lakes. Her eyes followed his sketch carefully.

When he was done, he looked up at her and pointed at the map, then at each of them. He placed his finger approximately where he thought they might be: somewhere just to the west and south of Lake George. Then he placed his finger near his starting point and traced it across to their current location.

She studied the map with a serious expression on her face, but Logan couldn't tell if she understood the symbolism. She'd probably never even heard of the concept of maps. She looked up at him, then pointed at herself, and drew a line from the coast north of Tampa Bay eastward to the point where he'd started his line representing their journey together. Then she thoughtfully sketched in a rough circle to the south of the Harris Chain that apparently represented Lake Apopka.

His mouth dropped open. She went back to their current location and traced a very light line down between the Harris lakes and Lake Apopka, then from there directly over to the area on the Gulf where she'd indicated she'd come from. Finishing with a little flourish of her finger in the air, she turned to Logan and watched expectantly.

Logan looked at her with appreciation. Not only had she understood the map, but she'd also just explained where she'd come from and where she was leading him. A sudden realization caught his attention. She was most likely heading for the Crystal River area. After all, it had been in more or less continuous use for thousands of years. Perhaps her people had camped there.

He turned to her and nodded his understanding. She placed her hand on his cheek again and gently pulled his head over to hers. They kissed. Then he moved closer to wrap his arms around her. Another kiss and the mammoths were totally forgotten.

Their breathing became deeper. Logan found himself shaking. His skin seemed abnormally sensitive. Every touch of her hands seemed to leave raised hot spots on his neck, face, and sides. Serensaa was breathing heavily also. Suddenly, she pulled back and simply pulled her buckskin shirt over her head. Her breasts hung free.

Logan tentatively touched one. It was silky smooth. Her nipple tightened under his fingers. She leaned forward and kissed him. This time, there was even more heat than he'd felt possible. He fumbled at his shirt, finally getting it off. He then pulled at the thong that tied the waistband of her pants.

She helped and then helped him pull his off in turn. She rolled onto her back, and he moved over her. There was resistance, then a yielding. Serensaa moaned. Logan kissed her again, and her arms pulled him down against her.

He kissed her, his mouth open. He couldn't get enough of her. He'd come into the past to find her, and now, at this moment, his desire for her was like a flash of lightning illuminating his mind to reveal new knowledge. He wanted to be with her forever. He couldn't envision living without her.

Their tangled bodies moved in an increasingly urgent rhythm.

⸺◆⸺

The light rays slanting into the alcove through the vines gradually slid lower and lower as the day progressed. The two were sleeping in each other's arms.

As the night approached, Serensaa disentangled herself and went to the edge to look down. Logan joined her. The swimming mammoth was not moving now. The unfortunate creature had become exhausted and drowned. It was floating near the middle of the pool. Its side was the only part that broke the surface. All was quiet from above. Perhaps the herd had given up.

Logan leaned out and looked upward. There was no sign of anything above. He pointed up, intending to indicate that they should climb out, but Serensaa signaled negatively.

She shook her head in what he'd come to recognize was her 'No' motion, a quick sideways nod, usually to the left. Then she pointed at the lengthening sun rays, lowered her hand to roughly the level of the horizon, then pointed at the east, after which she pointed up.

Logan understood. He'd become so used to trying to understand her without language that even cryptic signs from her conveyed information.

She wanted to wait until morning to climb out. That made sense. If they climbed up, there was still a chance that the mammoth herd would be in the area and resume the chase. Even if the mammoths were gone, the two humans would still have to find a safe space for the oncoming night.

His understanding was punctuated by the distant sound of some kind of cat screaming. In rage or fear, he couldn't determine. He glanced at the girl. She smiled at him, then took his hand and pulled him back into the depths of the overhang.

Neither of them had bothered to dress, so this time, when she initiated another bout of lovemaking, things progressed more quickly.

They slept afterward and woke again in the middle of the night. Logan surprised himself. He was more than ready to go a third time, and Serensaa obviously approved.

⚬

Daybreak found them still tangled in each other's arms, drowsily kissing.

Logan felt that they should get moving again, but somehow it didn't seem important. Her kisses were far more compelling.

Chapter Fourteen

The Forest

Hunger and thirst drove them out of their little paradise in mid-morning. The water below was green and wasn't very attractive. The dead mammoth, now beginning to bloat, making it even less so.

There was nothing to do but climb up the rock wall and hope for the best. They needed to continue moving. If they waited around, their pursuers would eventually close the gap between them, provided, of course, that they were as good at tracking as Logan assumed them to be.

⸻◆⸻

Once out of the enclosing stonewalls, the two scouted around cautiously. Branches had been broken off many of the trees in the general confusion, and there were a great number of mammoth tracks intermixed with dung piles. As for the animals themselves, there was no indication that they had remained in the area.

Serensaa was looking for something on the ground. She made an exclamation, stooped, and gathered up three spear shafts. She'd discarded them before she jumped.

Logan had worried that the mammoths would hang around trying to rescue their comrade. When he looked down for the last time, the drowned mammoth wasn't really visible. All that could be seen from the edge of the pit was a soggy lump of hair, floating in the green water with some of the fallen vines. Perhaps the herd hadn't recognized it.

The two set out, Serensaa, as usual, leading the way. She headed away from the sunrise and now seemed to be favoring a slightly more southerly path.

Logan followed her closely. He'd been fascinated by her before, but now his feelings had risen exponentially to a new level. He found her amazing, both physically and mentally.

He understood that she had some kind of built-in compass. He thought they were approximately in the area of modern-day DeLand, but he wasn't really sure. She, on the other hand, once again seemed to know exactly where she was going.

Logan didn't know their destination for sure, but what he did know was that they were walking through an area of sandy uplands. The trees were spaced a little farther apart, save for areas around the various streams they encountered, and there was a different type of coarse grass growing in the open places. He even saw cactus, something he was careful to avoid brushing against. The spines looked fierce.

Hunger was a problem. The tiger meat was still soaking in the sinkhole with the drowned mammoth. They had no opportunity to hunt since there were herds of mammoths scattered around. They sidetracked several times to avoid them, but there didn't seem to be any smaller creatures that might be possible prey.

Logan was relieved when Serensaa discovered an opossum ambling along the ground a little before noon. She grabbed the unfortunate animal's tail and swung its head against a tree trunk. It went "clonk," and the possum ceased hissing.

She tossed it to the ground and prepared to make a fire. They had been walking along the edge of a pine forest but were far enough from the litter of needles that a fire wouldn't spread out of control.

Logan helped her gather sticks and the filmy bits of pine bark from the inside layer of the shed pieces. She cranked on her drill for a few minutes, ending with a tendril of smoke. A little blowing and she had a flame.

He'd been arranging small sticks in a rough tee-pee shape while she worked. She turned and poked the flaming wad of bark and grass under the pile. A little more blowing, and they had their fire.

Logan turned to get the opossum. It wasn't there. He stood up, looked around, and saw its tail end as it trotted slowly around a tree on its way into a thick clump of palmettos. He pointed and said, "It's getting away."

Serensaa dashed after the escaping creature, returning a moment later, swinging it by the tail. She whacked it against a tree to stun it again, then quickly cut its throat with one of the stone spear points. Logan had observed that she used these implements as convenient knives as well as spear tips.

She skinned and cut up the beast, then jabbed a slender stick through the body. She stuck the stick into the sandy soil, arranging it so that the carcass was directly over the flame.

It wasn't long before the smell of roasting meat made Logan's stomach begin to churn. When he felt like he couldn't wait any longer, she sliced off a hind leg and handed it to him.

Before, she'd always started eating first, only handing him food when she realized he was watching her. Now her attitude had changed. She was far more companionable, walking mostly beside him rather than leading. He'd noticed that she smiled at him a great deal more often, too.

It was nice to see that she felt at least a little similar to the way he felt about her. She'd suddenly transformed from a good-looking girl, similar to ones he'd previously only dreamed about, to an amazing being who was incredibly dear to him. He wanted to be near her all of the time, and he was prepared to fight to the death to defend her.

That idea led him to move closer to where she was sitting. She glanced up in surprise from her dedicated eating. Seeing his expression, a slow smile crept over her face. She tossed the possum bone over her shoulder and grabbed him, pulling him close and smearing possum grease over his face as they kissed.

He kissed her back tenderly. She said something softly and indicated the rest of the animal. There were only a few bites remaining. It had been a small opossum to start with. Now that both hindquarters were gone, there wasn't very much usable meat left.

They picked at the carcass until they finished it off, after which she buried the fire with sand.

Logan wanted to start another session of lovemaking and she seemed to be tempted. They kissed repeatedly. Finally, Serensaa kissed him firmly, then pushed him away and indicated that they should start walking. He sighed, knowing that they'd eventually have to stop for the night. He hoped they could find another secure location. He couldn't quite imagine making love to her in a tree, although he was quite willing to attempt it.

They found a small lake and washed the possum grease off of their hands and faces. The lake was dark with tannin but quite clear. Logan could see fish swimming under the surface. He pointed them out to the girl. She nodded affirmatively, rubbing her stomach as if to indicate that they were good to eat.

The two went around the lake and found that it overflowed into a swampy area. They followed the edge of the swamp to the south for nearly the rest of the day before they found a spot where they could cross to higher ground.

By late afternoon, they had arrived on the bank of a swiftly running stream. The water was crystal clear and cool, indicating that it had welled up from underground. Logan tried to think of what stream it might be. He had believed they were near DeLand, but now he was completely unsure. They might be farther south as far as he knew. Then the course of streams and even their existence might have changed from her time to his. His geographical knowledge, which was spotty at best, was probably not very useful in his current time.

Logan felt like they'd walked forever. He had no yardstick to indicate how far they had come. It might have been twenty miles or more a day.

He missed the ease of his motorcycle, even as cranky as it was. On the other hand, he was happy that his legs had grown accustomed to walking. He was not suffering from the hike the way he'd been for the first couple of days.

Regardless of where they were, it was getting dark and not just because the sun was ready to go down. There was a huge, black wall of clouds welling up from the northwest, and another storm front looming in the east.

Logan had lived in Florida all of his life, and he knew what was to come. The wind from the Atlantic and the on-shore wind from the Gulf were piling clouds high over the center of the peninsula. A huge thunderstorm was in the making. He drew Serensaa's attention to the clouds. She nodded and turned towards a more open area where there was a sizable stand of palmettos.

The girl began cutting some of the large fan-shaped leaves free from the small palms. Logan pulled his knife and cut more. Seeing that he had understood, she cut some straighter branches from a tree. Then she stripped long fibers out of the palm fronds, quickly rolled them into thicker cords between her hands, and then used them to tie the branches together to make a low, tent-shaped framework.

They used fibers to tie some of the fronds to the branches, then interlaced the stems together, making a mat of overlapping leaves that would shed water. It didn't take as long as Logan had feared, which was fortunate, for the first large drops of rain were falling by the time they had finished.

Serensaa crawled inside, and Logan followed. With the two of them inside, their improvised shelter was full. The two lay side-by-side with no room to sit up. He put his arm over her, and she turned to kiss him. As she did, the storm hit full force. The wind picked up, blowing hard gusts of rain across the leaves. The drops made a racket as they struck the firm palm fronds.

Serensaa broke off the kiss and grabbed at a corner of the structure. The wind was gusting so hard that it threatened to lift the shelter and destroy it. Logan grabbed another stick and held it in the ground. The shelter flexed and rattled under the impact of the heavy rain and the wind.

There was a sudden flash, followed by a huge "boom" and the smell of ozone. Lightning had struck nearby. Central Florida was subject to very heavy lightning. Being out in the storm wasn't something Logan wanted to experience. However, there was nothing else he could do, nowhere else to be.

A second bolt struck, farther away, followed by a third, then a whole cluster of strikes all around them. Then there was a pause, followed by more strikes. The thunder cracked and rolled through the dark sky. The last lightning strokes seemed to be a little farther away, and Logan relaxed a little. The wind gusted harder as the trailing edge of the storm passed, then faded. The rain now fell directly downward softly, shedding off the palm leaf shelter.

They hadn't escaped the water, though. They were lying in a puddle. It was amazing how cold the rainwater was. The day had been sweltering, but now the two were shivering, trying to raise their body warmth.

Logan looked out of the shelter. The rain had changed to a sprinkle, and the wind was almost completely gone. Serensaa was shivering uncontrollably, as was he. He turned to her and wrapped his arms around her slender body. She dug her face into the side of his neck and cuddled as tightly as she could.

The cold was miserable. Logan cynically wondered if their shelter had actually helped, or would they have been just as well off out in the weather?

He decided that it had helped a little. They would have lost heat more quickly if they'd been in the direct rain. As he concluded that thought, he found that he was starting to feel warmer. Their body heat and the small, enclosed shelter were combining to create a warm space as the evening grew darker.

After a while, Serensaa lifted her head, stared into his face, then laughed quietly. They kissed again. That activity seemed to warm them even more, or perhaps it simply helped them to ignore their discomfort.

The tight space wasn't conducive to lovemaking, but the two did their best. They wriggled out of their sopping clothes and held each other close. There was a little difficulty getting started, but they worked at it, and presently, they became oblivious to everything but each other and their immediate sensations.

It was nearly full dark, and the two were resting in each other's arms. They both jumped as something crashed in the bushes nearby. There was a bleat, followed by a ragged snarl, then more noises that sounded like a struggle. Then there was silence.

Logan had pulled his knife, now holding it towards the opening in their shelter. Serensaa fumbled at her pouch, then came up with a spear point that she mounted in one of the socketed spear shafts.

Logan considered trying to get his clothes on, but that would likely be noisy. He caught up another spear shaft, holding it so that the girl could mount a point in its socket. She did, quickly and without fumbling. Then she slipped quietly forward, out of the restrictive shelter into the nearly complete darkness. Logan gathered their clothes, shoved them out before him, and followed.

It was almost too dark to see. The clouds overhead had thinned, but it was still overcast, and the sun was completely down, leaving just the final dregs of the dying light to filter through the trees. Logan listened with every nerve cell in his ears tuned for any sound.

All he could hear was a steady dripping sound as the water fell from the trees. He relaxed a little. Maybe whatever it was had run away.

There was a sudden burst of snarls, then the sound of fighting, followed by a screaming hiss. The activity wasn't too far away. Whatever it was, it now sounded like there were more than one of the things, and they were disagreeing over how to divide up the prey animal that had bleated.

He jumped as a warm hand grabbed his arm. Serensaa pressed two fingers against his lips to ensure he was quiet. They gathered their clothes, and she led him away from the sound. There was a nearby stand of low, scrub oaks, and she headed directly for them. The clump of gnarled branches made a threatening shadow in the rapidly increasing darkness.

They slid through the closely spaced trunks, finally coming out on the other side. A larger tree was growing there. Logan could see its branches against the slightly lighter sky. The sun's afterglow chose that moment to provide a little more light, and he could see it was a laurel oak.

Serensaa was already up the tree and perched on the first branch. Logan prepared to climb after her. A sudden crash of foliage behind him caused him to spin, presenting the spear he was carrying as a flimsy defense.

A large form leaped out of the darkness with a snarl, struck the spear, and knocked him back against the trunk. Something slashed past his face, and there was a flash of brilliant pain across his upper chest and shoulder.

He fell to a sitting position, gritted his teeth to keep from crying out, and stabbed with the knife at the furry bulk. It thrashed and then screamed. He stabbed, again and again, pulling the knife hard sideways as each thrust went home.

He could feel the sharp blade cut through flesh with each stab. There was a sudden thick smell of feces, mixed with blood. The creature was slowing in its struggle. The wounds were having an effect.

He rolled, trying to get clear. As he did, he bumped into Serensaa's legs. She'd climbed down the back of the tree, and was leaning over him, stabbing with her spear at the dark form of his attacker.

He jumped to his feet, and she grabbed his arm, pulling him around the tree. His shoulder wound made it hard to climb, but she pushed at his backside until he managed the first low branch. From there, it was easy to climb higher. She followed along right behind, moving more surely and quickly than he could. They moved steadily higher in the branches.

The wounded creature below was breathing raggedly in great gasps. There was another snarl, followed by a roaring scream. Another of the beasts had arrived. It clawed at the tree, and Logan realized that it was coming up. It climbed to the first limb but then seemed to have difficulty and dropped out of the tree, snarling.

The two sat in the high branches, shaking as the adrenaline worked its way out of their systems. The creature below paced around the tree, snarling and sometimes rearing against the trunk with a scratching noise from its claws. It didn't try to climb again, though.

Logan had lost all sense of time in the darkness. After what may have been a few minutes or an hour or so, it grew quiet.

Serensaa had somehow managed to bring their pants up with her. How she had the presence of mind to do so amazed Logan. He gladly worked his damp pants over his legs, then pulled them up while balancing on the branch. The fabric made sitting more comfortable.

He was sitting on a level branch, his legs dropping into space, while he leaned forward to rest his right shoulder against another parallel branch. The whole left side of his upper chest burned and dripped blood. That was painful enough, but the tree bark grinding into his posterior was almost unbearable. He tried shifting to get more comfortable, but the bark ground at his skin, no matter how he moved.

Serensaa had been quiet, apparently waiting for the animal below to leave. Now she worked her way around to be close to him. Her hand touched his face, felt it, and then slid down his neck and onto his chest. There was a brief flash of more intense pain as she found the wound. Her fingers carefully explored the gashes.

Logan had been clawed, and he knew he'd been lucky. The spear he'd shoved forward had struck the animal, somehow blunting its charge. It had barely missed his face with one slash, striking his shoulder with the second. From the pain and the dripping blood, it was bad. He'd been trying to forget it, but her probing was impossible to ignore.

Serensaa's fingers slid along the wound from his upper breast to the tip of his shoulder. It was difficult for him to visualize how bad it might be, but the pain wouldn't allow him to relax.

She didn't say anything at first. After a moment, he could hear her picking at the branches surrounding them. She moved away, plucking at something that made a soft ripping sound. Then she was back sitting next to him again.

He could feel her movements as she worked at something in her hands. She quit, then reached for him again. Her fingers searched for the wound and pressed something soft and fibrous against it. Whatever it was, it had the effect of stopping the dripping blood. Some drips still ran down his chest, but the fibers had blocked the wound enough that it seemed likely to clot.

Logan felt a little light-headed. He was worried that he'd lost too much blood, and he was also terrified that he'd get some kind of infection. He'd avoided that with his other wounds, but this one could be different. Without any antibiotics, he might easily die here in this primitive wilderness. He shifted uncomfortably until he found that resting the right side of his bare chest against the supporting limb eased the pain.

———————◆○◆———————

It was a long night. They didn't dare climb down. It was impossible to see anything on the dark ground, so they couldn't tell if the second beast might still be hanging around.

Eventually, the clouds thinned, then parted into fluffy cotton balls that floated by quickly overhead. Stars shined through the holes momentarily as the clouds blew past. The moon wasn't showing, but it seemed much lighter now that the overcast was gone.

———————◆○◆———————

Logan gradually became aware that birds were chirping somewhere in the trees. He lifted his head from where he'd had it cushioned on his right arm.

His eyes were bleary and he felt like warmed-over dog food. Something moved nearby, and he turned his head to face Serensaa. It was light enough to see her face and she looked concerned. Her concern made him feel worse.

He flexed his left arm, experimenting with the pain in his upper chest. It was still bad. Even so, he felt he could climb down with no problems, but he was slow. By the time he'd managed to work his way to the ground, it was full-on daylight.

Serensaa had wadded a mass of dry Spanish moss against his wound, and it was stiff with clotted blood. There was no question in his mind about the fact that the wound was full of bacteria. There had probably been a lot of filth on the beast's claws, and the Spanish moss wasn't likely to be much better.

He dropped the last few feet out of the tree, lost his balance, and fell, landing on his back. Serensaa helped him to his feet and then led him around the trunk.

There, lying on its side, was a large hyena-like cat-creature. It had saber teeth, and its hind legs were shorter than the front ones. He glanced at the claws. They seemed to be duller than what a cat would have; maybe more like those of a dog. That was why the other one hadn't been able to climb the tree easily.

The protruding canine teeth were about two inches in length. Impressive, but not as long as those of the saber tooth tigers he'd seen previously. The cat's body wasn't as large either. Logan had never seen anything like it. He wasn't enough of a paleontologist to even hazard a guess as to what it was.

Serensaa's eyes were shining. She showed him the spear he'd thrust. The shaft was broken, but the foreshaft, with its attached point, was embedded deeply in the animal's chest. That lucky placement had saved Logan from a worse mauling.

He'd done a good job with his knife during the struggle. There were several large gashes in the animal's chest, some of them actually cutting through the ribs. He could see pinkish lung tissue through one of the wounds. Another knife wound had opened the creature's stomach, and its intestines had spilled out in a coiling pile. The smell of blood and feces was thick.

They gathered the rest of their clothes, which were scattered around the tree trunk, and pulled them on. Logan had some difficulty with his shirt, and she helped him, settling it across his back. The matted Spanish moss made a lumpy, diagonal ridge across his upper left chest.

Serensaa hacked into the cat-thing, using his knife. She removed both of the animal's backstraps. Logan understood. It was food.

She sliced into the abdomen, cutting through the skin and exposing the liver. Then she sliced off several thin slices and handed one to him.

Logan paused, unsure about the raw organ meat. She indicated he should eat. When he paused a little more, she cut off a bit and ate it herself. He grimaced but then chewed at the bloody liver, making another face at the heavy taste.

Something in the meat seemed to fill a need that his body had. It knew better than he did that the liver would help him heal. He paused, looked at the meat as he readjusted his thinking then ate several large chunks. Perhaps it would help him replace the blood he'd lost, he was unsure about that, but it was good. He quit eating when his stomach felt full.

Serensaa showed no inclination to stay around any longer. Logan understood the odor would probably draw scavengers. He didn't think he was up for another fight at the moment, and he was glad when she started off.

They headed westward, away from the carcass. Logan wasn't too fast. His shoulder hurt, and his lower back still hadn't recovered from being perched in the tree all night. His back had been strained in the fight also, and that made it difficult to walk easily.

He limped along behind her. She was obviously looking for something, but he didn't know what. She investigated patches of weeds as they walked. Finding what she was looking for, she exclaimed, then picked a bundle of what looked like weeds to Logan. She motioned to him that they'd stop there.

Logan was happy to lie back on the pine litter and rest. He found a comfortable position and went to sleep while Serensaa busied herself with the plants she'd picked. He woke for a moment to see her off through the trees, gathering something else.

After an hour or so, she woke him. He hadn't pulled his tee-shirt off to check his chest and then didn't want to pull it back over the wound without her assistance. She made him get up and led him through the trees to a small stream. It was flowing quickly and looked like it might be a branch of the stream that they'd been beside before the storm had struck. It was so cold that it almost certainly was spring-fed.

She gathered more dry Spanish moss, soaked it, and then went to work on his wound. He flinched as she picked the clotted mess off. She washed the wound gently with the clean moss. Then repeated the operation, stopping at times to pick some dirt and debris out of the gashes. She finally seemed satisfied that it was clean.

It was bleeding slightly again, but Logan felt better about the possibility of infection. At least she'd gotten most of the dirt out. What came next puzzled him.

She took the weeds she'd gathered and chewed them into a mashed-up, pasty wad, after which she rinsed her mouth repeatedly at the stream. Then she took the paste and smeared it into his wound, covering the gashes from one end to the other. She carefully worked it into the cuts, making sure no area was left untreated.

Logan had feared it would be painful, and it was at first. He found that something in the herbs had a numbing effect that gradually set in. That was probably why she'd rinsed her mouth so often. Whatever it was, the wound didn't hurt the way it had. He sighed in relief and smiled at his beautiful primitive nurse.

She responded by taking his head in her hands and pulling him forward for a long kiss. As hurt, as he was, he could feel his body respond. When he tried to kiss her again, she shoved him in the center of his chest, pushing him down with a laugh while shaking her head in her 'no' gesture.

She seemed pleased with him in some way. Logan thought about that while she built a small fire, then roasted some of the cat meat. Eventually, he concluded that she was proud of him for killing their attacker.

It really didn't seem like something of which to be proud. Instead, he had a feeling that he had been stupid, perhaps fatally so. If his wound rotted, it was a good bet he wouldn't survive. Cats had notoriously dirty claws.

After they ate, she kept the fire going, building it up as a defense so they could sleep by its side. Logan lay back and tried to fall asleep, hoping to recover from the long night.

Chapter Fifteen

The Sand Hills

The memory of the attack worked to prevent Logan from sleeping. He replayed his actions over and over in his mind. There might have been something he could have done that would have prevented the cat's slashing attack from striking him, but he couldn't quite figure out what it could have been unless he'd been able to hurl the spear rather than just pointing it in the right direction. He tossed around fitfully, finally settling his mind by watching Serensaa as she sat tending the fire.

He eventually started to drop off to sleep. An owl called, deep in the woods. He rearranged himself, took a deep breath. The pleasant odor of burning pine lingered in his nose. His last waking memory was of her profile highlighted by the yellow and red flames, contrasting with the dim outline of the foliage against the dark sky.

He awoke to a soft pressing on his lips. His eyes opened to the site of Serensaa's face hovering over his with her lips barely touching his. Her long hair brushed against his cheeks and neck. He reached to hold her, and her eyes closed as the kiss deepened. His breath shortened. She slowly pulled back and smiled at him. Then she sat up, pressing on his chest as he started to rise.

He relaxed and lay still as she cleaned his wound and repacked it with the herb poultice, taking the same care as before.

He felt better about the wound after that. The gashes had not shown any signs of rotting. There was some redness around the edges but no heat. He touched the surrounding skin, wondering if he might be lucky enough to avoid infection.

Serensaa set a slower pace during the morning. Logan had no difficulty keeping up. His chest hurt and was stiff, but it wasn't too painful. The poultice she'd applied had some property that seemed to calm the aggravated nerves.

Following up on his idea of throwing the spear, he had searched through her pack, and finding one of the fore-shafts with a damaged point, he had appropriated it. As they walked, he practiced with the spear thrower. He didn't care if he broke the flint tip. It was already flattened on the end.

He'd pick a clump of grass or a weed, a suitable distance ahead, and then chuck the spear at it with his right arm, retrieving it as they passed. The spear-thrower allowed him to throw the light shaft farther than he could have with just his arm alone.

Serensaa was amused at first but then grew interested and began to practice; alternating turns with him. He was surprised that she was no more accurate than he was. Perhaps she hadn't had an opportunity to use the atl-atl. She certainly seemed capable enough using a hand-held spear, and she was obviously an expert at using the points to cut up meat.

He tried to query her about her apparent lack of experience but to no avail. She'd just smile and shake her head, more or less randomly to his questions. Finally, she turned to him and said several sentences filled with a sequence of rapid sounds that he could barely distinguish as separate words.

It was her gestures as she spoke that hinted at what she was saying. He understood her meaning partly. In her tribe, women were not allowed to use spear throwers. That tool was reserved exclusively for hunters. She knew how they were used, but had never experimented with one.

Logan enjoyed throwing the spears. He used their spear practice to work on their language problem by saying, "Good" when either one of them hit their target and "not good" or "missed" when they didn't. She quickly got the idea behind the words, so he started saying, "Throw the spear," prior to throwing. That was a little puzzling to her at first, but once he helped her understand the word "spear," she mastered that also.

After that, he added the words "grass," "weeds," and "tree." "Hill" was another easy one. "Up" and "down" followed from that.

By the time the sun was passing the zenith, Logan was tired but happy. The morning's journey had passed more quickly as they occupied themselves with language and spear practice.

<hr>

They had reached an area of low, rounded sandhills interspersed with forested areas. Cresting a higher hill about midday, they saw a large lake extending to the south. It looked miles across. Logan believed that it was Lake Apopka. Its general shape and size seemed correct. If that were so, they were nearing the middle of the Florida peninsula.

The afternoon wasn't nearly as easy as the morning. It was exhausting. They slogged up and down over the hills. None of the slopes were very steep, but the sandy soil and long, tough grasses interspersed with woody weeds made walking difficult. Some of the weeds had small orange flowers on them.

Logan didn't care for those. If they were bruised, they emitted an unpleasant scent that reminded him of sweaty socks. He circled around them whenever he had a chance.

It had taken several hours to pass the large lake. It was behind them, to the east. They'd veered slightly southwest and were now climbing the highest hill he'd seen so far.

He tentatively assigned the name "Sugarloaf Mountain" to it. That might not be what it was, but since he remembered that was one of the highest points in the middle of the state, and since it dominated the western side of the lake, he figured no one would argue with him over the name.

They gradually worked their way up the eastern slope of the steep hill, passing through some copses of trees, mostly scrub oaks. The yellow flies were thick in these. The pests had a stealth mode allowing them to fly up silently and land on an exposed part of his anatomy. They'd quickly bite, causing a sharp stabbing pain. He mimicked Serensaa and pulled a clump of long grass that he swished ineffectually at the insects.

Once they exited the trees, the flies dropped off their trail, possibly discouraged by the stronger wind in the open.

They crested the hill, walked several hundred yards to the north, and looked down into a long valley. There was a herd of tan-colored animals strung out below. They were grazing while gradually making their way towards the southwest.

As the two humans watched, a pack of wolves charged down from one of the opposite hills, panicking the animals into a brief stampede. The wolves rapidly pulled down a slower animal. The herd ran on a few hundred yards then slowed to their normal pace, the ambush already forgotten.

Logan wasn't sure what they were, but they looked somewhat like larger llamas. He decided they must be new world camels. They didn't seem particularly bothered about the wolves. Attacks must be a commonplace event. Once the predators had their victim, the rest knew they were out of danger for the moment.

Serensaa drew his attention to a stand of trees to the west. If they hurried, they could reach the trees, make their way through, and end up close to the herd's path, giving them a chance to ambush one of the animals.

Logan thought that was a great idea. He was anxious to try out the spear-thrower on something besides grass clumps. He was hungry, and their small store of cat meat had drawn so many flies that they'd ditched it under a bush some miles back. Camel meat for supper would be good.

Serensaa broke into a jog, and he followed. They trotted until they reached the tree line.

The scrub oaks formed a thick screen with a lot of brush under the twisted branches. She led him in a winding path, ducking under low branches and brushing through the hanging Spanish moss. In this way, they came out a little ahead of the oncoming herd.

She took his arm and pulled him down in the tall grass. They crouched and hastened to a smaller bush that was out in the open, trying their best to stay out of sight. The camels were too far away to notice their passage and continued moving in their direction, unalarmed.

Logan was shaking; he was so excited. He'd killed both men and animals during his time in the past, but it had always happened so quickly that he hadn't had the time to think. Now that he was actually lying in ambush, hunting, his nerves made him twitch.

He stretched to loosen his muscles, and his chest twinged a little in response. He'd almost forgotten the wound. It hadn't bothered his throwing practice, so he didn't worry about it.

The camels came closer. To Logan, it looked like they were moving in slow motion. The sun was now brushing the tips of the trees to the west. If only the herd would hurry up. He didn't want to try to kill one in the dark. He'd have to postpone until tomorrow if they didn't get here soon.

Somewhere back in the rear of the herd, there was a roar. The camels broke into an immediate run, heading directly at them. Some larger predator, it sounded like a saber-tooth, had attacked, spooking the grass-eaters.

Logan took the spear and mounted a fore-shaft with an extra-long point. He looked at the edges of the flint. It had been carefully knapped and was sharp, with a beautiful leaf-like shape. Serensaa prepared two other spears for throwing in the time he'd fitted the fore-shaft into its socket.

He carefully placed the slightly hollowed butt of the spear against the matching nub on the throwing stick, then, holding the spear and stick level in his right hand, drew back his arm for a throw.

By now, the leading edge of the camels was nearly upon them. The herd would pass within a few yards of the bushes in which they were concealed. Logan drew his arm back further, then paused, belatedly trying to remember what he'd learned about throwing the spear.

As the camels passed, he skip-hopped forward and threw as hard as he could. He instantly realized that he'd made a beginner's mistake. He'd thrown at the herd, not at an individual animal. The spear passed over the near line of camels. It arched down and luckily struck an animal that was several rows back in the group. The camel made an odd, groaning cry that was all but lost in the general noise of the stampede. It ran on for a moment, then stumbled, and went down. The others immediately behind it strode over its body. The bulk of the following herd diverged to pass on either side of their fallen comrade.

Logan wanted to rush out directly to his victim, but Serensaa grabbed his arm and pulled him back into the bushes. She gave him another spear and said, "Logan, throw the spear."

He did a double-take at the beautiful girl. She'd really been learning during their language lesson. He stood up to throw, but she suddenly pulled him down again. He looked at her in surprise. In return, she pointed towards the rapidly approaching end of the herd.

He looked in that direction, but there was nothing to be seen. When he looked at her inquiringly, she held up two fingers so that they mimicked a saber-tooth's fangs. Then she said, "Piskata," and pointed again.

Logan didn't like that idea at all. If the saber-tooth tiger or tigers, he didn't know which, came their way, he felt their best option was to climb a very tall tree. He was worried that throwing a flimsy spear at one of the big cats was likely to be a fatal act.

The camels passed, creating a dust cloud that hung in the air. When the herd was gone, the floating dust stirred to the vague gusts of wind that descended into the valley. The thudding of padded feet that had sounded like distant thunder had faded into the distance. After the noise of the stampede, the valley seemed eerily silent.

As the dust gradually settled, the two could see a downed camel far back along the herd's trail. It was struggling to rise but being held down by a large, heavy-shouldered cat. Another of the tigers came charging up to sink its six-inch fangs into the camel's neck. The llama-like head dropped as the fangs severed its muscles and blood vessels.

Logan looked at Serensaa. She looked at the camel he'd struck, then back at the tigers, obviously trying to decide if they were far enough away not to notice the two humans.

Abruptly, she dropped to her stomach and began to worm her way out into the open, moving toward the dead animal. Logan immediately followed suit but had so much difficulty trying to keep his wounded chest from dragging that he fell far behind.

The girl slid up to the camel, pulled the spear free with several tugs, and then began to hack at the beast's back with the spear tip. In just a few minutes, she'd removed both back-straps. Laying them on its dusty ribs, she moved around to the other side, opened the abdomen, and sliced out a large chunk of liver.

Logan had arrived at the kill by this point, and she handed him the spear. Then she grabbed the pieces of meat, rose to a stooping position, and began to hurry back to the bushes. He followed.

There was a distant roar. He glanced down the beaten track. One of the tigers was trotting towards them, followed by a second. There were now seven or eight of the stripy beasts clustered around their kill. The two coming their way had apparently been turned away by the others and now were intent on claiming the human's prey.

Serensaa rounded the bush, rose to her full height, and started running, her long hair streaming behind her. Another roar caused a shot of adrenaline to rush through Logan's blood like a bolt of electricity. He put on a burst of speed and caught up to her.

He glanced at her. The crazy girl was laughing. She actually enjoyed this. He couldn't help but laugh with her, even though it made running difficult.

She was so loving, so competent, and yet, so incredibly wild. That was the only word for it. She seemed suddenly very alien to him. He couldn't imagine any of the women of his time finding being chased by saber-tooth tigers exhilarating.

They had covered several hundred yards before they paused to look back. The two tigers had stopped by the dead camel and were now ripping chunks of meat off and gulping them down. Chasing the two humans was apparently the farthest thing from their minds. Eating came first in the brutal calculus of survival.

Serensaa had recovered herself somewhat. When she finished panting, she looked at him and started laughing again. Logan grinned tentatively, then laughed along with her after he caught his breath.

It was strangely funny. They'd risked death and gotten away with supper. Not too bad a trade. So what if the saber-tooths had the main bulk of the camel? They had come away with more than enough to eat for the moment, and that was all that counted. Meat didn't keep long anyway.

She led him toward the setting sun until they reached a lower area surrounding a small lake. The trees were bigger near the water, and they picked one they could climb that was large enough to offer shelter for the night.

There was a lot of dry wood in the area. A tree had fallen and ripped branches off in the process. They gathered a sizable pile of wood before it got too dark.

Serensaa used her fire-starting rig to get a blaze going. They sliced off pieces of liver and tenderloin, speared them on some sticks, and broiled them over the coals. It was a great supper.

⸺◈⸺

They'd finished eating. Now, the fire was banked, and there was plenty of wood. They were sitting, a little apart, watching the flames, and Serensaa seemed lost in thought.

Logan was in a good mood. He'd made his first kill using the state-of-the-art weapon system of the time. He'd initially believed that using the spear-thrower would be difficult. It wasn't, although accuracy would likely take a lot of practice.

During the day's journey, he'd learned that he could throw the slender spears an incredible distance. The throwing stick gave a two-foot extension to his arm and allowed an amazing increase in throwing speed. He was confident in the device's use, although he cautioned himself that it wouldn't do to become overconfident.

The constant presence of the girl had become an indispensable part of his life. He looked to her for all of his cues. Life in the here-and-now was hazardous, and she'd shown that she was capable of avoiding most of the dangers. Since they'd become intimate, Logan had developed a deep desire to protect her. Mastering the spear-thrower was directly related to that desire.

Serensaa interrupted his reverie. He became aware that she was looking at him questioningly. He cocked an eyebrow at her in response. She said, "Logan," and held up one finger.

He nodded, and she then held up a finger on her other hand, simultaneously saying, "Serensaa."

Logan puzzled over that for a moment. She'd identified them as two separate individuals. That wasn't what he wanted.

He used her gestures, holding up the index finger on both of his hands spaced a little apart. He identified his left finger as Serensaa and his right as Logan, then slowly moved his hands together so that the two fingers were side-by-side.

She watched closely. Inspired, he hooked the fingers together, making loops with his thumbs. He tugged, showing the two were now inseparable.

She hesitated, and then her eyes widened as his meaning sank in. She smiled up at him, relief apparent in her expression.

He scooted over beside her, then wrapping his arm around her slender shoulders, he marveled that she could be so competent and yet so intensely feminine.

She leaned into him and pressed her palm on his heart, looking upward a little at his face. She asked, "Logan, Serensaa?"

He nodded firmly and pulled her face to his. She sighed in response. Apparently, he'd fully answered her question about their relationship in a way that she approved of.

He lowered his face to hers slowly, holding just short of a kiss. Her breath felt warm on his lips.

She kept her eyes focused on his, then moved a little so that their lips touched. The sensation of fire was instant. Logan focused entirely on her, the scent of her, the heat of her skin, the soft feel of her hair against his arms. The kiss went on for an infinitely long time ending slowly as they pulled apart.

Serensaa's chest was heaving with her rapid breathing, and her eyes were wide. Logan was confused. They'd already become intimate, yet this moment was almost like it was happening for the first time. His heart was racing with urgency.

He reached out to her with shaking hands and undid the lacing on her top. She lifted her arms to help him slide it off over her head.

He pulled his ragged shirt off, tossing it aside carelessly. She came into his arms again, her perfectly formed breasts pressing hard against the muscles of his chest. The pain of the scabbed-over claw marks was totally forgotten.

They kissed again, their hands sliding over each other. She moved one hand to the back of his neck and pulled his mouth firmly against her lips while her tongue touched his. The fire crackled and sent up a spray of sparks. The shadows moved against the nearby trees in response.

Logan couldn't wait any longer. He backed away a little and pulled off the rest of his clothes. Serensaa's mouth was open, and she took deep breaths as she took off her buckskin pants. A moment after that, they were entwined in a slowly moving tangle. Their movements gradually became rhythmical, then increased in speed. The fire projected their moving shadows against the foliage.

The sensations were so intense that Logan could barely think, but he had a fleeting feeling that he'd found his destiny. Serensaa was the one he'd waited for all of his life. He didn't care that he was somehow lost in time. Everything was fine as long as he held her in his arms.

⊶◆⊷

Later, they made love again. This time it was less frenzied, but just as deeply satisfying as before. The mosquitoes had thankfully left them alone because of the slight smoke from the fire, so they hadn't dressed, lying in each other's arms by the fire's warmth.

A little after they'd finished, there was the faint, far-off scream of a panther. It came echoing eerily through the trees, putting a punctuation mark on their lovemaking. Serensaa sighed and stood to pull on her clothing. Logan watched her, admiring every nuance of her form against the flickering light.

She knew he was watching and took her time, stretching to highlight her beautifully proportioned body as she pulled on her clothing.

He dressed while she built up the fire.

He was worried about their safety, spending the night by the fire. A predator might attack them. There were obviously plenty in the neighborhood.

The saber-tooths were out there somewhere, hopefully sleeping off full stomachs. And, he remembered the wolves they'd seen also. Then there was the cat that they'd just heard screaming. There was plenty of danger, yet, somehow he felt at peace here by the fire with her. He glanced at her and felt a strange stir in his heart, something like, yet different from the intense passion she aroused in him.

That puzzled him at first, but then, suddenly, everything about his feelings clicked. He loved her! He hadn't quite come to that thought before, but now he knew. He loved her with a deep and abiding love.

Without thinking about their communications difficulties, he said, "Serensaa, I love you."

She instantly came to him and held him tightly. It was obvious that she understood his meaning perfectly, if not his precise words.

He looked into her face and said, "I love you."

She smiled and repeated the words back to him. "Logan, I love you."

Logan laughed joyfully, nodded, and hugged her tightly, only belatedly realizing that she'd frozen.

He looked at her, startled. She was looking off into the darkness.

She slowly pushed them apart, then bent and handed him one of the spears and the throwing stick.

There was some threat out there in the darkness that he hadn't as yet sensed. Her senses were so finely tuned to her world that she was aware of danger long before he could detect it.

He separated from her a little, preparing the spear-thrower for action. An idea struck him. He caught her attention and gestured for her to climb the big oak.

She shook her head negatively. Apparently, the tree offered no sanctuary from whatever was out there.

There was a movement in the darkness followed by a rumbling growl. He focused intently. There was something out there moving closer.

The vague, threatening form became clear, and he saw that it was a bear. Something about it didn't look right to him. It was larger than he'd thought it would be, certainly larger than the Florida black bears that he'd seen before. It was possibly the size of a grizzly, but he felt that a grizzly was unlikely to be here. Then he saw that its muzzle was truncated. It had a short, bulldog-like face. That, paired with its extra-long legs, made it look almost alien.

Shrugging his shoulders in puzzlement, Logan drew back his arm. The bear walked slowly towards the fire. It didn't seem even slightly fearful of the flames, only puzzled by the light. The two humans moved slightly until the fire was directly between them and the approaching animal. It hesitated and peered, trying to make out what caused the movement. It seemed at least partially dazzled.

When it had approached nearer and was fully illuminated by the flames, Logan launched as hard a throw as he could. The spear flew straight but struck the bear's shoulder hump, burying itself deeply next to its neck.

The bear roared and reared up, slapping with its long arms, trying to come to grips with the thing that had bitten it.

Logan held out his hand, keeping his eyes glued on the angry beast. Another spear was slapped into his palm. Serensaa knew exactly what was needed. He glanced quickly at her. She was holding a third spear ready in one hand and a flaming branch in the other.

He fitted the spear to the throwing stick, trying not to shake with excitement. Then he stepped back from the fire, sprang forward, and launched the second spear.

This time it struck directly in the bear's chest. It would have been difficult to miss. The animal was standing only about twenty feet away.

The bear dropped its head and grabbed the spear shaft, snapping it in half with a quick bite. The fore-shaft came away, remaining embedded in the creature's chest. It swiped ineffectually at the stub but only succeeded in moving the sharp spear point sideways inside its lung. Logan hoped it had severed something vital.

The bear roared in response to the increased pain, then dropped to all fours and ran directly at the fire.

The two humans jumped aside as the bear came right across the blaze, kicking embers all over the place. It roared in pain at the flames but continued blindly forward, passing to Logan's right.

As it passed, he lunged with his tanto, driving the knife deeply into the bear's neck and dragging it hard in a cutting motion. He was rewarded by a gush of blood. The bear whirled towards him, and he skipped back to distance himself.

Serensaa ran forward from behind the animal and shoved her spear directly into its backside. Logan couldn't see where she struck, but from the bear's reaction, it was somewhere extremely sensitive. It jerked around, roaring in pain and trying to bite her spear shaft. She dodged back behind the thick oak trunk.

As it whirled, Logan could see that she'd planted the spear deep in the bear's rectum. It ignored him as he danced forward, looking for a chance to slash with the tanto.

Before he could bury the knife again, the bear broke and ran for the darkness, roaring in pain with each step. It disappeared.

They could hear it for a short time, but the roars suddenly became choked, and then there was a distant gurgle.

Serensaa cocked her head on one side, listened, then said, "Tode." The context made the word unmistakable. The bear was dead.

Logan sheathed his knife, trying to regain control of his nerves. They could easily have been killed.

The bear had taken three of their spear points away with it. By his count, they only had two more in her pouch. They'd taken three from the man that they'd killed. Those plus the three from the men the saber-tooth tigers had killed made six, and he'd used the broken one for practice until it was completely destroyed. They needed to recover those points from the bear. Two were not enough for defense.

He grabbed a flaming branch and started forward. Serensaa made a cautioning sound but came beside him, carrying her own branch and one of the two remaining fore-shafts that she held like a knife.

They walked slowly along the direction the bear had retreated. Logan glanced back to see the fire shining faintly in the distance. As he did, Serensaa made a soft exclamation. He jerked his head around. There was the bear.

It was not quite dead. Having lost much blood, it could no longer run, but it had managed to stand, leaning its back against a tree. It snarled feebly at its two adversaries and took a slow step forward. Its massive strength chose that moment to give out, and it dropped onto its chest.

Logan cautiously moved forward. The still-living bear tried to crawl to meet his advance. He stepped quickly to the side and drove the tanto deep between the bear's ribs in the exposed lower part of its chest. The sharp blade struck something vital, and the bear made a convulsive flinch, gasped, and then stilled in death.

Serensaa came forward, deferentially held out her hand for the knife, and, when he gave it to her, she knelt and quickly cut off several large chunks of meat.

Logan watched, bemused. This was primitive life at its best and worst. The bear would have cheerfully eaten them. Now it would serve as their next meal. He resolved to be more alert. It was not his ambition to become lunch for some hungry predator. If he had any say in the matter, it would be he who did the eating.

Chapter Sixteen

Separated

B ear meat for breakfast was good. Logan finished, feeling quite stuffed. The meat was a little greasy, but he wholeheartedly approved of the taste. It was something he hoped to have again.

He sat watching Serensaa cut up and cook a few last bits to be eaten later. When she was finished, she wrapped the steaming meat in some palm fronds, making a neat package that she put into her pouch. Then she stood and kicked dirt over the fire, still holding his tanto.

Logan stretched and began to gather the spears. He saw her feet stop kicking dirt and wondered why. The fire was still smoking. Looking up, his first impression was that she was terrified. Her face was pale. She was standing stiffly, looking into the trees, holding her arms at her sides.

He jumped to his feet. There was a bearded man standing by a tree staring at them. No, staring at Serensaa.

The man said something low and harsh. Serensaa answered an angry tone in her voice, then spat on the dirt. The man laughed, shook his head, and started forward. She turned to run but drew up instantly.

Logan began to turn but was grabbed from behind by a strong pair of arms that came around his chest, pinning his arms to his sides.

His Tae Kwon Do training was triggered by that unexpected attack. Without thinking about it, he stamped hard on the attacker's foot. The grasp loosened in response. Logan caught one of the man's arms with both hands and bent into a throw that flung the attacker to the ground.

The man landed on his neck and flopped limply for a moment. Taking no chance that his assailant might recover, Logan kicked him under the chin, slamming the man's jaw shut with a "clack."

A third warrior grabbed at Logan's arm. He twisted into another throw, using the man's forward motion against him. That one, too, ended on the ground but rolled quickly away and jumped to his feet.

Logan looked around, trying to see where the next attack would originate. Serensaa was sprinting away through the trees with the bearded man in hot pursuit. He started to yell at her, but a fourth enemy presented himself.

This one was armed with a spear that he apparently intended to stick in Logan's guts. He came forward at a run and lunged with the spear held low.

Logan desperately twisted, and the point grazed his side, cutting a hole through his ragged shirt. The fabric twisted and bound, trapping the spear as the man tried to pull it back.

Logan grabbed the foreshaft, pulling it free with one hand while he yanked on the spear shaft with the other. His attacker didn't release the shaft and stumbled forward a little. That was all Logan needed. He swung the short fore-shaft upward in a rising strike and drove the flint point directly into the man's solar plexus. It went deep. The man's eyes rolled up. He dropped to his knees and then fell forward on his face, unmoving.

Logan had released the fore-shaft when the man fell and now turned to face two more attackers. These men were more cautious, having seen him dispose of three men almost instantly. They separated, raising their spears as if to throw. He jumped towards the nearest one, striking the spear upwards as he closed. The man grunted as Logan struck his neck with his knuckles, then grabbed the infuriated youth in a bear hug.

As Logan started to break free, the second man kicked him in the back of his knee. He fell backward, dragging the hugging man down on top of him. The second man dove down to help.

Logan was holding his own until the man that he'd previously thrown away got his hands around Logan's neck. The grip tightened until Logan started to see black closing in. With the last of his strength, he wrenched one of his arms free and caught the choker's left thumb. A twisting motion snapped the digit like a twig, and the choker let go with an inarticulate cry.

The other two men managed to flip Logan onto his face and sat on him. One of them had a piece of hide that he used to tie Logan's wrists, and that was that. He was captured.

Logan lay still, breathing heavily and trying to recover. His mind was moving at high speed. If he could regain his feet, he'd attack with kicks. He started to pull his knees under him, but when he moved, one of the men began to whack him viciously with a spear shaft. The blows hurt and didn't cease until he lay still. When he moved again, he was struck instantly.

He relaxed. There would be another chance. It was up to him to be prepared when it came. He hoped that Serensaa had gotten away.

Then a question struck him. Were these the men that had been trailing Serensaa when he first saw her? The ones they'd been fleeing from across half of Florida? He visualized the instant of attack. Serensaa had recognized the bearded guy. That was for certain. She hadn't been happy to see him either.

The first man, whose jaw he'd kicked, regained consciousness slowly, finally sitting up. When he saw Logan, he climbed to his feet and came forward, drawing a stone knife. One of the others said something, and the man stopped. He yelled something back at the speaker.

The two argued for a moment, then the kicked man put his knife away, moved up to Logan, and kicked him in the ribs. Logan grunted but made no attempt to move. The man drew his leg back for a harder kick.

That was what Logan had been waiting for. He bent at the waist, scissored his legs hard, and swept the guy's supporting leg, bringing him to the ground. Logan scrambled around, rolled over, then brought his heel down hard on the nose of the fallen man. There was a loud crunch, and the man went limp.

The others were on him again, beating him with spear shafts. Logan tried to shield his head but ended up curled in a fetal position, simply trying to endure until they tired of hitting him.

They quit after a bit. He lay there gasping in pain, trying to recover.

They beat him some more after they determined that his last kick to the nose had killed his final attacker.

Logan endured it with grim satisfaction. He'd killed two of his five attackers, broken another one's thumb, and given the last two men some serious bruises. They were likely feeling almost as ill-used as he was. He'd gotten in some hard strikes while they rolled around on the ground, including kneeing one in the groin.

The three remaining men sat and watched him, talking among themselves. When Broken-thumb saw him looking at them, he said something to Logan in an ugly tone, then dragged his finger across his throat in an unmistakable threat.

Logan didn't respond; he was re-evaluating himself. He hadn't realized that he could fight so effectively. He'd always been tentative and fearful of hurting others before. Of course, his instructor had emphasized that they shouldn't strike full force. It wouldn't do to have students injured in a university-sponsored class. Nevertheless, Logan's self-image was changing.

He'd won the love of a beautiful woman whom he'd never dare to approach in his own time, and now he'd demonstrated that he was a deadly hand-to-hand fighter. In addition, it seemed that he was stronger than he'd thought he was. All that carrying shingle-bundles up ladders had given him muscles he didn't know he had.

There was a hail, and the men stood up. The bearded guy came through the trees. Logan rolled over, unnoticed, and saw that Serensaa had gotten away. The bearded man was obviously winded and angry. Logan was happy that she was so fast. With her free, perhaps there would be a chance for him to escape, provided they didn't kill him outright.

Logan's three captors showed a degree of deference to the bearded man. From that, Logan gathered he was their leader. The four engaged in a heated discussion for several minutes, pausing to gesture at the two dead men and at Logan.

Not knowing the language wasn't too much of a handicap, Logan thought. The bearded guy asked what had happened, and the others made up some kind of story that inflated their fighting prowess culminating with capturing Logan.

The only thing was, the bearded leader didn't buy it. He laughed derisively at something one of them said and then gestured at the two dead men.

Logan imagined he was saying, "Those two were better fighters than you, and he killed them. If you hadn't gotten lucky, he would have defeated you too. Look at you! You're all beat up."

His imagined statement was probably close to the truth. The three looked embarrassed when the leader was finished with them.

The men discussed Logan some more, ending with one of them yanking his bound hands until he managed to get to his feet. The thong had been tied tightly and had been cutting off his circulation, but it loosened slightly with the tugging. He hoped it would loosen more. He surreptitiously twisted at it, trying to stretch the poorly cured leather fibers.

They set off, one of them shoving Logan along. The leader headed along Serensaa's path, following her tracks. Logan moved slowly, just trying to avoid making them angry enough to beat him again. His bruises had bruises, and walking was difficult. His knee was sore from being kicked, and he limped a little, favoring it.

He looked down at his waist and felt a shock of loss. His tanto was gone. For a moment, his mind was blank, and then he remembered Serensaa had been holding it last, cutting the last few pieces of bear meat to save for later. He hoped she still had it. His captors certainly didn't, although they'd been careful to pick up the spears he'd been carrying.

Spears were to be preserved. They weren't that easy to make, and they broke often. The men's action was completely understandable.

The leader wanted Serensaa. That was obvious. He carefully followed her tracks. They came to a place where the trail faded out, and the leader and Broken-thumb cast about for a long time before Broken-thumb found a faint trace of her passage. Then they were off again.

The hunters ate some jerky or dried meat during the day but didn't offer any to Logan. He trudged along stoically, his stomach making complaining noises.

The path led through pine forests, interspersed with scrub oak. The long-leaf pines were thick in the valleys but gave way to sand pines near the crest of the low sandy hills.

Logan's back ached from walking with his hands behind him. It seemed like the men would never stop. He walked through the pain from his knee, and it gradually grew better, but by the time the sun was setting, he was moving in a gray fog of exhaustion.

He didn't know what they were going to do with him. By now, he felt it would almost be a relief if they killed him. His main concern was for Serensaa's safety. He wanted with all of his heart for her to escape. Whatever the leader had in mind for her, it wasn't something Logan wanted her to be forced to endure.

The day faded unceremoniously into an overcast night. The clouds had gathered during the late afternoon and were now a solid mass from the east across to the far western sky. He could only tell the sun was low by its faint glow through the cloud cover.

The leader selected a campsite and directed the others to gather wood. Broken-thumb complained that he couldn't carry wood, shaking his hand in the leader's face. The leader pointed at Logan, and Broken-thumb came over and grumpily settled down to guard him.

The men had a fire going before the last light faded. They'd gathered a lot of wood, something Logan was glad of. He didn't fancy fighting off any predators with his hands bound. Climbing a tree was out of the question, too.

The bearded leader came over to Logan and asked him several questions. Logan could make no sense of the words and just shook his head "no" using Serensaa's motion. This seemed to anger the man. He slapped Logan twice and then walked back to the other side of the fire, where he sat, glaring at his captive.

—◆—

Night fell, and the cloud cover made it pitch black. The leader and two of the men were stretched out, sleeping. Logan was lying on his side, facing the fire, while Broken-thumb sat guard and tended the fire. The man was drowsing. Every so often, he would almost nod off, but then he'd catch himself with a jerk. He'd raise his head, look around alertly for a moment, and then start to fall asleep again.

There were no night noises, save for a young barred owl that flew into a tree a hundred yards away. It laughed like a maniac for a bit and then flew off, pausing to laugh again much farther away. Broken-thumb ignored it, drowsing by the fire while the others slept.

Logan was nearly asleep himself when he felt a slim hand grasp his hand. He jerked slightly but then lay still. There was a dragging sensation at his wrists.

Serensaa had wormed up behind him and was cutting the restraining thong. There was a brief sensation of pain as the knife nicked his skin. She was using his tanto. The cutting motion was smooth instead of a jagged, rough feeling that one of the flint tips would have caused.

His hands came free. He fought an almost irresistible urge to pull them in front of him. The muscle pain in his upper arms and shoulders was intense and called out for relief. He lay still, watching his captors.

Imperceptibly, the sense of Serensaa's presence faded. She was moving away. He chanced a look over his shoulder. The crazy girl was working her way around behind Broken-thumb. The man, head slumped on his chest, was nearly asleep now.

Serensaa rose up behind him, grabbed his mouth with one hand, pulled his head back, and slashed his throat. He jerked and started to struggle. Blood was pouring over his chest, but he wasn't dead yet. One of his feet struck a log that was partway in the fire, making a sound.

The leader raised his head and yelled. All three of the remaining men jumped to their feet in alarm.

Logan was well into the darkness by then. He couldn't run very fast, his knee was still sore, but he was moving as quickly as he could. There was shouting behind him.

He glanced back. Serensaa had dashed forward and slashed the leader's face with the tanto, then had run in exactly the opposite direction that he'd taken. The men were yelling in confusion. The leader shouted in anger and gestured for the two to follow Logan. Without waiting to see if they followed his order, he turned and set out after the girl.

Logan had no doubt that she'd escape his pursuit. She'd already shown that she could easily outrun him, and it was so dark that she couldn't be seen.

The main fear Logan had was of running headlong into some predator. Or a tree, he thought, as he barely avoided a looming black trunk. He slowed in order to avoid trees and move silently.

The two men chasing him had set out at an angle to his course, so he turned more to the left in order to diverge from their path. He kept going until his knee gave out, then he limped along as quickly as he could, trying to keep from groaning with the pain at each step.

His hands had regained their circulation, and when he stumbled over a suitable broken branch, he carried it along. It was better than no weapon at all.

He hoped that Serensaa still had the tanto. She'd probably need it. He tried not to think of his own condition. He didn't know what he would do with no weapon and no fire. It was too much to consider at the moment. He was exhausted, but he forced himself to keep moving.

⸺◦◦◦⸺

Morning found Logan far away from the events of the night. He'd reached a large lake and had circled around it, moving to his left, reasoning that he was headed westward as he did. He stumbled along blindly until near dawn.

The clouds had opened up in the middle of the night and washed everything with heavy rain. It had been chilly, and he was still shivering, but he was glad for the rain. He hoped that would be enough to cover his trail. He'd been crashing along, probably leaving signs that a blind man could read. The rain might have been enough to wash away any footprints he'd left.

The clouds were gone, and there was some light in the east when he climbed an oak tree. He moved upwards into a thick patch of leaves, then wedged himself in a fork. He had to get some rest, and the tree was convenient.

He woke hours later. An osprey had landed in the upper branches and was bitterly complaining about his presence. The large hawk peered down at him, unwilling to come closer. He moved, and it took off in alarm, flapping heavily as it rose.

It had carried a fish into the branches and had been preparing to eat when it noticed Logan. Now the fish, forgotten in the bird's urge to fly, dropped through the branches. It slid past Logan's perch and fell to the ground.

He was down the tree in an instant, his sore muscles protesting all the way, but overruled by the growls of his stomach. Raw fish never tasted so good.

The fish was gone, all but the head, and even that looked good. Still, the edge was off of his appetite.

Now Logan was again worried about Serensaa. He knew roughly where he was, but he had no idea where she might have fled. They hadn't had time to make plans, even if they could communicate.

He knew that she'd been insistent on her westward course. The idea had come to him that she was headed for the Crystal River site.

Without him, she'd probably continue in that direction. He couldn't imagine that she would spend too much time wandering around trying to find him in the pines. She had to know that he would head westward also. After some thought, he glanced at the sun, oriented himself, and set out westward.

He looked for a better weapon as he walked. There were some shoots that were nearly the same thickness as a spear. He worked at one until he broke it off. A little later, he found a piece of coquina stone. It sufficed to allow him to grind the thick end of the shoot into a crude point. Then he found another limb on an oak that he might be able to use as a makeshift spear-thrower. He got it off and sized to the right length. When he tried the rig, it worked. Not as well as the one they'd had, but enough so that he felt more confident. He might be able to injure one of the men, should they find him.

He kept moving, looking for something, anything to eat.

Chapter Seventeen

Westward Alone

The second day alone, Logan found the partially rotten carcass of a turtle. It wasn't much, but there was a little meat on the stinking thing that hadn't yet turned. At least it wasn't so bad that he couldn't swallow it. He worked it loose with his fingers, then closed his eyes and swallowed. It hit like a leaden chunk, cold and nasty in his stomach.

About an hour later, he knew that eating it had been a mistake. He was struck with a horrible case of diarrhea and vomiting. The meat hadn't been as fresh as he'd assumed.

He decided that it was something that he'd get rid of quickly, but by mid-afternoon, he knew that wouldn't happen. He was running a fever and feeling very dehydrated. He staggered on until he came to a swampy area.

There were pools of water here, and he stopped to drink. The water was clear but dark with decaying vegetation. It was full of little mosquito fish, and their friendly presence let him know the water was safe to drink.

He drank, then immediately vomited. He drank again. This time, the water sat in his stomach and seemed to soak into his parched tissues. After a short time, he drank some more. Then he had another run of diarrhea. By now his intestines were almost totally cleaned out, so it was mostly water.

After that, he was exhausted. He was still feverish, too.

There was a thick stand of reeds that were growing in a sandy bank. The water was down a little, and the reeds were exposed and dry. He crawled in, leaving a winding trail, and then lay down in the center of the reeds. After a time, he fell asleep.

When he woke, it was nearly dusk. He felt a little better but thirsty. He didn't want to leave a clear trail into his hiding place, so he crawled along a different path towards the pool, threading through the thick stand of reeds. He reached the water's edge and drank again.

During the night, he crawled to the pool for another drink. By the time the local red-winged blackbirds were singing from their perches in the reeds, he was feeling almost well enough to continue his journey. He lay for a while, watching the puffy clouds travel by overhead and thinking that it was a good thing that he'd gotten those preliminary inoculations for the dig.

The reeds were full of dragonflies. These jewel-colored insects would sit on the top of a reed, resting, and then shoot off to grab a passing mosquito or mayfly. The dragonflies were so thick that their wings made a low humming sound that he found relaxing. They were undoubtedly responsible for the lack of mosquitoes in what was prime mosquito territory. He was grateful for their presence.

Hunger drove him out of the reeds in the early afternoon. He'd lost the entire contents of his stomach and was now feeling weak and terribly hungry. He didn't have much hope of food, but as soon as he reached the edge of the reeds, an opossum ambled by.

That was lunch. Logan didn't much care for the raw meat, but he couldn't seem to match Serensaa's knack of starting a fire easily, so raw had to do. The calories were welcome, and by evening he was starting to feel more optimistic. Maybe he'd survive after all.

He resorted to climbing a tree to spend the dark hours. There were wolves somewhere around. He heard them howling on and off through the entire night. Nothing came by to bother him, and he slept fitfully in his perch, moving occasionally for relief from the uncomfortable position it imposed.

◆

What had developed into an enjoyable journey now had become a depressing slog. Logan missed Serensaa. He missed her daring humor, her smiles, and, most of all, he missed her loving embraces. Just the sight of her shapely posterior walking ahead of him had seemed to make the time and miles go faster. Now, on his own, he found that he was incredibly lonely. The only solace he found was in imagining that she was somewhere just ahead of him and could possibly show up at any moment.

To compound matters, he wasn't absolutely sure where he was going, save that he was generally headed west-northwest. He hoped that would put him near the Crystal River area by the time he hit the coast. He was pessimistic, though. He had some difficulty assuming he would live that long on his own.

That assumption had become a constant worry in Logan's mind. He felt lost without Serensaa's knowledge and guidance. She knew so much about surviving that he didn't know. A lifetime's worth, in fact. He tried to be more cautious. Now, on his own, he felt even more acutely just how much he'd relied on her sharp senses and ability.

The higher elevation of the Mid-Florida ridge gradually gave way, and with the lower altitude, the land became swampier. Logan had believed the Green Swamp was far to the south, but the sound of frogs and the flocks of wading birds said otherwise. In response, he veered northward.

A day of walking put him back in more sandy territory. The pines grew more sparsely here, making the visibility slightly better. There were small hills, and when he found one that was not overgrown with trees, he could see for miles.

Late in the afternoon, he heard a low rumbling noise. The sound instantly sent shivers down his back. It sounded like mammoths. The memory of his last experience with the huge beasts sharpened his senses as he tried to localize the sound.

The direction of the rumbling was difficult to pin down, but Logan finally decided it was coming from a thick stand of trees that were in a small depression that likely held a pond or sinkhole. He turned and walked away from the spot, hoping to avoid any sign of the creatures.

A crash behind him made him look back. An elephant-like animal had broken through the trees, knocking two askew. It was big but definitely wasn't a mammoth.

He ducked behind a screen of brush and peeked under the foliage. The animal had turned and was stripping branches off a deciduous tree as it browsed. Its head was shaped differently than a mammoth, as was its body. It wasn't quite as tall as the larger beasts, although it was easily as large as most modern elephants.

It came to Logan that this must be a mastodon. He knew their teeth were commonly found in some areas in Florida. If that was what it was, it could go on with its feeding. He didn't want anything to do with either mammoth or mastodon.

He slipped farther back, then turned and jogged away, gradually turning in a large circle to regain his direction of travel. The mastodon trumpeted behind him, a sound like someone blowing through a spit-filled trombone. The trumpet was answered by a second from farther away. If there were two of the beasts, there might be more.

Logan sped up, leaving the area quickly.

———◇———

He was hungry that night. He'd found a sizable tree to climb and wasn't too worried about predators. It even had a comfortable fork with limbs so broad that he wasn't concerned about falling. The main problem was his stomach. It was prowling around in his gut, looking for something to eat. He resolved to find food in the morning, even if he had to delay his trek.

A chuck-will started calling in the small hours of the morning. The dratted bird must have found a nearby location that it favored because it kept at it. Logan found it impossible to sleep with the loud calls repeated every second or so. He tried counting them, but lost count started again, and lost count again.

He woke to a cardinal singing cheerfully a few trees over. Its liquid notes were far more pleasant than the chuck-will's boring love song. The sun had cleared the horizon by that point.

Logan looked down, checking the ground below for potential threats. He could see nothing, so he descended.

He'd seen a pond the night before while locating the tree. It was only a few hundred yards away, so he headed there for a drink.

After water, food was next on his list. He was quite pleased to see that there were duck potatoes growing in the shallow edge of the pond. There didn't seem to be any gators nearby, so he waded into the clear water and scuffed the tuberous roots out with his feet. They floated to the surface, and he washed each one, pulled the thin roots and main plant stem off, and ate the tubers.

They tasted like a combination of potatoes and chestnuts. Not the best breakfast, but at least he was able to give his stomach something to work on besides its own lining.

He gathered more and stored them in the remains of his shirt. It was just about at the end of its usefulness as a garment. Torn and rent from climbing trees, claw slashes, spear holes, and all, it barely had enough strength to hold another meal's worth of duck potatoes.

As a precaution against biting flies and mosquitoes, he smeared mud across as much of his torso as he could reach, then set out, heading west-northwest.

The walk was much like that of the day before: a seemingly endless trek through pines mixed with scrub oaks. There were no animals in evidence, save for numerous small gray squirrels that were mostly up in the trees.

They'd slide around the trunk as he approached, carefully keeping the bulk between themselves and the two-legged intruder. A few chucked at him, and that was company of a sort. None were careless enough to give him a chance to throw the stick he was carrying.

He kept watching for a chance. Even a small squirrel would be welcome meat.

He'd passed through a great stand of smaller pines and scrub. It was littered with downed trees that showed signs of an old fire. He didn't know if it was caused by lightning or human action, but the dead trees made travel difficult.

On the other side, the taller pines thinned out into grassland. This bothered him. He could see farther, but, in turn, he was far more visible to any lurking pair of eyes. He circled the area, trying to stay just inside of the bordering trees. After a time, he had reached a place where the grassland trended away to the south.

He came around a thicket and stopped. There was a man tied between two saplings. He ducked back into the thicket's edge and looked again, more carefully. The man was unmoving and covered with blood. Any others who might have been there once had apparently moved on.

Logan came out and cautiously walked up to the man. It was a grim sight. The stranger had been tortured. There were cuts and gashes all over his torso. His face was mutilated, and his fingers were gone.

Logan felt the man's arm. It was cool. He was quite dead. Logan wasn't sure if he should untie the body in order to salvage the strips of hide that held the wrists. That was the only thing that was salvageable. The corpse was otherwise naked.

He inspected the back of the body. There was a wound with a bit of stick protruding. He bent down to look. Someone had stabbed the man with a spear, striking his kidney area. The fore-shaft had carelessly been left in the wound.

Logan grasped at the stick. It was slippery with blood and didn't come out freely. After working at it for a few minutes, it pulled free. The spear-point was intact.

This was a real find! The lack of any weapon save the stick he had been carrying had weighed on his mind, making him nervous and timid. Now, with the simple, hand-made stone knife, he felt more of a man. Maybe not quite ready to tackle anything, but still a lot more confident.

The dead man wasn't one of those that had attacked Serensaa and him. The man was of a different physical type. His hair was long and black, and he had a distinct Roman nose along with darker skin color.

That meant there were two different groups of humans living in the area. The tortured man seemed to mutely imply that the two were at war. Or, at least, hostile towards one another.

The possibility of being caught between two groups of warring tribesmen added an additional sense of danger to the situation. It wasn't that Logan felt particularly friendly towards the men who had pursued them, but the possibility of a new tribe to watch out for made him even more nervous.

His studies had given him a little understanding of how cruelly the Native Americans often treated members of other tribes. The horrendous torture that had killed the man was probably representative of what he could expect. He wished Serensaa were present. He could certainly use her guidance.

He worked the bindings loose, letting the corpse slump to the ground. He might need the thongs. Certainly, the spear-point was too good a weapon to pass up. He was happy to have discovered it.

After that, he kept on the lookout for another sapling that could be converted into a spear shaft. The one that he had wasn't really straight enough to suit him. He wasn't quite sure how he would create the socket for the fore-shaft, but maybe he could tie the two together with one of the thongs should he find a suitable sapling.

———◆○◆———

That night he camped in a hollow log. There were no climbable trees about, so when he found an uprooted hollow tree in a depression, he cautiously worked his way inside. He wriggled around until he found a comfortable position. Then he gradually dropped off to sleep. He'd eaten the remains of the duck potatoes, having found nothing else all day. They had made a moderately filling, if uninspired, dinner. Now his stomach was full enough to let him rest. He hoped he'd be able to sleep through the entire night.

———◆○◆———

Logan awoke. There was a noise from outside the log. Something, some beast, was sniffing around. It made a low, rumbling, growling noise. It sounded more like a bear than anything else. He felt for the spear-point and prepared to defend himself.

The dim outline of the opening was suddenly blocked. There was a growl in the darkness, and he heard the creature scrabble at the opening. Looking closely, he could barely make out gleaming, reddish eyes and a mouth full of teeth.

Logan shifted to a crawling position, holding the knife in front of him. If the thing crawled in with him, it would restrict its forepaws. It could bite him, but maybe he could jab its eyes and make it retreat.

He moved slightly and jumped with a curse as his hand came down on a snake. The reptile wasn't large, but any snake was a bit too much in this situation. He started to back away as the bear shoved its head and shoulders deep into the log.

Inspiration struck, and Logan felt for the snake again. He yelled, then snatched the reptile and flung it directly into the bear's opened mouth as it roared in return. The bear snapped down on the writhing creature then shook its head violently.

The bear continued to shake its head but then made an odd noise and backed slowly out of the log. Logan moved deeper, carefully feeling for any other serpents. The bear made a low, moaning noise from outside. It had seemingly lost interest in coming into the log.

Logan felt suspended in the darkness, waiting for a resumption of the attack. Minutes passed with no sound. He crawled slowly forward, pausing between each movement to listen. Finally, he reached the opening and carefully peered out. There was no sign of the attacking bear. Maybe it had gone elsewhere.

He backed into the log nervously, worrying about the bear and about any other possible snakes. It took him a long while to calm down, and he was unable to fall asleep again. He lay awake through the hours until dawn, nerves tingling, alert for any sound.

⦿

The light had imperceptibly gathered until the hollow log's opening was more clearly defined. Logan couldn't wait any longer. He was tired, sleepy, frightened, and needed to relieve himself. That last urge was gradually winning over the fear.

He crawled out, trying to peer around the edges of the opening for an ambush. Once out, he quickly did his business and then started up the side of the depression. He found the bear just over the edge. It had made it that far and died.

Completely amazed, Logan investigated. The animal was dead, and he didn't know why. Suspicion struck him, and he turned back to the depression. He found the remains of the snake near the opening. He hadn't noticed it before.

It was brightly colored with rings in a repeating pattern of red, yellow, black, yellow, and red. Logan shuddered, thinking about picking the thing up. It was amazing it wasn't him lying dead, rather than the bear.

It was perhaps a little over two feet in length, which was large for a coral snake. It must have struck the bear on the lips or nose. The snake's venom was a nerve toxin of high potency, and there had been a lot of it. The bear hadn't made it more than a few steps before the venom reached its brain.

Logan's stomach reminded him of another issue. Bears were good to eat. Had the coral snake venom poisoned the meat, or could he risk eating it? He wasn't sure.

He rationalized that the bear had probably succumbed to a bite on the face, and the venom most likely wouldn't have circulated throughout the animal's body. It was a large black bear, far larger than it should be. Florida black bears were usually fairly small. This one was easily over four hundred pounds. More like a grizzly bear in size, he thought.

Finally, hunger decided him. He used the spear-point to haggle through the hide and cut out some of the muscle from a rear leg. That was the part of the bear that was farthest from the bite, so if any part were safe, that would likely be it.

He walked off, cautiously chewing on some of the raw meat. It was greasy and not as pleasant as it had been when Serensaa cooked it. He only ate a little and then waited for over an hour to see if he noticed any effect.

He felt fine, and there were no odd sensations, so he ate some more as he walked along.

Chapter Eighteen

A Fox

During the next two days, Logan walked over a seemingly endless upland area with grasslands interspersed with low, rounded sandy hills. The travel was boring, long, and hot. Despite the cool nights, the days heated up quickly. The weather seemed to have gotten hotter.

He had worked as a roofer with his dad, and he understood how to survive in the heat. He drank plenty of water and made sure to rest during the hottest part of the day. For the most part, animals left him alone. The sole exception was a gray fox that trailed him for over a day.

Logan was crossing a spacious grassland. The tall grass whispered around his legs as he headed for the distant tree line. He was uneasy. The grass-covered area seemed to stretch for miles both north and south. It had seemed expedient to cross it, but now he was again worried about being seen. There was no nearby shelter from predators or enemy warriors.

Before starting the crossing, he checked the bindings that secured his spear-point to the shaft he'd made. The lashings weren't as effective as the normal socket mounting, but they'd remained tight. He'd used the rawhide he'd salvaged from the tortured man, soaking it in water before he tied it. The leather had shrunk as it dried and now formed a firm bond, holding the foreshaft and point against the sapling.

He'd first tried walking crouched low to minimize his profile, but after fifty yards of this, his back let him know that it was a bad idea. He stopped in an area where the grass didn't grow, stretched, then came to the conclusion that it would be better to meet any danger with his ability to move unimpaired by cramps.

A stronger feeling of being watched struck him as he started moving again. He glanced around. There had been a surreptitious movement at the edge of the barren area. He looked away and then looked back. There was a gray fox looking at him.

He snorted – another fox. Well, it wasn't a threat unless it was rabid. He looked at it closely.

The fox sat there calmly, looking directly back at him, its eyes shining in the sun. It didn't seem to be sick. It wasn't doing anything unusual, except sitting in plain view, watching him.

That wasn't the way foxes acted in Logan's experience. They always avoided humans. He wondered if that was the case in the prehistoric past. Maybe foxes here and now didn't view humans as much of a threat. Maybe they were bolder.

He shrugged, then turned and continued. After a few minutes, he saw the fox off to one side as it crossed some shorter grass. Then, about half an hour later, he saw it waiting for him near the sole stand of trees in the plain.

He detoured to investigate the trees. The fox ducked into some bushes as he approached. The clump of trees was not very big, but it was dense enough to provide a hiding place for a predator. The fox's presence seemed to indicate that there was nothing there, but Logan proceeded cautiously.

There was a sudden rustle in the bushes that grew between the trees. Logan halted, raising his spear. A deer broke cover to the right of him. It limped rather than bounded as it tried to get clear of the bushes. Once it got into the open, Logan could see that the animal could barely walk. Something had attacked it, leaving deep gashes on its rear quarters. It wobbled as it turned away from him.

He felt a surge of pity for the creature, but the cold necessity of survival took over in his mind. He ran forward, caught up with the injured animal, and stabbed it in the neck with the spear. It bleated, then fell over, its eyes wide and frightened. Blood poured out of the spear wound. The deer thrashed, trying to regain its feet. Logan quickly moved away.

It stopped kicking as he disappeared in the grass. He sat there for a while under the sun, sweating and waiting, determined to give the creature a chance to die peacefully rather than to continue to terrify it by standing close.

After a while, he stood up and checked. The deer was dead. It wasn't moving. The fox was already eating some of the flesh exposed by the hip wounds. Logan wondered if the fox had known where the deer was and had tried to lead him to its location with the idea of getting a free meal. If it had, the strategy had worked.

The fox reluctantly left the deer and retired some distance as Logan walked up. He used the spear point to haggle off some meat for himself. He'd have to eat it raw. He really missed Serensaa.

He sat and ate as much as he could, then cut off more for later. When he had as much as he needed, he cut off another chunk and tossed it towards the fox. The small gray canine snapped it up, carrying it into some shade to devour.

Logan picked up his meat and started off. He still had over a mile to go before he was across the prairie, and he wanted to be in the trees by night. He had no desire to spend a night with no shelter and no fire.

That worry was confirmed as he continued. There was a wide beaten-down path in the grass. A herd of some kind had passed by recently. He looked both ways along the track. There were bones lying in the crushed grass not too far to the south. Some predator had made a kill there. He moved closer to the bones, curious as to what kind of animal it had been.

Its skull was that of a bison, but a huge one. Logan took a little time trying to estimate the behemoth's size. The bones were scattered around, but from the thighbone and pelvis he found, the bison had possibly stood seven or eight feet high at the shoulder.

The pelvis was that of a heavy creature, and he wondered how much it had weighed. It was at least half again as the bison of his modern world.

He turned up a scapula. It had been gnawed on, and the tooth marks were large and deep. This reminded him of where he was.

Logan turned towards the tree line and trotted across the remains of the track. He continued towards the distant trees, alternating his stride. A hundred steps walking, then a hundred steps at a slow jog. The trees grew closer, and his sense of worry increased.

Logan stopped a few hundred yards away from the tree line, inspecting the shadows carefully. After considering, he ducked into a patch of taller weeds and then moved towards the north, keeping low and out of sight.

If there was an ambush in the trees, he wanted to avoid it. After passing a long distance through the weeds and grass, he turned, wincing as his back complained, and crept towards the tree line. The grass grew a little shorter at that point, and he moved more cautiously until he saw the fox again.

It was still with him. This time it was sitting right out in the open, near the forest edge. It seemed completely unconcerned. Its attitude somehow seemed to Logan to be one of supercilious amusement, almost as if it were laughing at his efforts to go undetected.

He grinned. He must look like a total klutz to the fox if it knew what he was doing. He stood up, trying to act nonchalant, and crossed the remaining space. He stepped quickly into the cool shade when he reached the trees.

Once through a thin screen of brush, the trees opened out. He oriented himself, picked out a distant tree to head towards, and continued moving. There was no sign of the fox.

⸺◆⸺

By nighttime, he was exhausted and ready to stop. The ground had gradually gotten damper until he realized that he was approaching another swamp. There were large cypress trees about, but nothing that offered him a chance to climb to safety. He continued walking.

The night was setting in seriously when he found a standing, hollow cypress. It was a large tree, and in the darkening gloom, he could see that there was plenty of space inside. The opening was narrow, and that promised safety, provided he could get through it.

It was so tight that he finally resorted to stripping off his pants to slide through. Once inside, he pulled them back on and stirred through the litter with his spear. The lesson of the coral snake was fresh in his mind, and he didn't want to repeat the experience.

It was lighter inside than he'd thought it would be. There was an opening high overhead that let in the rays of the setting sun, which illuminated the dust particles he stirred up.

His search didn't turn up any snakes or anything else except for a couple of large millipedes. He stomped on those, not wanting to experience them crawling over him as he slept. Then he sat and ate the remains of the deer meat.

It was warm and strong-smelling. Not a great supper, but filling, nonetheless. There was a little left that he was preparing to choke down when he noticed the fox peering in through the opening at him.

Logan was startled but glad of the company. He didn't want the rest of the meat, and it went to the fox.

The little creature caught the tossed piece and disappeared into the dusk. Logan arranged himself as comfortably as he could, hoping that he'd see the fox in the morning. It seemed as if it had tied its fortunes to his for the moment and it had proven its worth, leading him to the deer.

He fell asleep and dreamed of Serensaa.

⊸◦⊷

The night passed softly. There were no animal noises other than the distant grunting of gators to wake him, but Logan's sleep was fitful.

In his dream, he was walking along a beach, hand-in-hand with Serensaa. Somehow they'd conquered the language problem and were having an involved conversation. Her movements continually distracted his attention. He wanted her with all of his being. She'd say something that made sense, but then he'd notice how her hair hung down over her breasts, and the words she said would sort of fade away.

At a certain point, the conversation became clearer. Serensaa looked at him and said, "I'm trying to get back to my people by the west sea."

Logan asked, "Will I be welcome?"

She looked away for a moment and then returned her gaze to him. She answered, "Perhaps. I'm not sure. There is one who will not welcome you."

He asked a second question, "Do you want me to come with you?"

She smiled and said, "You know the answer."

His attention turned to her lips, and he forgot what he was going to ask. They kissed.

He moved in his sleep, making a low sound.

The small waves rolled up the dream beach, and Serensaa turned away, saying, "The pursuers are dangerous. They want me. The bearded man wants me for his own. Watch out for him. He is a great fighter."

Logan moved again, on the verge of waking.

Serensaa's form was fading, turning misty and vaporous. As she faded, she seemed to say, "Come to me by the river. The quickly flowing river."

Something brushed past Logan's face, and he sat up instantly. It was the fox. It had come into the tree. It jumped away, alarmed, but then composed itself and sat near the opening, watching him. He lay still, watching it in return.

It was still dark, although the moon's light was now illuminating the interior of the tree well enough. The fox slowly lay down and wrapped its fuzzy tail around, partly covering its face. He had the feeling that it was still watching him through the fur, but it seemed to mean no harm. He was content to have the company.

Fox or no fox, he wanted to be back with Serensaa. He had many more questions to ask her, and then he had other things he wanted to speak to her about, such as their future together. He closed his eyes and tried to sleep, saying a small, disorganized prayer for her safety as he drifted off.

The fox was gone when he woke up. There was a woodpecker hammering on the hollow trunk over his head, and the racket was enough to wake anyone.

The bird seemed intent on knocking its brains out against the wood.

Logan wanted to yell at it. He had a severe headache. The dust and mold in the hollow cypress had given him a headache. His sinuses seemed to be blocked and the front of his head wanted to come off.

He worked his way back through the narrow opening. It seemed a little easier to get out than it had to get in.

The crow-sized woodpecker apparently didn't care for his presence. It quit pecking, gave a loud cry, and flew off in long swoops, squawking at intervals.

The sun's slanting light filtered through the tall trees, the rays pointing in the direction he needed to walk. His dream was still in his mind, and it somehow reinforced his need to hurry and reach Serensaa's people.

He was now sure they were at the Crystal River site. Deep in the back of his mind, Logan realized that was probably irrational, but he told himself he had nowhere else to go. His only goal was to find her again, and if she'd told him, even in a dream, that she was going to be on the coast, then that would be where he would go.

———◇———

Shortly after the sun indicated midday, Logan came to a wide river. It lay across his path and posed a barrier that he would have to cross.

The fox had been around on and off during the morning but had gone off somewhere. Logan didn't worry about the small animal. He'd enjoyed its company, silent as it was, but he also recognized that their partnership was unlikely to last for long. He wasn't surprised when it didn't show up during the rest of the afternoon.

He set himself to the task of making a raft. He didn't feel comfortable swimming the entire river. It wasn't safe. He'd seen several large alligators as he worked. The entire river was full of them.

Several of the larger ones had been attracted to the commotion he made assembling the raft and now hovered around offshore with what he thought was a hopeful look in their eyes.

It was nearly dark by the time he had gathered enough branches and pieces of wood, woven them together in a kind of mat that was reinforced by some tough vines. He decided that he'd wait for the sun to be high the next day before he attempted to get across.

Meanwhile, there was shelter for the night. He'd found a thick tangle of vines that allowed him to climb into a tall tree. It wasn't an oak. He didn't know what it was, but it was a long way up to the first branches, and the height alone offered security.

The vines held, and he scrambled around until he found a moderately comfortable position. He was extremely tired due to the lack of sleep the night before, and he worried that he'd probably fall off the branch.

After a little work, he improvised a safety line around his middle with some smaller vines. They would keep him from moving too far, and their pull would wake him before he fell. That would have to do.

He looked hopefully at the ground for his friendly fox, but the animal hadn't returned from wherever it had gone.

⚬

In the morning, he took his time about getting ready. Gators feed in low light, both in the evening and morning. He didn't think they'd be as motivated if he waited until mid-day. In addition, they'd be easier to spot.

He thoughtfully removed the stone spear point and fore-shaft from the sapling and tucked it into his pants. If he had to swim, he couldn't carry the spear, but the fore-shaft wouldn't be a burden. There was no way he would leave it behind.

He gathered a couple of leafy branches to use as paddles. The second was an extra, in case he lost one. Pushing the raft off was difficult. It was heavier than he had planned, but he finally got it moving.

The next problem was that the raft just wanted to spin around and around. He couldn't paddle very effectively with the branch. He finally settled on pushing the mat along with a sort of sculling motion. That worked well enough that he could see he was making progress, but it was terribly slow.

He had neared the opposite side when a massive gator decided that he was just too good an opportunity to let pass. It lunged up and started to climb over the edge of his raft, overturning the woven mat instantly. Logan leaped forward as far as he could as the raft flipped.

He hit the water with his arms churning and swam the remaining thirty yards at Olympic speed. There was no sign of the gator as he clawed his way over the bank. He moved away a few yards and took a moment to recover, glancing at the water in case it was planning another attack. Then he set off with the idea of putting as much distance between himself and alligators as possible.

Now began an ordeal of wandering through a confusing area that was covered with interconnected lakes and ponds. Much of the land was covered with water, and the grass was so tall and thick that it was difficult to see if a strip of land was a peninsula that dead-ended into a pond or if it was an isthmus that provided a pathway between adjacent lakes.

The day passed slowly. Logan was getting tired of wandering through alternate patches of cypress trees, watching for alligators, and pushing through tall grass. His arms were bleeding from saw grass cuts, and he was sick to death of the mosquitoes that hovered around. He had smeared mud all over his torso to keep them off, but his sweat washed it off in rivulets, providing targets for the aerial bloodsuckers.

By early afternoon, the swamp was being left behind. He had reached an area of low, sandy woods. Walking went faster here, and he made good progress. He kept up a steady pace, filling his stomach with more duck potatoes he'd gathered in the swamp as he walked.

By dusk, he was beside the bank of a swiftly moving river that flowed across his path. He recognized it. He'd arrived near the head of Crystal River, where it turns northwards prior to turning towards the Gulf.

He wasn't sure how much farther he had to walk but figured it was probably less than five miles. He'd do that in the morning. There was no sense blundering around in the dark and possibly alarming men who might think he was an enemy. Besides, he had heard the scream of a panther or some kind of cat off in the distance. Night was not a good time for humans to be out in this land.

Chapter Nineteen

Crystal River

Logan descended from his tree in the dawn light. He was getting so used to climbing that he was starting to question the theory that humans evolved on the ground. At the minimum, he was now a far better climber. He could see that his arms and chest had developed more muscle than he'd ever had before. It was a satisfying feeling to flex his arm and feel his biceps press on his tight pectoral muscles.

He stretched, got a drink in the nearby river, and then started northwestward along the bank. The trees and undergrowth forced him to diverge from the bank occasionally, but he always returned to the water's edge as soon as he could. He felt that following along the verge of the fast-moving river would ensure that he didn't miss any camps or settlements. The convenience of the clear, running water would be hard for primitive people to resist. They'd probably camp within a few hundred yards of the banks.

Eventually, the course turned more to the west, and, as it did, Logan became more and more nervous. He knew that directional change meant that he was getting close to the Gulf of Mexico. The idea of meeting Serensaa's people impacted him strangely. He felt a kind of performance anxiety. What if they didn't like him?

He hoped that Serensaa would be there already and would help with his introduction to her people. He was so anxious to see her that he almost forgot that she might not be present.

That might be inconvenient. He'd envisioned her telling her tribe about him, but if she wasn't there, they would have no reason to welcome him or to treat him differently than they normally treated strangers.

His experience with the people in this primitive world had not been of a nature to encourage confidence. The only men he'd met so far had been hostile and mostly determined to kill him. He hoped that wouldn't be the case this time.

He sensed something indefinable in the air. In response, he stopped abruptly and looked cautiously around. There was nothing to suggest an ambush. The only thing he could hear was the river sounds. Even so, his anxiety took a leap upwards, and he started to move back into the shadow of a tree. There was a sudden rush of feet paired with screams.

Logan backed against the tree. There were about twenty men surrounding him, all with their spears ready. There was no chance to fight. He wouldn't survive. He bent and laid his spear point on the ground, then straightened and held his palms out towards the men.

One of them said something brief in a commanding tone. At that, another man moved cautiously forward to retrieve Logan's weapon. He kept his eyes on Logan's face as he did.

Logan tried to smile, but it was difficult. He was about as tense as he could remember ever being.

The other men jumped forward, grabbed his arms, and forced him down onto his belly. They twisted his arms back and tied them behind him.

They grouped around him as they led him farther on down the river. The trees opened up, and there was their camp.

It didn't seem very imposing to Logan. There were maybe twenty skin tents, some chikee structures, and a central fire. Children came running out as the group approached.

The children clustered around Logan, laughing and talking to each other. One of them tried to poke him with a short stick but was discouraged by one of his guards. The guard knocked the stick down and said something harsh to the boy; after that, Logan was treated well enough.

When they reached the center of the tents, there was a long discussion that apparently focused on what to do with him. The men seemed to be roughly equally divided. One group was more or less friendly, while the others wanted to string him up, or at least that was Logan's interpretation.

The argument ceased as a medium height man with black hair stepped out of one of the tents. He strode over to the group, his forehead wrinkling in an aggressive scowl. He looked Logan over, up and down, with a hostile expression. Seeming to find nothing that met his approval, he barked a question at the others.

One of Logan's guards answered. That man had been relatively considerate and had even helped Logan a couple of times on the walk.

The newcomer shook his head, then stepped forward, looked into Logan's eyes, and then swung his right arm in a powerful blow. It was aimed at Logan's face. Logan was startled, but he managed to slip most of the force. It was still strong enough to rattle his teeth.

He staggered, then straightened and glared at his assailant. He shook his head a little and said, "What kind of man strikes a helpless prisoner?" As he did, he turned slightly, displaying his tied wrists.

His words were doubtless unintelligible to the group, but his meaning was clear enough. Black-hair's face reddened at the implied criticism. He raised his arm and swung again. This time Logan was ready. He stepped back slightly so that the strike missed completely.

A couple of men laughed but quickly stifled themselves when Black-hair glared at them.

Black-hair turned back to Logan and spat, hitting him on the chest. Logan smiled calmly. He was raging inside, but showing emotion wouldn't do in this circumstance.

Black-hair made a brief speech, waving his arms, while he gave directions. Two of the men turned away, muttering. It was obvious that they didn't agree with the orders. Some of the others grabbed Logan and hustled him over to a post that was set in the ground near the fire.

Logan began to be really concerned. This didn't look good, especially since there were stains on the post that could only be blood.

The men tied a thong to his wrists and tied the other end to the post. It was long enough so that he could sit, but his tied wrists precluded his escape. The thong was tied higher than he could reach on the post. He hoped that he might be able to work it loose with his teeth, but there was no opportunity for that as long as he was in plain view.

One of the men plopped down nearby. Logan inspected him, hopefully. The man had the attitude of someone who had been assigned a boring task. He looked like he had been told to act as a guard but didn't relish the job.

Some of the children came up and made noises and faces at Logan, but he ignored them. They became more intrusive, finally throwing small stones and litter. The guard yelled at them, mostly because he was trying to sleep and their noise was disturbing his nap. The man didn't really care if the kids tormented Logan.

Logan was resting with his back against the pole in a sitting position. His mind was working overtime, trying to figure out a strategy that would allow him to escape.

The black-haired guy passed by several times, and each time he glared at Logan. Maybe he should have let the guy knock him down. Making fun of a powerful enemy when you were a captive wasn't a very good idea. He wished his pride hadn't taken over at that point.

He looked up. There was some kind of commotion on the west side of the camp. Suddenly a group of women came walking through the tents, led by Serensaa. He jumped to his feet, anxious to greet her.

He was disappointed when she turned from her course towards him to go and meet Black-hair. The man put his hands on her shoulders in a possessive fashion that made Logan see red.

Their relationship wasn't entirely smooth, however. Serensaa shrugged his arm off her shoulders and, while pointing at Logan, gave a long and passionate speech. Logan watched quietly.

She was arguing some point, but he couldn't figure out what it was. If she told the truth about their adventure together, the tribe should view him favorably. He'd helped her avoid capture and travel across the peninsula. That was positive.

On the other hand, if she told them about their commitment to each other, the men might not take it very well. For all he knew, women in this tribe might be promised from birth to some man. Maybe he had trespassed on someone else's presumptive property. Perhaps Black-hair. He acted like he had some kind of claim on her.

Black-hair argued, but Serensaa was eloquent and long-spoken. Finally, the man threw up his arms in frustration. Then he turned to some of the bystanders and gave an order. Shortly after, Logan was cut free.

He stood by the fire, rubbing his wrists. His circulation hadn't been totally cut-off, but it had been impaired. His wrists were numb, and he couldn't move his hands well. He was still worried. So far, Serensaa had ignored him.

She'd gone in a tent for a while, then come out to help the other women prepare some food. They'd come to the camp from down by the seashore. From the preparations, it looked like they'd been gathering some kind of shellfish, perhaps scallops or clams. They were busy, and Logan didn't want to presume on his conditional acceptance by the tribe. He had been imprisoned and set free. He didn't want to convert to a prisoner again, simply because he offended someone. He kept glancing at Serensaa surreptitiously, hoping that she would look at him, but she kept her attention on her work, ignoring his presence. From that, he judged that he wasn't entirely safe.

It grew dark, and people wandered up to eat. The clams, for so they proved to be, had been cooked with hot stones that were deposited in the water held in leather containers.

Logan sat and watched without trying to get anything to eat, even though his stomach was rumbling.

Eventually, a young woman, little more than a girl really, brought him some clams on a piece of wood. He blew on them until they were cool enough to eat, then chewed up the rubbery meat systematically. They were good but could have used some salt and pepper.

The camp settled down after that. People mostly ignored him and proceeded with their nightly rituals. There were fewer people moving around. Most of them had retired to tents or the chikee huts. Logan was wondering if he could sleep by the fire, but most importantly, he was wondering if Serensaa would acknowledge him. So far, she'd studiously avoided looking his way.

He finally lay back and tried to get comfortable. It wasn't like he was unused to sleeping on the ground. It was better than a crotch in a tree. He watched the stars overhead.

The sky was clear. It had been cloudy earlier in the day, but the puffy clouds had all retired somewhere, and now the stars showed brightly. It was quiet, except for the distant call of a chuck-will and the crackle of the fire. Once a man came and threw more wood on the blaze, but it had now burned down to a bed of glowing coals. The camp was dim and quiet.

There was a slight noise, and Logan turned his head to see its source. Serensaa was peeking around a tent. He rose and sauntered over, acting unconcerned, in case someone was watching. He didn't know what was going on, and he didn't want to give anyone grounds for complaint.

Her nearness was an irresistible temptation. He took her in his arms and kissed her. For a moment, she kissed him back, pressing against his body. Then she pushed him back and shook her head in a negative motion.

Logan again regretted their communication issues. He pointed at her and said, "Serensaa," then pointed at himself and said, "Logan," in the same way he had before. She smiled at that. Then he linked his fingers and repeated, "Serensaa, Logan." Her face sobered in response.

She linked her fingers and repeated, "Logan, Serensaa." Then she pressed her hand over her heart and said distinctly, "Here."

Logan understood. She'd learned more of his language than he'd realized. He had used the word 'here' with her several times, and it seemed that she'd been paying attention. Her next action was even more startling.

She pulled her fingers apart and said, "No Logan, Serensaa here," and waved her hand inclusively, indicating the camp.

Her meaning was clear. She held him close in her heart, but their relationship wasn't something of which the tribe would approve. To confirm, he linked his fingers and said, "Logan, Serensaa here?" Then waved at the camp.

She shook her head sorrowfully, then said, "No."

After a moment, she tried to communicate another idea. Linking her fingers loosely, she said, "Serensaa, Ulfa here."

Logan's heart sank. She obviously meant she belonged to another in this place. He didn't know if she was simply promised or was already married. In either case, though, there was no place for him.

His face fell, and he turned towards the fire and slowly walked back. His mind was spinning as he tried to grasp the situation. He hadn't quite reached the fire when her hand grasped his arm.

He turned to look at her. Serensaa was close to him, her expression agonized. Tears were trickling down her face. She pulled him back behind the tent. It was darker there, and they couldn't be observed. She came into his arms again, and he kissed her lips, her cheek, her forehead, followed by the side of her neck.

She shuddered and sobbed softly. Finally, she looked up and said, "Logan go."

It was like a slap in the face. She was telling him to leave. It seemed like she didn't want him to, but she had told him to go anyway.

He pulled her closer and said, "No. Serensaa, Logan, go."

She looked up again, a little hope in her eyes. She appeared to be thinking it over.

Logan realized that he had little to offer her. Here, with her tribe, she had a measure of security and a better place to live. With him, she'd only had trees and danger. He sighed. It would be better for her to stay here. He'd only lead her into danger. He sighed again, then said, "Serensaa stay, Logan go."

She understood his meaning. Her eyes opened wider, and tears again streamed down her face. Logan's cheeks were suddenly wet. He hadn't realized that he was tearful, but now that he had, he felt even worse.

He nodded his head affirmatively, then started to walk away, heading towards the edge of the camp, moving into the darkness.

She grabbed at his wrist and hastily said, "No." With an arm motion, she indicated the sun rising and said something he didn't understand, but which he interpreted as meaning, "Wait until morning."

He nodded and returned to the fire. When he looked back, she was gone.

He wasn't able to sleep. His heart was breaking. Seeing her again made him realize how much he loved her. He wanted her slim body next to his, and he wanted her cheerful, sometimes crazy personality near him. How could he face being lost in this primitive wilderness without her? His mind couldn't seem to come to grips with the problem.

◆

He was sure he wouldn't sleep, but perhaps he dozed a little. Morning seemed to come before he knew it. People were moving around when he opened his eyes.

A couple of men came up to the fire from the edge of the camp. Logan realized they must have been sentries. There was danger here, even for this large camp.

Women and some of the older children were preparing breakfast. They had built the fire up and were cooking fish. When the food was done, men came to eat. The tribe ate more or less randomly in clots of two or three people.

Black-hair came by, kicked some sand at Logan, and grabbed some fish away from a woman, shoving her as he did. She staggered away, almost falling.

Logan was abruptly very angry with the guy. He considered his options. Aggressive action didn't seem to be a good idea, given his tenuous position. He wanted to get out of the camp, but he hoped to leave with at least a few weapons. It would be good if he could have a spear thrower and several spears. That would give him a chance at survival. Antagonizing the man who seemed to be the power in the group wasn't a good idea.

He looked down as Black-hair glanced at him.

Black-hair finished his fish, then got up from his position by the fire and strutted over to Logan. He unceremoniously kicked Logan's foot. Logan looked up and watched as the man said something.

Based on the gestures, the guy wanted Logan to either leave or to go gather wood. Logan couldn't figure out which. He stood to face the man.

Black-hair's face darkened. Apparently standing was the wrong response. Logan didn't care by this point. He had decided to leave, weapons or no weapons. The idea that Serensaa wouldn't come with him hurt so much that he didn't worry about offending the man.

Black-hair yelled at him. Logan shrugged and started walking away.

Without warning, Logan was struck heavily on the side of his head. Caught by surprise, he fell, disoriented. He rolled to see Black-hair standing over him, his face bright red. The man yelled at him again.

Serensaa came running up. She spoke softly, almost placatingly to Black-hair. He spoke harshly to her, then motioned towards Logan. She said something else, followed by the word, "Ulfa."

Logan supposed that she was arguing that he should be allowed to leave. Then the import of the last word sank in. This man was Ulfa. He was the one Serensaa belonged to in the tribe. He couldn't believe it. She was going to stay with this man rather than go with him.

He said, "Serensaa?"

She looked at him.

He pointed at Black-hair and asked, "Ulfa?"

She nodded slowly.

Ulfa was looking back and forth, trying to follow what was going on.

Logan said, "Serensaa, Ulfa?"

She flinched a little. Her response seemed to imply that she didn't want the man but was somehow promised to him. Logan wasn't sure if that was correct, but that was what it looked like to him.

Several warriors had walked up and were watching the show. Logan figured it was probably the most entertaining thing that had happened in their camp recently.

Ulfa, looking back and forth, seemed to read something into her gaze that he didn't like. He spoke viciously to her. When she didn't respond, he struck her hard. She fell, holding her face.

Logan exploded into action. He grabbed Ulfa's arm, spinning and lifting in a judo move, to throw the man to the ground in turn. Ulfa landed on his shoulder, grunted with the impact, rolled over, and came to his feet, murder in his eyes.

Logan looked over his shoulder, checking for obstructions, and then moved to his left, away from the fire. The ground was flat with no obstacles, an ideal place to fight.

Ulfa drew his knife slowly. Logan hadn't paid any attention before, but now he was outraged to see that it was his tanto. How had the man gotten it? Serensaa? He was glad to see it hadn't been lost, but now he wanted that knife back.

Ulfa yelled a war cry and started forward. He lunged at Logan with the knife held high.

That was simple to counter. Logan blocked with his arms crossed, grabbed Ulfa's wrist, bent the black-haired man's arm into a lock, then took the knife away from him by pulling it back against his fingers. An elbow to the face knocked Ulfa backward, staggering towards the fire. There was a collective groan from the crowd.

The black-haired man caught himself then turned towards Logan, moving more cautiously, with a calculating attitude.

Logan indecisively looked down at the knife. If he used it, the tribe would be angry. Better to keep the combat bloodless. He reluctantly tossed the tanto far away, between two of the tents.

He faced Ulfa. The two circled each other for a moment. Then Ulfa jumped forward.

Logan sidestepped and simultaneously snapped a kick into Ulfa's mid-section. Ulfa made a gasping noise and staggered backward. The kick had been a hard one.

The onlookers were silent for a moment but then began to mutter while shooting dark looks at Logan.

Logan backed away, waiting to see if that would be enough. Ulfa faced him again. This time, rage seemed to overtake his caution. The heavier man lunged at Logan, swerving at the last moment, then dropping to catch Logan's knee.

It was a clever move but too slow. Logan danced away in a spin, simultaneously swinging his right leg around in a perfect crescent kick. The heal of his foot impacted Ulfa's cheek with a crack. The black-haired man went down flat and lay, unmoving, for a moment. There was an angry outcry from the onlookers.

A group of additional men had come up and now encircled the combatants in a ring that was two or three deep. They were jockeying for position while looking at Logan with expressions of mixed antagonism and amazement. Apparently, they hadn't expected him to stand against Ulfa for more than a moment.

Ulfa was back on his feet. He pressed forward and, almost by chance, caught Logan with a heavy fist against the side of his neck. Logan staggered stunned, then rolled in a backward somersault and came up to his feet with a yell in a ready position. His yell was all but drowned out by the spectators who seemed to be cheering for Ulfa.

Logan's head was spinning. The blow had been really hard, and he wanted to gain a moment to recover. Since the best defense was a good offense, he jumped forward with a low sidekick. It wasn't very powerful, but he caught Ulfa's left knee at the very end of the kick, causing the man to stagger and fall.

The crowd was silent. Logan could see that the men directly behind Ulfa were watching attentively.

He moved back, still somewhat stunned. He glanced to the side to see Serensaa, her face white and her mouth open with both hands pressed to her heart. She was looking at Ulfa.

Logan was hurt more by that than by the blows he'd received. She was afraid he was hurting the man. He drew back farther, then, with a feeling of irony, he bowed slightly. It was just a simple nod of the head intended to acknowledge his opponent, nothing more.

Ulfa looked at him, his mouth open, panting.

Logan turned and started to walk away. Ulfa shouted something, and several of the other men yelled and jumped in front of Logan, their spears ready. He stopped and turned to face Ulfa again.

Ulfa had grabbed a spear from one of the men. Now he was coming forward. Logan saw that the black-haired man meant to kill him. He looked at the other men. No help there.

Serensaa dashed forward, grabbed a spear from one of the men, and tossed it to Logan. He caught it, grinned, and swung it up, knocking Ulfa's thrust away.

Logan spun the spear. He'd had some lessons with the staff. While he wasn't a master by any stretch, he felt fairly competent with the moves he knew.

He spun the spear, moving forward, and slapped the shaft into Ulfa's spear. Instantly reversing the direction, Logan brought the other end of his spear shaft down on the top of Ulfa's head with a "Thwack." Ulfa's eyes closed for a moment.

That was all Logan needed. He leaped forward and delivered a front snap kick to the man's chin. Ulfa's jaw snapped closed, and his head flew back, blood splattering from his mouth. He flopped onto his back and laid still, his arms involuntarily held in a rigid position indicating that he was unconscious.

Logan watched him for a moment. Ulfa was still breathing but showed no signs of recovering consciousness.

He turned, holding the spear, and started to walk away, but an older man stepped into his path, holding his hand up in a halting motion.

This man had been present but had never seemed to have any authority over the battle or Ulfa. He'd been in the back of the circle as the two fought.

Now he said something, not to Logan, but to the assembled men. They rather reluctantly answered. The older man moved close and placed his hand on Logan's shoulder, simultaneously saying something that sounded complicated.

Logan's puzzlement must have shown. The man moved closer, still holding Logan's shoulder, then smiled and said something else while waving his free hand inclusively over the entire encampment.

Logan tried not to pull back. The guy's breath was terrible, and he was speaking directly into Logan's face.

The man continued speaking for some time, ending by clapping Logan on both shoulders.

Logan was at a loss as to how to respond. He didn't want to give offense. Finally, he stepped back a half step, then bowed a martial arts bow. Deeply, with his hands at his sides.

The man said something, so Logan looked up. The old guy was beaming, so the bow must have worked.

Logan straightened and looked for Serensaa. She was standing at the back of the crowd, her face positively glowing. When she saw him looking at her, she looked even happier.

Logan motioned to her. She threaded her way through the men, who rather grudgingly moved out of the way.

The girl walked up to him, eyes bright, chest heaving with emotion.

Logan wasn't sure of her now. He'd feared she had been worried about Ulfa, but now her actions seemed to say otherwise.

He glanced at the elder. The man was watching the two young people with a neutral expression. Logan couldn't tell if he approved or disapproved.

Deciding it didn't matter to him, Logan asked the girl, "Ulfa, Serensaa?"

She looked at Ulfa. He still hadn't regained his senses but was moving a little where he lay on the ground. Some men were standing beside him, but no one was helping or administering aid.

She shook her head negatively, then linked her fingers together and said, "Logan, Serensaa," in a firm tone that admitted of no doubt.

The old man asked something, and she answered with a minutes-long speech.

Logan figured that she was now telling everyone how they'd crossed the peninsula together and, he hoped, how brave he was. She gestured towards Ulfa and then kicked some sand in his direction.

This started a heated discussion among the spectators, but then the elder raised his voice, silencing the crowd. He spoke some more, then grabbed Logan's arm with one hand and Serensaa's with another.

He pulled the two together in front of him and asked Logan something. His formal attitude somehow reminded Logan of a justice-of-the-peace. Logan wondered if this meant the man was marrying the two of them. He had a momentary qualm. Was this what he wanted? To be bound to this primitive girl for the rest of his life.

Then he looked at Serensaa. Her face was aglow, and she was almost breathless with anticipation. That was all it took.

Logan nodded his head, raised his voice, and said, "Yes!"

The old man smiled at him and then turned to ask Serensaa the same thing.

She looked down for a moment as if thinking it over.

Logan could see that she was looking at him out of the corner of her eyes. He whispered, "Please."

She instantly raised her head, saying, "Ayeaah."

That was all it took. The old guy pulled them close together and placed her hand in Logan's.

The crowd, which had now grown to most of the tribe, including the women and children, made a loud cry of affirmation, then dispersed, talking about the events in a flurry of conversation.

The old man unceremoniously turned his back on the couple and walked away, stopping to say something to Ulfa, who was now sitting up.

The black-haired man spat some blood out of his mouth and replied while staring directly at Logan. His look promised revenge.

The old man made a sharp statement, apparently telling him to leave the couple alone.

Ulfa started to protest, but the elder had already turned and was walking away. The black-haired man slowly rose. He staggered, caught his balance, and then started for where Logan had thrown the tanto.

Logan was not in the mood to let him have it. He snapped, "No!" He pulled Serensaa over to the knife and picked it up while Ulfa looked on indecisively.

Logan had never taken the sheathe off of his belt, and now everyone could see how the knife slid perfectly into it, identifying it as his. Ulfa grunted at the sight, then turned away and limped off towards his tent.

The new couple walked through the remaining people, and Serensaa led him to a tent. She indicated it and said, "Serensaa, here."

Logan had been afraid that she was sleeping with Ulfa. He felt relieved that she had her own shelter.

They entered, the girl leading the way, crawling through the low opening. Inside, there were few possessions. Some pouches were hung on one of the supporting poles, and there were a couple of flint knives lying on a small piece of tanned skin.

A rectangular piece of rawhide was staked over a crude framework with some pine boughs shoved underneath. The boughs filled the space and made the hide bulge upwards. The presence of two tanned furs tipped him off. This was her bed.

Serensaa didn't give him time to inspect it. She turned, grabbed him, and was instantly all over him with kisses.

He was more than happy to reciprocate. He'd first been worried that he'd never see her again. Next, he'd been terrified that she belonged to Ulfa. Now that their relationship was formalized, he was filled with joy.

He didn't waste any time thinking about the problems the future held. In a matter of seconds, the two were undressed and embracing on the bed, the scent of pine needles filling the air.

Chapter Twenty

Attack

The first part of the night seemed to last forever to Logan. He couldn't get enough of Serensaa. Her passionate embrace, her kisses, and her hot breath on his neck as they made love all combined to place him in a timeless state of ecstasy.

Filled with the afterglow, they recovered themselves quietly. Logan held her in his arms. He knew she couldn't understand him, yet he repeated over and over, "I love you, Serensaa," until it became a kind of chant. She snuggled closer to him, content in his embrace.

When he paused, she answered in turn. It seemed to Logan that she said she loved him with all of her being. He kissed her, a long and tender kiss. They lay still for a time.

Eventually, Logan felt his body stir. Serensaa moved in response, positioning herself over him. He reached up, running his hands freely over her slender body as she worked. It was a wonderful experience, transporting him to heights of ecstasy that he could never have imagined. His heart beat so violently, he felt it must come out of his chest.

At last, she collapsed, falling forwards into his arms. They lay there, breathing heavily. The universe seemed to come to a complete stop, which suited Logan perfectly. He wanted to remain there forever.

Still, time went by. The two eventually fell asleep in each other's arms. Logan woke twice during the night to change position, moving carefully so as not to disturb Serensaa. She murmured something and rolled over the second time he moved.

They were awakened slightly before dawn by an uproar followed by a series of war cries from the edge of the camp. Logan jumped, coming awake instantly.

He pulled on his pants and shoes, belted on the tanto, and crawled out of the tent, with Serensaa following right behind.

The camp was stirred up like a hornet's nest that had been struck by a rock. Armed men and women were running everywhere. The men were mostly headed for the east side of the camp, some still rubbing their eyes from sleep.

The sun wasn't quite up yet, but its preliminary rays were casting long, faint shadows across the camp. A spear arched over one of the tents and stuck, quivering in the ground directly in Logan's path. He snatched it up, then began looking for Serensaa. She wasn't visible, and he started to panic.

She popped out of a nearby tent, dragging two more spears and carrying a throwing stick. There hadn't been any weapons in her tent last night.

Logan hadn't remarked on that fact, but he'd noticed. It seemed to be the custom for only the men to have weapons. The women now were either carrying rocks or sticks, along with flint knives, some little more than sharp stones.

Serensaa gave her load to Logan, and he gratefully placed a spear against the throwing stick. Then, carrying the other two in his left hand, he ran forward through the camp until he could see what was going on.

The eastern edge of the camp was a battlefield. There were several men scattered on the ground, either dead or dealing with spears that had struck them.

The attackers had come out of the sunrise, hoping that the light at their backs would make them more difficult to see. There were still some men running toward the camp through the trees. Logan picked one out and threw his spear in a trajectory that he hoped would end where the man would be in a moment. The spear arched down, unseen by the oncoming man, and struck him in the torso.

Logan was gratified but didn't waste any time. He reloaded and threw his second spear at a fighter on the edge of the melee. The attackers looked exactly like members of Serensaa's tribe, but his target had identified himself by attacking the elderly man with bad breath. Logan saw the old guy was making a good attempt to defend himself, jabbing with a spear.

Logan had fond feelings for the old man who had given him Serensaa and a place in the tribe. His spear struck the attacker in the leg, dropping him as he lunged forward at the old man. The elder warrior finished his opponent off with a spear stab to the side of the neck, then glanced at Logan and nodded in approval.

Logan switched the spear-thrower to his left hand, moving the last spear to his right. He could use the throwing stick to parry with, although it wasn't heavy enough to be a useful club. He moved forward, cautiously, seeking to engage another enemy.

A man came running through the fighters, heading for the tents, then, catching sight of Logan, he veered in his direction with a loud scream.

Logan wasn't intimidated by the noise. He answered with his best martial arts yell, a chest-deep "Hyah", and sidestepped the man's thrust. He moved sideways, spinning in a full circle to club the warrior on the back of the neck with his spear. The man staggered forward with the blow.

Logan hesitated. The last vestiges of his civilized being clung to him for a moment, then expediency and survival took over. He thrust his spear deep into the warrior's back. The man screamed and fell forward.

Logan whirled, barely in time to slap his spear-thrower down to block a knife thrust from a second warrior. He jumped away from the man to give him time to ready his spear.

A fist-sized rock flew by Logan's head and struck the knife-wielder on the chest, making a hollow "thunk." The man staggered back, gasping. Logan jumped forward and stabbed him in the abdomen, drawing his spear back instantly as the man tried to grasp it. The wounded warrior plopped down into a sitting position, then bent over, holding his middle. Blood was pouring from the wound, running over the stricken man's legs and making a red pool in the sand.

Logan recognized it as a fatal wound. Probably hit the aorta, he thought, as he moved forward looking for another opponent.

The battling warriors suddenly resolved from a confused, screaming tangle into numerous smaller groups. Now it could be seen that the attackers outnumbered the defenders. Logan saw Ulfa, recognizable by his long black hair and muscular body, grab a man's arm, simultaneously slashing his throat with a stone knife.

An enemy came up from behind, with a club, and swung it at Ulfa's head. Logan hastily threw his last spear, striking the club swinger's arm neatly in the biceps. The club bounced off Ulfa's head in a glancing blow that had no force.

The black-haired warrior spun with a yell and stabbed the offending man in the stomach. Entrails spilled out on the ground as the man went down.

Ulfa followed the spear's path and saw Logan. His eyes lit up with hatred, and he charged, crossing the yards between them in a breath's time.

Logan dropped into a front stance, yelled, and launched a sidekick. It was, perhaps, not the ideal counter for a rapidly charging opponent. It struck Ulfa in the middle, knocking the wind out of him, but Logan was knocked backward by the impact.

He scrambled to his feet, barely in time to sidestep Ulfa's continued charge. The man was still gasping for breath but not wasting a moment in his attack. Logan could see he had murder in his eyes. All thought of a simple fight vanished.

Ulfa spun and grabbed Logan's right arm, moving to stab him in the side. Logan slapped him in the face with the throwing stick and twisted away, trying to avoid the thrust.

The knife glanced across his ribs, leaving a deep slash that felt like someone had struck him with a red-hot piece of steel. Blood instantly poured down his side, feeling hot and wet.

Yelling in anger, Logan spun on his right foot and delivered a hard back-sidekick to Ulfa's thigh, knocking him off balance. He followed up with a left-handed strike at Ulfa's knife-hand. The throwing stick went flying as their wrists met. Ulfa grabbed at Logan's wrist, preventing him from distancing himself.

A simple hapkido move broke the warrior's grip, allowing Logan to step back. Ulfa paused, re-evaluating his foe. Logan quickly drew the tanto.

The black-haired man's eyes widened. He knew from experience how deadly that knife was.

Struggling men suddenly surrounded the two adversaries. The battle had rolled over their position. Logan was struck from behind by a body crashing against his knees. He went down, and Ulfa jumped on him.

The two rolled back and forth, each trying to stab the other. Logan's knife arm was forced down against his side, out of action, while he desperately tried to control Ulfa's knife-hand.

Logan's blood-covered side provided unexpected assistance. The blood slicked his wrist. With a massive effort, he wrenched his arm free and stabbed Ulfa under his jaw. The tanto penetrated up and through the man's skull with a loud crunch, remaining embedded there.

Ulfa continued to glare at his foe, still straining to kill him. As Logan held him off, the life leaked slowly from the man's hate-filled eyes. They faded, turning to the dull opacity of death.

Ulfa collapsed. Logan heaved the body off of his torso and began to rise, in a rush to regain his knife. He tugged at it, trying to pull it free.

Some feet came into his vision, and he looked up to see the bearded man that had pursued Serensaa. The man grinned in triumph as he struck at Logan's neck with his spear shaft.

Logan dodged, wrenched at the tanto, and yanked it free. His attacker twisted his spear, presenting the point for a thrust. Logan brushed the shaft aside, straightened, stepping close while slashing upwards with the blade.

A thin trail of red appeared across the warrior's chest. The man yelled in anger, then lifted the spear again. As he did, the slice opened to reveal the ends of severed ribs. The bearded man wheezed, then faltered with the spear held high. His severed chest muscles refused to pull it down in a fatal stroke. He thrust downward weakly.

Logan blocked the thrust, sweeping his left arm across and grabbing the spear as he did. They tugged back and forth for a moment, the bearded man trying to regain control of the spear with the remainder of his strength. His breath made a whistling sound through the deep cut.

Logan struck again, this time planting the tanto in the center of his antagonist's chest. The man dropped instantly, pulling Logan slightly forward.

He broke free to stand there, panting. As he did, he was struck on the back of the head. There was a flash, and all went dark.

Chapter Twenty-One

Alone, Again

Logan opened his eyes painfully but could see little. It was dark. His head throbbed. Then he remembered the battle. He tried to sit up, groaned involuntarily, and looked around, moving his upper torso so that he wouldn't have to twist his neck. That seemed to be the source of the pain he felt.

It was quiet. His heart beat faster as he searched for the attackers. He'd lost his knife somewhere. He groped for it in the darkness. Everywhere he felt there was grass. He paused, confused. The camp had been used for such a long time that the surrounding area was mostly barren and pressed flat by the constant coming and going of the tribe's people.

Logan sat still, trying to understand. He'd been in a battle, been triumphant over both of his primary enemies, but now he was somewhere else. He wondered if he had been killed. This didn't seem like the afterlife. He wasn't quite sure what that would be like, but sitting in a dark, grassy area didn't match any account that he'd ever heard.

He looked up. There were stars overhead. His head spun, and then everything clicked. He was sitting on the ground in a grass-covered clearing, and it was night.

He – he paused as the conclusion struck his conscious mind. He'd moved in time once again.

A cry of grief came from his mouth. Serensaa! Where was she? Had he lost her forever?

A distant roar came from somewhere to the north. It came again, faintly through the encircling trees. The saber-tooth roared a third time, making Logan's heart leap with hope. He was still in the past. Perhaps he hadn't moved far. Serensaa might be close. He had to find her.

The pain in his skull washed up again, making him feel dizzy. The world seemed to spin, and he fell sideways into a fetal position.

⋯⟡⋯

It was daylight. Logan had been lying there, barely conscious, thinking or dreaming of Serensaa.

Heavy wingbeats and a squawk made his eyes snap open. There were three vultures inspecting him from a close distance. He moved his arm weakly.

"I'm not dead yet, you vermin. Shoo!" he said. His mouth felt dry. He moistened his lips with his tongue and repeated, "Shoo!" The vultures hopped away a little.

He sat up. The birds evidently decided that he wasn't yet ready to be breakfast and took flight, landing in the spreading branches of a nearby oak.

Logan shakily got to his feet. He had to find Serensaa.

He looked around. The camp had disappeared. The entire area was covered by grass and low scrub. It looked as if it might have been used, but long ago. He walked to where the fire had been.

There were some disarranged stones scattered around. He kicked through the grass. There was a piece of burned wood, its end charred to a black stub.

The conclusion was inevitable. He had moved in time to a point where the tribe no longer used the area. He looked around hopelessly, searching for something, anything that would link him to Serensaa.

Maybe the people had moved closer to the seashore. He started to walk in that direction, but then a feeling of being watched made a sudden shiver run up his back. He looked around, searching for the source of the feeling.

A gray fox was sitting at the edge of the clearing, and its eyes were focused on him. He gasped in astonishment. Was it his fox? The one that had followed him before? But, no, it couldn't be. That was probably years ago. Foxes don't live very long.

The fox stood and yipped at him.

He smiled. Silly little thing. He turned back towards the shore.

The fox yipped again.

Logan turned back. The fox stopped yipping and looked at him expectantly.

He walked toward the creature. After four steps, he stumbled over something in the deep grass. He recovered and bent down to see what it was. There were some rib bones there. Closer inspection showed him that it was a human skeleton scattered about. Animals had chewed on some of the bones. They were splintered and showed teeth marks.

His eye caught a glint. There, buried in the grassroots, was his tanto. He worked it out and held it up to inspect it.

There were stains on the blade, and the rubberized grip was filthy, but other than that, it was almost as it had been. The skeleton must be that of the bearded man.

Without a further thought, Logan replaced the knife in the sheath that was still belted to his waist. When he looked up, the fox was gone. The event seemed otherworldly to Logan. It almost seemed that the fox had known about the location of his knife. He had a warm feeling for the furry animal. Even though it couldn't be the same one, it had proven helpful.

He looked for it again, scanning the bushes, but it was definitely gone. After a final look, he started back towards the shore, walking across the grassy area and pushing through a screen of brush.

There were some palms that he walked through, then some low dunes covered with sea oats. At the base of the dunes, there was a large stone that someone had stood on end.

It had been buried partway in the ground and was firmly planted. It seemed familiar. He moved closer. It was the stele stone. He'd seen it farther inland, under the chikee hut at the archaeological park.

Logan checked both sides. There was no carving. That was strange. It must have been carved later in time.

Leaving the stele behind, he climbed the dunes. There was the Gulf, stretching out in both directions. There was no sign of humans anywhere. He sighed in disappointment.

◆

Logan camped near the old campsite. He'd constructed a small shelter with palm fronds at the base of the large oak.

He'd climbed the oak once to avoid a saber-tooth. It had hung around for nearly a day. Logan had become so thirsty that he was deliriously considering trying to kill it with just his knife.

The cat eventually grew tired and left. Logan waited for an hour or so and then climbed down to drink from the river. Later, he walked along the beach, finding and eating some clams.

◆

He'd searched the entire area, both up and down the shore and inland. There were no people to be found. There were some signs that they had been here once, but they had gone.

His hope of finding Serensaa had slowly faded. It had taken a long time to go, but now there was only a faint shred left.

Logan believed that the people might come back to the area. If he left, searching for her, he might miss her if she returned with them. Finally, a solution occurred to him.

He spent two days carving her likeness in the stele, tapping at the limestone with the butt of his knife and some pieces of flint he'd found.

If she came back, she'd recognize herself. It was irrational – he knew that. His carving only vaguely resembled her. The main likeness was the long hair. An impartial viewer would have known that the figure on the stone was female, but that was all.

To Logan's grieving mind, it was a work of art, painstakingly carved to resemble his lost love. He hoped she'd see it and wait, understanding that he'd return.

Some days after finishing, he set out eastward along the fast-flowing river. Maybe he'd meet some people farther inland.

—◦—

Days passed as he searched the area around the head of the Crystal River. He didn't want to go too far from the stele.

Logan had salvaged a few spear points from the old campsite. He knew enough now to understand how to make his own spears and spear thrower. With those implements, he made a slim living, hunting when the opportunity presented itself. He was careful, avoiding any run-ins with predators, sleeping in trees for security.

—◦—

He was walking through a clearing in the trees with hunger gnawing at his stomach. He'd killed nothing for days. There had been nothing to kill. All of the game had apparently moved out of the area.

There were some mushrooms growing in the clearing. He paused, considering. He didn't know much about mushrooms, only that some were deadly, and some were edible.

A wave of despair washed over him. He'd been wandering in a gray fog of depression, searching for any sign of his beloved, but now the fog darkened to almost pitch black.

What did it matter if he lived or died? If he lived, he'd have to live with her memory and the knowledge that he'd lost her irrevocably. If he were dead, perhaps it wouldn't hurt so badly.

He plucked a handful of the small mushrooms. Their caps were a pleasing golden-brown, and the larger ones were almost completely golden. They were round in shape with a prominent nipple in the center.

He gathered five of them, selecting the most perfect and rejecting any that showed signs of having been nibbled by insects.

As he plucked the last one, he noticed that the stems were turning blue. The ones he'd picked first were the bluest.

"That's funny," Logan said aloud. He'd taken to speaking to himself recently. "Maybe it hurts when I pick them. They're bruising."

He selected the very nicest one. It was a larger specimen and almost completely golden. He nibbled at the edge of the cap. It didn't taste unpleasant. No acid or burning taste.

He looked around suspiciously as if someone might be watching and disapprove of his action. Then returned his attention to the mushrooms. His stomach was growling, and the small bit of food had increased rather than decreased his discomfort.

"What the hell?" he said, shrugging his shoulders. He quickly ate the entire batch.

"If that doesn't kill me, maybe it will at least get me through until I can kill something to eat," he muttered.

He stood up and resumed his journey. He'd have to keep moving to cover more territory. He'd never find Serensaa's people if he didn't keep moving. Here his thoughts stopped and returned to repeat the phrase: never find Serensaa. The words seemed to echo in his mind, again and again, making ripples across the sky as it repeated. He felt depressed, and his hunger was making him light-headed.

He walked on for a few minutes, crossing the large clearing, then stopped. There was a leaf on that oak over there. It was picked out by a ray of light that made it seem...made it seem...almost magical. The leaf shimmered with a rainbow of light around it.

Logan finally tore his gaze away from the fascinating, magical leaf. The sky was full of clouds, and they were saying something to him. He couldn't quite make out their message, but he knew it was for him. If he could just interpret their deep voices...

Looking up made him dizzy. He wanted to rest for a bit but couldn't find a tree to climb. No, he was wrong. He didn't need a tree. Anything that attacked him would die. His tanto would cut it to shreds.

A portion of his mind told him that he wasn't making any sense, but he ignored it.

The world was swirling around him now. Everything was covered with rainbow light making even the weeds seem like things of beauty. Something in the woods caught his eye. It was a yellow cat spotted with black patches. A jaguar. He liked its look.

It was friendly and came to him. He looked down at himself. He was spotted also. Black and yellow gold. He was a jaguar. Together the two of them ran through the trees, stalking deer. They killed a deer and ate, then the jaguar looked at him. It was Serensaa.

They mated in rainbows of love and lust. Afterward, he lay in the grass, panting and looking at the rainbow sun. The jaguar disappeared, and he cried out mournfully for his lost love.

A dragonfly came near, hovered over him for a moment, and then flew away. Logan's eyes tracked it. It looked huge, as large as a real dragon. He could see himself riding it across the forest, looking for Serensaa. He was suddenly sure that the dragonfly knew exactly where she was.

He got to his feet. The ground was moving and didn't want to cooperate. It made it difficult to walk, but he managed to move slowly until he started to glide over the ground.

He moved effortlessly, gliding above the surface, pursuing the dragonfly. It led him a merry chase, first here, then there. It was aggravating; it was so indecisive.

He called out to it to stop, but it flew away without looking back. He paused to grieve. He'd never see it again. It was so pretty. It was lost to him throughout all time.

Now there was a buzzing sound that grew quickly louder. He ducked as a deer fly flew past. It circled, rapidly gaining in size. It was horrible. A huge, hairy monster with bulging eyes that zoomed across his vision, first near, then far. He shrieked then ran as it pursued, striking at his head and face, inflicting painful wounds. He was escaping. He was elated.

There was a loud, jarring bump. He'd tripped on something. It caused him to fly slowly through the air, the rainbow-colored air, slowly arching downward.

The arching flight took an incredibly long time. The grass grew larger and larger in his vision. He was intrigued by the way the individual stems swelled and grew. They beckoned to him. He wanted to move closer to see what they wanted.

Suddenly the grass jumped at him, and he struck with a thunderous crash. Everything flickered, rainbows flashed everywhere. The world disappeared. It was black.

◄O►

A blue dragonfly darted through the air in pursuit of a mosquito. The insect hovered briefly over the spot where the man had fallen. Relieved of Logan's weight, the bent grass stems were gradually straightening themselves. A squirrel chucked from the crown of a nearby magnolia. Other than those two signs of life, the clearing was empty.

Chapter Twenty-Two

Back

Everything was dark. Far away, in the darkness, there was a series of sounds that rose and fell. Logan wished the noise would quit and just leave him in peace to die. Life without Serensaa wasn't worth the effort.

A flash of light struck his eyes, making him squint. He lifted his arm to block out the light, muttering in a feeble protest. Then a voice said, "Roll over and put your hands behind you. Move it, or I'll tase you."

Logan tried. He couldn't move very well. His arms seemed disconnected and uncooperative. He gave up the attempt.

Suddenly there was a spasm of pain. His muscles tightened incredibly, making him cry out. As the pain faded, he was roughly dragged onto his face. His arms were twisted behind him and bound in some fashion.

Fingers fumbled at his waist. His tanto. He tried to stop the theft, but his hands were locked behind his back.

Someone grabbed his wrists and lifted hard, pulling his arms upward painfully. He managed to come to his knees, then his feet, trying to relieve the agonizing pain in his shoulder joints. He cried out again, incoherently.

The voice said, "Damned homeless druggers! Now I'll have to run him into the hospital for treatment, then on to the facility to write him up. I should be heading home right now. My shift is over. Damn it!"

Logan was aware of movement. He was sitting in a comfortable spot, swaying slightly. It was more comfortable than he'd been in many, many days. He was, he suddenly realized, seated in the back seat of an automobile.

His head hurt. There were lights passing outside. They were glowing with tinges of rainbow around them. He closed his eyes and slept.

Logan woke. He vaguely remembered a confusion of glaring lights and people talking, saying things he didn't understand. Now, he saw that he was in a hospital room. He moved his arm, and it made a clanking sound. His wrist was handcuffed to the bed. A woman in a nurse's uniform was doing something with a clipboard at the foot of his bed.

She looked up and saw his eyes were open.

"Well, well, well. So you've come back to the world. Can you understand me?" she said.

He nodded slowly and answered, "Yes. Where am I?"

She shook her head disapprovingly. "We pumped your stomach. It's a wonder you aren't dead. You ate enough cubies to kill most people. I'll be surprised if you don't have recurring psychotic episodes from this. Whatever possessed you?" she asked, not answering his question.

Logan was thinking and not really listening to her. His mind was remarkably clear. He looked at the wall. The clock said it was ten-fifteen. From the light, it must be mid-morning.

"Am I in a hospital?" he asked.

"The alternative would be jail," she said. Then she added, "Yes. This is a hospital."

"I know this will sound strange," he started.

She snorted, making him look at her. "You couldn't surprise me. I've seen it all, working here."

He shrugged, "What's the date?"

She scoffed and said, "You call that strange? It's August 21st."

Logan's mind was still trying to understand what had happened. After a bit, he asked, "Of what year?"

The nurse smiled. "That's better. Now you're getting stranger. It's the same year it has been since January 1st: two-thousand and sixteen."

He was back! Logan felt dizzy. He was back. Did he want to be back? He wanted Serensaa – that was the only thing he was sure of. His eyes watered.

The nurse said, "Don't get all sad on me now. I can't help what year it is. Why do you want to know?"

He pulled himself together, then answered., "I was just checking. I was so disoriented by the – What did you say I ate?"

The nurse sighed. "Cubies – psilocibe cubensis. They contain a very strong hallucinogenic. You overdosed. And, what happened to you? You've got a freshly healed wound across your chest. If I didn't know better, I'd say claws made it. What was it? Also, what caused that nasty, jagged slash on your side?"

He shook his head negatively. "I think I was maybe...I mean I think I ran into a sharp branch or something. It was dark."

The nurse snorted again in response, then said, "You're lucky you weren't hurt worse. The cops can't figure where you've been. It's only been three days since the archaeology students left. They said you were one of them."

Logan thought about that. When he didn't respond immediately, she asked him again, "Where were you?"

He said, "I was wandering in the woods. I guess I was lost."

"Look, young man. I don't know what kind of a fool you take me for. There are houses all around there. You couldn't have gone too far without running into someone who could help," she said with a frown.

This was getting too detailed for Logan. He grinned, trying to charm her out of her bad mood. "I must have been walking in circles."

Then, before she could think of a suitably cutting remark about his lack of intelligence, he shook his wrist, rattling the handcuff against the bed. "I need to go to the bathroom. Can you unhook me?"

The nurse didn't answer, but she showed her opinion of him by the set of her face. She went to the door and said something. After a little time, a policeman came in.

"Are you back in the real world?" the man asked, with a hint of humor. He seemed to be in a good mood.

Logan was grateful for that and didn't want to make him angry. He answered, "I'm fine, only I really need to go to the bathroom. Will you please unlock me?"

The officer cautioned, "No tricks." Then unlocked the cuffs.

Logan climbed out of the bed, belatedly realizing he was wearing a hospital gown. He reached behind, gathering it together where it gaped open, then walked slowly into the bathroom. The officer allowed him to relieve himself in peace.

When he came out, the man was still there. He said, "I'm assuming you're okay. I'm going to check you out of here. You'll have to come down to the station to be booked. You'll probably be charged with public intoxication. You don't seem like a habitual drug user. Ever do this before?"

Logan shook his head from side to side. "No. I was hungry. I found some mushrooms, and I ate them. Things got really weird after that. Did I get tased? My back muscles hurt."

The cop said, "Yeah. I read the report. You were uncooperative."

Logan replied in a level tone of voice, "I couldn't control my arms. You didn't have to tase me. I wasn't going to do anything."

The policeman grinned at him again. "It wasn't me. That guy went off-shift. He recognized you, though. Said you were one of those archaeology students that were working at the Crystal River site. I thought you all left three days ago."

Logan's mind whirled. Three days ago. The nurse had said that, but it hadn't really registered. He had returned to the present, but the time that passed here didn't seem to match up with the time he'd spent in the past. He mentally suppressed an image of Serensaa. It wouldn't do to show his grief. They'd think he was having some kind of episode or something.

Thinking about the time discrepancy made his head hurt. He smiled back and said, "I got lost in the woods. I think I learned a lesson. I'm never going to eat anything that I don't know what it is ever again. That was a horrible experience."

The cop said, "Life is hard, and it's even harder if you do stupid things, but you'll probably get over this one with no real damage."

———◆○◆———

They released him from the hospital in the afternoon. Someone came up with a tee-shirt from somewhere. His pants were ragged and stained, but they were still wearable as were his sneakers.

The police weren't really busy. He was quickly charged, booked, and placed in a holding cell for the night. There were some drunks that were brought in a little after midnight, but they didn't bother him much. One basically passed out, and the other just sat with his head resting in his hands.

His arraignment was the next day. It was unexpectedly brief. The judge looked him up and down, then referred to Logan's paperwork.

"It sounds like you did something stupid, Mr. Walker. Have you ever done drugs before?" he asked.

Logan shook his head and said, "No, your Honor. Uh – I mean, I drink beer sometimes." He quickly added, "But I don't drive when I do."

The judge chuckled. "You'd better not, either. If they'd brought you in here with a DUI charge, I wouldn't be sympathetic. Incidentally, I wouldn't have believed you if you'd said you didn't drink."

Logan nodded and said, "Yes, Sir."

The judge said, "'Your Honor' is the approved term. Mr. Walker, the police force, and the prosecutor want to make an example of you. I don't think that's necessary. I'm minded to give you a warning and let you go. You won't do this again, will you?"

"No, your Honor. It was a horrible experience. I didn't know what was happening. I just thought the mushrooms looked good, like the ones in the produce section at the grocery. I like those, but these things made me wish I was dead."

"Well, young man, from what I read on your medical report, it's somewhat lucky that you aren't dead. Keep in mind that there are more poisonous plants than not out there in the woods."

He slammed the gavel down with a loud "klonk," and said, "We'll dismiss this one. You're free to go."

Logan couldn't believe it. This was far better than he'd expected.

⊰•◦O◦•⊱

He'd been given a chance to call his father from the police station before being transported to the courthouse, now he was waiting outside the courthouse. There was a small park there, and he was sitting on one of the benches.

His dad had answered the phone after a couple of rings, sworn some, but ended by saying, "Alright. I guess the guys can work without me. I'll be there to get you as soon as I can." Then he slammed the phone down.

Logan held the phone away from his ear and looked at it curiously. His father seemed angrier about missing work than worried about where he had gone. He wished that he hadn't called him.

⊰•◦O◦•⊱

The sun was hot, even though the sky was filled with small, fluffy clouds. There was a mockingbird singing somewhere in the trees. He closed his eyes and imagined that he was with Serensaa. There had been moments with her where he wasn't exhausted or worried about pursuers or animals. Moments just like this. She seemed close. If only...he sighed deeply.

———◆———

"Are you gonna sleep all day? Get in the truck," his dad said.

He opened his eyes. His father had arrived. He walked over to the pickup and got in. His dad immediately started driving.

"Now, I gotta get us moving. I need to get back to work." Only then did his father look at him and ask, "And where the hell did you go? Cheryl said that you disappeared. She said you ate one of her brownies and wandered out into the front yard. She said you fell in the ditch, and when she looked, you were gone. What gives you the idea you can just go off somewhere? I needed your help. We got behind until I found someone else to work. I'm still playing catch-up because'a you."

Logan wearily said, "Sorry about that. I wandered off, and I don't know what happened, really. That brownie was bad."

"Bad? I'll say it was bad. You've been gone for a couple'a weeks. You can stay tonight, but it'd probably be better if you get your stuff and head back to school. Larry got kicked out of his rental, and he's sleeping in your room now. All's I got is the couch."

That pretty much ended their conversation. The drive east was long and quiet, with only a few words spoken.

Logan tried to catch up on sleep. His mind still felt abused from eating the mushrooms, and his thoughts kept circling around to Serensaa. He tried not to think of her because it was too painful, but somehow her image kept returning. Her slender form danced through his dreams as he napped.

———◆———

He had deflected all questions posed to him at his father's house. When they realized he had nothing to say, they left him alone. He gathered up his things with the intent of leaving early in the morning. His cell phone was there, but the battery had discharged. He put it on the charger, so it would be ready to go in the morning.

Fortunately, Larry had broken up with Cheryl, and Chelle was out of town, so the nightly debauch was limited to a couple of beers apiece for his dad and Lar.

Logan made up a bed on the couch, said he was tired, and lay down while the two men were still talking in the backyard. He lay there thinking about his life. He finally understood the pain he'd suffered from his mother's suicide. Now, he realized that his father, too, hadn't outgrown her loss.

His dad had never been a hard worker when Logan was little, while his parents were still together. He remembered the two of them fighting over money and his dad's drinking. Now William was far more interested in working than in any problem Logan had. That lack of interest had bothered him initially, but he'd mostly overcome it during the time they were working together.

His recent experiences had changed him, giving him vastly more insight.

His dad had only been interested in Logan as long as he fit into the life William had created for himself. Logan's value was in how well he worked and how much beer he could drink. College, anthropology, and even police problems meant nothing to the man.

In a way, Logan understood. He was a living symbol of his father's failed attempt at marriage. His dad had to have mixed feelings for him.

He pulled up the light blanket and rolled to a more comfortable position. He had his own problems now. Serensaa, and the ethics hearing. Of the two, the ethics hearing was by far the least important. But, then, again, if he graduated, he'd have plenty of money. Perhaps that would give him the chance to figure out how he'd traveled in time.

He'd jumped in time, somehow covering thousands of years. If he'd done it three times, he could probably do it again. Only, how would he know he was coming to the precise time where he'd have a chance to meet Serensaa? That was the point where his mind always stuck. How would he ever find her again? If he couldn't, then how would he live without her?

Logan finally slept, the dried tracks of tears on his cheeks.

He was on the road before Larry, and his dad had rolled out of bed. He didn't say goodbye to them, just left a note on the table that said, "Thanks for everything. Good Luck!"

The old motorcycle made good time, running smoothly in the cooler morning air. His mind was busy as he rode. The ethics charge against him hinged on his discovery of the tanto. How could it have been in the ground, obviously deposited there thousands of years before Larry had given it to him, and how could he have it now?

There had been a critical decision point that made the difference. It happened when he had been on the verge of going towards the shore. If he'd walked that way, he probably wouldn't have returned. Discovering the stele near the shore had taken all thoughts of exploring the old campground out of his head.

The fox had made the difference. Its yip had led him to discover the dirty knife buried in the grass stems.

Maybe, just maybe, the universe had divided into two parts at that point. In one universe, the knife went undiscovered until the dig. In the other, he found it; still had it as a matter of fact. The police had given it back to him once he'd been released.

The question of the knife faded from his mind as he accelerated around a slow-moving car driven by an old man.

It was still early in the morning when he reached Gainesville. It was Sunday, and the traffic was light. He stopped for some donuts and coffee, used the restroom, and then got back in the saddle.

He was heading for the university when he noticed a Chrysler convertible that looked familiar. It was sitting in a driveway behind another car. It might be Dameron's. He circled the block to make another pass.

As he turned the corner to come by again, he saw someone coming out of the house. It was Dameron.

Logan stopped and rolled his motorcycle into the space between two cars parked on the street. He straightened so that he could just see over the top of a car.

Dameron got halfway to his convertible but turned back when Mandi appeared at the door and called to him.

She was barely covered, wearing a thin nightie and nothing else. Dameron looked her over. Logan clearly heard him say, "I've got to get to my office. Janice is coming to pick me up for lunch, and I need to look like I've been working."

Logan didn't hear what Mandi said in return, it was low and soft, but it obviously was something seductive. Dameron came back to her like a dog with his tongue hanging out at the sight of a bone. The two kissed in the doorway.

Logan took the opportunity to snap a couple of pictures with his cell phone.

Such a sight would have made Logan incurably jealous in the not-so-recent past. Now it just seemed tawdry and cheap. He wasn't interested in the woman. What he'd originally believed was beauty was only a more common sort of prettiness. She was no competition for Serensaa.

The two disappeared into the house, shutting the door.

He figured that meant he had at least a half-hour before Dameron would get on the road. He backed his motorcycle out and headed for the Archaeology department.

———— ◆◇◆ ————

Dameron's office was unlocked. Logan looked around. There was no one in sight, anywhere. Even the graduate student offices were empty. He stepped quickly in and pulled the door shut.

The man's office was full of crowded bookshelves. There were some artifacts hanging in the little available wall space, and there was a credenza behind the desk. Both the desk and credenza were covered with a litter of papers.

He sorted through the papers on the desk, hopefully, but to no avail. There was nothing there that seemed relevant. He replaced the pages exactly as they had been, then accidentally bumped the computer mouse as he started to turn away.

The screen illuminated. The machine had only been asleep, and there wasn't even any security. Dameron was pretty trusting. Logan snorted. Even freshmen knew enough to secure their machines.

He looked at the display. It appeared that the professor had walked away while reading an email. The text was still there. He glanced at it, cursorily, then shrugged his shoulders and turned away.

He started for the door but then jerked and looked at the screen again. Yes, he'd been correct. The email was from Schmitzke. It was addressed to someone named " Samuel Friedholm," with a copy sent to Dameron. Logan scanned the text and printed it. He tucked the email in his backpack.

He started to check the credenza, but then noise coming from the hallway told him that time was running out. He cautiously opened the door, assured himself that no one was in sight, stepped out, pulled the door shut, and then ran the other way, lightly moving on his toes to minimize any noise. He ducked into the men's room, went into a stall, and sat down on the seat for a few minutes. Then he exited the room, turned, and walked normally to the stairs.

The sound he'd heard was the janitor. The man was working his way down the hall, collecting the trash. Logan grimaced. The man might have discovered him.

The janitor had a wheeled trash bin. He systematically parked it by each office door, went in, and returned with the occupant's wastebasket, which he dumped into the bin. Then he replaced the wastebasket before moving to the next office. Logan watched speculatively.

When the janitor had dumped Dameron's trash, Logan walked by and glanced into the bin while the man was replacing the wastebasket.

There was a page with Dameron's name on it lying on the top of the pile. He grabbed for it, coming up with a handful of papers that he held tightly against his chest as he strode away.

One of the classrooms was open, and he turned in there to inspect his find. He poked through the papers. They looked like the start of a journal article. He picked one at random and read the title: Advanced Metallurgy and the Clovis Culture by George Dameron, Ph.D.

The abstract wasn't very specific, but Logan understood that Dameron was attempting to fit the pitted steel tanto in the context of the Clovis site.

The professor was trying to make the case that someone, possibly a wandering Japanese metal artisan, had migrated with the Clovis people and taught them how to make high-grade steel.

Logan snorted. As far as he knew, there had been no one on Earth ten or eleven thousand years ago who had any idea of forging iron, let alone making stainless steel. Certainly, his tanto had been a new thing to the people he'd met. He didn't think the idea would be well received.

Apparently, Dameron felt much the same way. The paper had been heavily edited, then wadded and thrown in the trash. Dameron had to know that this theory was ludicrous and unsupportable.

Nevertheless, it seemed the man was trying to figure out how to present the idea in a publishable form so that he could take credit for it. That meant that Dameron knew the knife was a legitimate find and that Logan hadn't planted it.

That was all that he needed to prove. If Dameron was going to publish the finding, then Logan obviously hadn't done anything wrong.

He grinned tightly. It was going to be difficult for Dameron to get any academic traction with the paper. No one would believe that the knife was in context when found. The only proof was on the cell phone that he'd recovered at his dad's. He grabbed at his waist to make sure that it was still there. It was.

———◆———

He got some coffee at the student union and sat at a table, thinking until the coffee was cold. Then he went to the library where he set up his laptop in a carrel.

He began to type, outlining the situation. He wanted to be prepared for the ethics hearing. He started and stopped several times.

He researched time-travel, but there was nothing that he could find that was very helpful. The idea of a paradox stuck with him, though. He paused and thought some more.

Was it possible that his knife, now stored safely in his backpack, was the knife that he'd found in the strata near a Clovis point? There certainly had been Clovis points in the camp area. Now, if he hadn't found his knife buried among the grassroots, it would have been lost. Not quite lost forever, just for about eleven thousand years or so. He'd still recover it, only to have Dameron take it from him.

What would happen now? Did Dameron even have the pitted knife? Yes. He must. The journal article that he was writing referred to it. So, the timeline hadn't made any correction, even though the knife hadn't been lost and was now essentially duplicated. There were two tantos, one old and pitted, and one new.

He snatched up his backpack and feverishly checked. Yes, his knife was in there. It would be bad if it had somehow disappeared.

He took a piece of paper and tried to diagram out the situation, but he couldn't make sense of it. There was no knowing what would happen in the future.

He let that puzzle go for the moment and turned to creating a short slide show, using the photos from his phone.

He took the journal article title page, which showed the title, by-line, and abstract, and scanned it to himself using one of the library's scanners. Then he added that page to the slide presentation with an appropriate title.

He considered, weighing the negative aspects against any possible advantage, before adding one of the pictures of Dameron kissing Mandi to the end of the presentation. He need not show it, but it might be nice to have if things went badly, even if Berensten wouldn't approve.

When he was done, he recalled the email. He pulled it out of his pack and studied the names. Then he ran several searches on the Internet.

It took some time to find what he was after, but using a variety of sources for public records proved fruitful. He identified Samuel Friedholm and found Dameron's wife's maiden name.

That discovery caused him to draw in his breath through his teeth.

"So that's why I've had such a hard time with Dameron," he whispered.

More searches, but no luck. Then he got the idea to try Friedholm's wife. She was almost a dead end, but while researching her, he discovered that she had a brother named Jeffery. Jeff's wife was the linchpin. There it was. Everything clicked together.

He incorporated that knowledge into his thinking. It was shocking. The idea that people would do what was implied by that email and his search results offended his sense of what was right.

The future became clear as he considered. He had to prevail in the ethics hearing. He felt relieved, but then a wave of sadness washed over him. None of this mattered if he couldn't find Serensaa. He feared she was lost in the distant past.

Tears came to his eyes. She had been dust for over ten thousand years. How could that be? He'd been with her. They'd made love on their wedding night just a few days ago.

Logan swiped at his eyes, trying to stop the tears.

He packed his stuff up and left the library, pausing by the exit to wipe his eyes again before putting on his sunglasses.

He needed somewhere to stay for a couple of days.

Chapter Twenty-Three

Ethical Behavior

The motel offered a continental breakfast. Logan found it consisted of some picked-over donuts and weak coffee. All of the cinnamon rolls were long gone. He figured he wouldn't need the sugar rush from the pastries anyway. It would probably make him sleepy, and he wanted to be on his toes for the ethics hearing.

He went down the street to a local cafe for breakfast. The food was good, but he was so nervous about the upcoming hearing, he couldn't concentrate on it. It went down, filling his stomach, but once he was on his motorcycle, heading for the university, he couldn't have told anyone what he'd eaten.

Professor Berensten wasn't in yet, and he had to wait. He found a spot outside, under a tree. His time in the past had made him feel confined whenever he was inside. It was better to be out in the fresh air.

After weeks outside, the heat and humidity didn't bother him as much as it had when he spent most of his time inside, in air-conditioned luxury. He shook his head disparagingly. People were spoiled. They didn't realize it, but they were.

Nine a.m. rolled around, and he went in to check on Berensten. She'd come in the back way and was in her office.

"Hello, Logan. Are you ready for the hearing?" she asked.

"Hi, Dr. Berensten," he answered. "Yes, I'm as ready as I can be."

She looked at him critically, one eyebrow cocked. Then remarked, "You seem different somehow. Oh, well. Never mind that. Just remember, I want you to have one thing clear. It won't help your case if you start throwing unfounded accusations at Dr. Dameron. It would be one thing if you had proof that he's having an affair, but even if you did, it really isn't related to your case."

Logan shrugged. His defense was based on the photos he took and evidence that he'd collected. He figured they wouldn't like the idea that he had been surreptitiously going through Dameron's office, but he hadn't actually found the article until it was in the janitor's trash bin.

He remembered reading that anything that had been discarded in the trash was no longer considered private property. Or something like that, anyway. That would be his defense for having the papers. He'd found them discarded in the trash.

The other information, the results of his searches, and the email weren't in his plans for the ethics hearing. Well, it was true that they showed Dameron's motive for making the complaint, but then he'd have to admit he got the email directly from the professor's computer. That wouldn't sound very good in a hearing about his ethics. He'd reserve that information for later when he needed it.

The two of them walked across campus to Tigert Hall. Dr. Berensten led him to the conference room. They were a little early, and none of the hearing committee members was there.

On the way over, Berensten had explained that the committee was composed of a mix of faculty and student representatives. In the event of an equal split, the hearing officer, the assistant dean of students, would have the tie-breaking vote.

Logan shut his eyes and tried to compose himself. It was easy compared to worrying about being attacked by a saber-tooth. The old value system he had painstakingly created now seemed trivial. He had changed, and not just mentally either. His body was harder, more able, and honed down.

He glanced at the people who were now finding their places in the room. They didn't impress him. They were uniformly out of shape, not fit to survive in the natural world, and yet, they were here to judge him. He exhaled, making a disgusted sound. Berensten glanced at him curiously.

He closed his eyes again, waiting for the hearing to start. He daydreamed a little, thinking of Serensaa and how he'd proceed with her English lessons.

———◄O►———

"Mr. Walker, you've been accused of fraudulently attempting to invalidate the data collected by your first summer session archaeology team. This is a serious issue. The archaeology department and our university cannot countenance such activity. This group has been convened to hear the evidence and decide what to do with you."

The speaker was someone Logan didn't know. He thought the woman held a position in Student Services or was, as Berensten had said, the assistant dean of students. As far as he was concerned, it didn't matter.

She paused, addressing the rest of the group. "As we commonly do, if anyone has any reason that they cannot sit on this panel, they should make it known now before we start."

A nicely dressed woman raised her hand. The hearing officer said, "Yes, Janice?"

The woman said, "I'm going to bow out. I have a personal conflict. I'll remain in the room, but I really couldn't judge fairly since I'm George Dameron's wife."

Logan straightened and looked at her with interest. She was a good-looking woman of about Dameron's age. What had he seen in Mandi? He shook his head, puzzled. Mandi was cute, but why not stay with your wife? Surely Dameron had more in common with her than a student.

He hoped for her sake that he could prevail in the hearing without his final piece of evidence. If he brought that out, things would get interesting.

The hearings officer said, "I understand, and it's commendable that you bring this up now. Now, I'd like to remind the committee that I have the final vote regardless of how the members rule. The university retains the right to decide any issues that impact its credibility."

She looked around at the members. They nodded. Then she looked at Logan. "Is that understood, Mr. Walker?"

He nodded.

She continued. "Do you have anything to say at this time?"

Logan looked directly at her. She held his gaze for a moment and then dropped her eyes. "No," he said. "Nothing more than a simple observation."

She waited, and when he didn't continue, she asked, "Well, what is it?"

He looked at the other people, acknowledging their presence, then said, "Your opening statement gives the impression that you've already made up your mind to find me guilty. Don't you think that coming to judgment prior to hearing both sides is a little unfair?"

She flushed in anger at his question before she responded. "You've been accused by your professor. He's been employed by this university for several years. I'm inclined to take his accusations seriously. He is a responsible member of our faculty."

Logan grinned. "You side-stepped my question. You haven't heard my version of what happened yet, and you're already defending my accuser. I repeat, don't you think that's unfair?"

She glared at him, obviously unused to challenges from an accused student. "We'll get on with this process without any more quibbling. We'll now hear from Professor Dameron. Professor, please explain what led to your complaint."

Dameron leaned back, obviously relishing the moment. He smirked a little at Logan then began.

"As you know, I've been teaching archaeology for years, and I was trained by experts during my academic career. I've been on numerous digs and have a number of published articles in various journals."

He glanced around and continued. "I'm explaining this so that you will understand that my credentials are impeccable. I know how to run an archaeological dig.

For the past three years, I've been teaching two summer sessions that provide my students with field experience. These are often on sites in the State of Florida but sometimes in other locations.

This summer, I decided to work on a site that holds minor value. This one is conveniently located near the university, over at Crystal River. The site itself is not considered to be terribly unique. It is in an area that has been well explored. The location has been in use by humans for thousands of years, although it was previously believed that it hadn't been a major center of Pleistocene activity.

We now have solid evidence that the site was in use by members of the Clovis culture. Our dig turned up numerous Clovis artifacts and signs of human use that dated to about 11,000 BCE."

He looked around, then added in explanation: "About thirteen thousand years ago. Needless to say, this data, while not radically startling, is still extremely valuable.

Based on the results, I've planned a series of papers that will be submitted to appropriate journals. This will greatly add to our department's reputation and will increase the already high prestige of our university.

The dig went well overall, but, as in every group, there were marginal performers, including some who, for one reason or another, were destined not to earn a passing grade. Others, such as my student supervisor, Mandi Thompson, performed on a stellar level.

Mr. Walker was, unfortunately one who didn't seem to understand why he was there. Ms. Thompson had to reprimand him repeatedly for failing to follow approved procedure in his work. He was also notably recalcitrant and insubordinate both to her and to me.

I watched his performance closely. He'd been given a grid square of little importance due to my doubts of his ability. He repeatedly failed to follow proper procedure in reducing the square to a contemporaneous horizon, uh, that is, for those of you unfamiliar with our science, digging every layer so that all artifacts from a particular time period are simultaneously exposed. This allows us to place the artifacts in context with each other, leading to an understanding of what the primitive human occupants were doing at any one time.

Mr. Logan, as I say, was reprimanded, not only for sloppy digging procedure but for failing to follow instructions on a field trip to the Crystal River Archaeological State Park on Pine Island. I found that he'd ignored the assignment to create a report about the mound site, and had, instead, retired to the bus.

When I discovered him, he gave an excuse about needing a drink. That and his general bad attitude constitute a point against him, but..."

He paused again, dramatically. "But not the main point. The final straw came when he approached me, saying that he'd discovered something unusual. I was speaking to Mandi – uh – Ms. Thompson at the time, and she will attest as to his actions.

We immediately investigated and found that he'd attempted to invalidate the entire dig by planting an artifact in his grid. He'd cleverly placed an old, pitted steel knife blade adjacent to a Clovis projectile point, assuming, I suppose, that I'd think they were contemporaneous.

Since I selected his grid on the basis that it was out of the inhabited area, even the presence of the projectile point is suspect. Such arrowheads can be purchased on the Internet, and this one might even be a replica, not an original artifact.

Due to this fraudulent act, I immediately suspended Mr. Logan and banned him from further participation. His grade, I'm sorry to say, will be a failing one."

Dameron looked around again, nodded to Berensten, and leaned back, signaling that he was done.

The hearing officer then turned to Mandi.

"Ms. Thompson, have you anything to add?"

Mandi drew herself up, swallowing nervously as she glanced at Logan. He stared back, and she, too, dropped her eyes for a moment but then glared defiantly at him.

"Logan, uh, Mr. Walker was a constant problem. When I had him remove overburden, he complained that he didn't have the proper equipment. His pre-dig instructions included a complete list of necessities, and he had no excuse not to have gloves. I allowed him to leave to get some, but that was just the start. He was always fooling around, being late to start, or starting too early, or anything to mess up the orderly progression of the dig."

Her face had been pale as she started, but now that she'd worked herself up into a righteous case of outrage, her complexion changed to a blotchy red.

She looked at Logan, then, speaking more quickly and shrilly, said, "He planted the knife and the spear point. It was a stupid thing to do. The knife would never be there. That's a paleolithic site. A stone-age culture, by definition, can have no knowledge of steelmaking. How he ever thought we'd fall for that shit is beyond me."

Belatedly realizing that she'd used a non-professional term, she put her hand over her mouth but quickly lowered it as she added, "Sorry. I don't have anything else to say."

The hearing officer looked at Logan with a grim smile as if she'd already pronounced judgment. "Mr. Logan, have you any response to these accusations?"

Logan took his time. He stretched, then opened his laptop and started the slide show software. He brought up a distance picture of the site that he'd taken. It showed the mess tent, and much farther away, over by the tree line, one could make out a shovel standing upright.

He turned the screen so that everyone could see.

"I'll deal with the accusations very briefly," he said.

"The mess tent is in the foreground. The shovel way over there is where my grid square was located. It was, as Professor Dameron has said, carefully selected so that I could be placed out of the way and not find anything valuable."

Dameron interjected, "Not mess up any valuable finds, you mean."

Logan glanced at him, then at the hearing officer. She was impassive. He asked, "Am I going to be allowed to make my case without interruptions?"

She lowered her eyebrows and said, "You make your presentation. We'll listen."

Logan shrugged and continued.

"As for the preliminary items that my accusers hold against me. Yes, I neglected to get gloves. I purchased some and didn't complain after that point, even though my hands were blistered raw.

As for the field trip, I felt that I was suffering from dehydration. I needed water, so I went to the bus and got some. Professor Dameron came driving up as I was exiting the bus and told me that I'd better turn in a good report, or he would be only too pleased to flunk me."

Dameron interrupted again, "I'd never threaten a student. That's a lie."

Logan looked at him, shook his head tiredly, and said, "That is my answer. That's what happened. After that, Mandi often criticized my work. Neither of the two ever provided me with any positive instructions, only criticism. I studied on my own in my tent at night, and that's how I managed to learn how to work a dig properly."

He continued. "Now to answer the main item. It seems that this part of the complaint can be divided into two separate issues. The simplest one to resolve is whether the knife was discovered in context."

He clicked the keyboard, advancing the presentation. "Here's a picture, a close-up, showing both the knife and the Clovis spear point embedded in the matrix, before they were touched by Professor Dameron."

Everyone leaned forward to inspect the picture. A couple of people got up and moved behind some of the nearer ones in order to see better.

Logan waited until everyone had satisfied themselves. "The picture shows the objects clearly and also shows no sign of disturbance of the overlying soil.

It might be argued that I stuck the artifacts in from the side. The next picture shows the knife blade, as it was first uncovered. All you can see is the middle of the blade. Both ends are buried. No one could have placed it there in that fashion without disturbing the soil at one or both ends.

You can see that it's untouched. By the way, the original photo files are available if you want to check them for photoshopping. You'll find there has been no manipulation. These two photos refute the claim that the knife was not in context."

Most of the student committee members were nodding their heads affirmatively along with some of the faculty members. It looked like they found his photo convincing.

Logan inwardly cringed as he prepared to show the next piece of evidence. He might lose some of his support here. He swallowed and advanced the display.

"The second part of the argument against me relies on the assumption that the Clovis culture didn't have metallurgy. That's a generally accepted fact that seemingly invalidates the photos showing the knife in context.

I'm not claiming that the prior research is incorrect. I don't believe the Clovis people knew enough about metals to create stainless steel. However, the problem raised by the knife requires some explanation.

The next slide that you see is a scan of the first page of a draft article that was written by Professor Dameron."

There was a murmur of incredulity, interrupted by Dameron shouting, "That's private property! He stole that paper!"

The hearing officer waited until Dameron quit, then said, "Mr. Walker, you've committed a gross violation by stealing the paper. We cannot countenance that sort of behavior. You're – "

Logan interrupted her. "I've done no such thing. That paper isn't private property according to commonly accepted legal precedent used by every police department in the United States."

The woman said, "What?"

Logan continued. "I found it in the department trash. It was not in the professor's possession. He had discarded it. It's an accepted fact that when things are discarded, they are no longer private property. This is the case here.

The page shows us two things. The first is that Professor Dameron was or is attempting to make a case for the knife to be a new discovery that will change the generally accepted scientific view of the Clovis culture. He makes the argument that the knife was in context. I ask you how could it be in context for his paper while he accuses me of planting it?"

Without waiting, he said, "The second thing is that Professor Dameron has placed his name on the paper as sole author, meaning that he intended or intends to take full credit for the discovery. How is it fair to accuse me of fraud, then take the purported fraud and claim it is a scientific discovery? That speaks more to his ethics than to mine."

The room became chaotic. Dameron was shouting incoherently, as was Mandi. The rest of the committee was loudly arguing the point back and forth. It took the hearing officer some time to regain order.

When they quieted, she said, "Mr. Logan, I find your accusation of Professor Dameron severely out of place. It's you who is accused here."

Logan sighed. She was probably going to force the issue. Some of the other people were nodding yes, while the rest shook their heads negatively. He couldn't decide if he was winning the case or not.

He said, "The paper that Dr. Dameron was attempting to write is based on a theory that some outsider taught the Clovis people about metallurgy. They apparently were supposed to have figured out how to create the knife without the use of any advanced machinery, machinery which would have undoubtedly have left its own mark on the archaeological record.

I'm considered to be a marginal student, but even I think that's highly unlikely. Can you imagine what a respected journal would do with such an article? Even if it got published, it would end up damaging this university's good name. I think it was in the trash because Dameron realized his explanation was totally unsupportable."

Dameron interrupted again, "And if my idea was unsupportable, exactly how do you account for the knife being where it was, Walker?"

Logan smiled. Now he knew he'd won.

He said, "That's a good question, professor. The answer is simple, but no one here will find it easy to accept. Before I give you the answer, though, I'd like to point out that you've just exonerated me. Your last question essentially admitted that you intended to take credit for the discovery and also that the knife was in context when found, which means that I couldn't have planted it."

Dameron stuttered, "But – but – uh – I meant – "

Logan raised his volume, talking over the man's protest.

"The fact is that the knife was mine. I lost it at that site somewhere between eleven and twelve thousand years ago."

There was uproar in the room. When everyone calmed down, Logan continued. "I know it's difficult to believe. I don't understand what happened to me either, but somehow I traveled in time. I can prove it."

The hearing officer said, "That would be a good trick. Exactly how can you prove it? And, take care about what you say; you're only digging yourself in deeper."

Logan snorted in wry amusement. "Was that a reference to the archaeological dig? No, don't answer that. My proof is simple, but there are two parts to it. The first is that I know the origin of the carving on the Crystal River stele."

Dameron and Berensten looked at him in amazement. She hissed, "Logan, don't pull tricks. They'll get you in even worse trouble."

Logan waved her off. "No, it's true. I carved a picture of my girlfriend on the stone. She's a Clovis woman and – " Here he choked up with emotion, finally gasping out, " – and I don't know what's become of her. She's back there somewhere."

Logan looked around. The group was staring at him with confusion. It was obvious that they understood he was upset but also placed no credence in his explanation. He sighed. Then he said, "That didn't help much. Anyway, the figure is female, not male. It had no religious symbolism, at least not while I was carving it. I can't speak to the beliefs of the people who came after me."

The hearing officer said, "As you said, that didn't help. You'd better have better proof than an imaginary carving."

Berensten interjected, "No. The carving exists, and it's true, no one really knows what sex it is intended to be."

Dameron couldn't resist a comment. "Walker first tries to get us to believe he lost the knife back in time. Now he claims to have carved an ancient artifact. I demand that he be expelled."

The hearing officer lifted her hand to rap on the table, simultaneously saying, "I agree with you, Professor."

Logan hastily said, "That's not the main proof. I have the knife in my possession, the new knife, not the old version that was found at the dig site."

He pulled his knife from his backpack, unsheathed it, and laid it down so the initials LW were visible. Everyone leaned forward to see.

"This is the original knife. You can see that my initials are stamped on the blade. If you look at the pictures, you can see the same initials, but they aren't very clear because of dirt and pits in the metal."

He backed the computer up two slides so that the blade was again visible. The marks on the steel that had puzzled him at first were suddenly identifiable as the letters: LW.

Dameron yelled, "That's impossible. I've got the real knife in my briefcase. Just a minute." He clawed the case open and pulled out the aged piece of metal, waving it around wildly. "This is it. There's no way this is the same knife as the one he has there. This is old. He must have bought that one and stamped it to make it look like this."

Logan said, "No. It's the same knife. A metallurgist could probably prove it."

The hearing officer rapped on the table to regain control. Everyone looked at her.

"Mr. Walker, I find this totally unbelievable. Your new knife cannot be the same as the old one in Professor Dameron's hand. There are two knives, not one. I find against you. This hearing's closed."

Logan stood up and shouted, "Not so fast! I have one more piece of evidence to introduce. It speaks to Dameron's character."

Professor Berensten put her hand on Logan's arm, but it was too late. He had advanced the computer to the slide showing Dameron and Mandi kissing in the doorway.

Logan said, "Dameron has been having an affair with his student assistant. This picture was taken early last Sunday morning at her house. He may have suspected I knew. I observed her going to his tent at the dig during the night. I listened outside. They were having sex."

A new voice pierced the uproar, "You said you were going to work early Sunday! How long have you been seeing this girl, George?" Janice Dameron was white and shaking. She rose to her feet and started to the door without waiting for an answer to her question.

The room had fallen into complete silence. Some of the committee were staring at Dameron. Others were watching Janice as she left the room.

Dameron quickly stood and said, "Baby, it was a mistake. I'm going to break it off with her. Just give me a chance. It won't happen again."

There was a wail from Mandi, "You promised, George. You promised, and besides, I'm pregnant."

Janice turned, glared Mandi into silence, then said, "Don't bother coming home, George. I'm filing for divorce as soon as I can call my lawyer. You're not welcome to come back."

Dameron, for once, was silent. He stared down at the knife in his hand for a moment and then shouted, "It's not the same knife. Look!"

He grabbed Logan's tanto from the table and held it up, bringing the old version of the knife close so that everyone could see the differences.

As the knives approached each other, they began to glow softly. Dameron looked puzzled. He appeared to exert himself, trying to bring the two together, pushing against some unknown force that was keeping the two knives apart.

The glow increased as he struggled with the knives, trying to move them closer together. Frustrated, he pulled his arms wide and slammed his hands together.

The blades touched. There was a brilliant flash, momentarily blinding everyone. There was no corresponding sound, except for a clink and a rattle as something fell. There were startled cries from the committee members.

Logan's vision blurred into negative images, then alternating flashes of black and white. When he could see again, Dameron had vanished, as had the old, pitted knife.

Logan's new knife was rocking gently on the conference table, where it had been dropped.

⸺ ◆ ⸺

The hearings officer refused to let anyone leave until they'd promised not to discuss the events in the room. Something weird and terrible had happened, but no one was sure what it was.

Logan suspected that Dameron was trying to learn how to avoid predators in the Florida of the Pleistocene. He hoped that the man wouldn't meet Serensaa, but, other than that, he was sorry for the professor. It wouldn't be easy to survive. He knew that from personal experience.

He was dubious that the hearing officer's suppression of the events would last. Janice Dameron was demanding to know where her husband had gone. Mandi, meanwhile, was in hysterics, crying uncontrollably over in the corner of the room.

Logan got Dr. Berensten's attention. "Professor Berensten," he said. "I assume that I'm exonerated from the charges against me. I'd like to meet with you to set up a plan that will allow me to graduate next year."

She looked at him with some wonder. "Logan, I don't know what just happened. I doubt that I ever will. We'll have to find George. What happened to him?"

She looked around rather wildly and then returned her attention to Logan. "I think you proved your case, although I don't want to consider time-travel as the proof. However, it looks like I'm going to have to accept that explanation. Just a minute."

She got the hearing officer's attention. "Ruth, you're going to allow Mr. Walker to enroll again."

Ruth said, "Uh, well, I guess so. He made some good points about the knife and the article. I'm not happy with the way he brought up George's affair, but that's actually a peripheral issue. Yeah. I don't think the case against him was well-founded, and we should just try to keep this whole thing quiet. Do you agree, Mr. Walker?"

Logan could see that she wanted his promise to keep quiet about the mess. He said, "As long as I get a chance to graduate, I'm not going to complain. The hearing is over, and I'm satisfied. I'll keep quiet about everything."

She sighed in relief and then turned away to speak to the other faculty members, who were now speculating that Dameron had slipped out the door using the flash as a distraction.

One of the older professors came up to Logan. "Mr. Walker, I'd like to speak to you further about the time-travel issue. I'm Professor Wolf from the physics department. I believe that you have information that might be world-changing."

Logan replied, "As long as the hearing officer approves, I'm happy to talk to you, but I think you'll find that I don't know much more about the issue than what you've seen today."

Berensten put her hand on Logan's shoulder and said, "Why don't we meet in my office tomorrow at nine a.m. I'll try to get creative. If you promise me, you'll work hard and not slack off. Perhaps there is a way to meet your grandfather's goal for you to graduate in four years. Now, are you sure you don't know where George is?"

Chapter Twenty-Four

Money Can't Buy You Love

Logan had to check back into the motel. He'd checked out, unsure whether he would be staying in town. It had depended on the results of the hearing.

He'd picked up a newspaper in the lobby as he was leaving with the key. He'd have to rent another apartment for the next year. If he could graduate, that would be the last apartment he ever had, he told himself.

The next morning, he turned up at Professor Berensten's office exactly on schedule. She waved him in and pointed at a seat, all the while speaking to someone on the phone. From the side of the conversation he could hear, Logan understood it to be about him.

"No, Henry, he's going to enroll, and I have his promise that he'll exert himself."

"No, I'll take responsibility for his grades."

"Yes. He better not disappoint me."

She glared at him when she made that last statement.

Logan nodded in agreement. She continued with the conversation.

"No, I'm not sure exactly what occurred yesterday. I was there, but it was so unusual that I think it was a previously unknown phenomenon."

"I know the police are investigating. They've already interviewed me."

"That's correct. I don't know what happened. I think Mr. Walker has a possible explanation. I had a conversation with Professor Wolf."

"Yes, that's him – physics department. He wants Logan to work with him. He thinks that might provide enough information for him to make some kind of a breakthrough."

She paused, listening to a longer statement, then answered. "Yes, I guess actually being present for the event convinced Wolf that there was something there worth deeper investigation. Mr. Walker is here now. I need to get him set up with his next session's classes."

"Okay. Bye."

She hung up the old phone with a thunk and turned to Logan.

"You've started a perfect firestorm of gossip, Logan. The police have been in already, wanting my account of George Dameron's disappearance. They'll want to interview you, I guess. I think they're talking to everyone who was present. It sounded like they weren't getting anywhere from the things they asked me. He's gone, there's no sign of foul play, everyone has the same story, and there's no corpse, so they can't really even come up with a crime," she said.

Logan said, "I believe he's somewhere back in the distant past. If he's lucky, he'll meet some people who will take him in. If he's not, well, there are a lot of hungry predators back there. It was all I could do to stay alive."

She shuddered. "Isn't there anything you can do to help him?"

He answered, "I'm sorry for him. I mean, I didn't like him, but I don't want him to end up as lunch for a saber-tooth either. I'd help him if I could, but I don't really have any idea how I traveled back and forth."

He wiped his eyes. They seemed to be watering somehow. "If I knew how to go back, I would. Serensaa – uh, I mean a girl I met back there, I – Oh, I miss her so much."

His eyes wouldn't stop watering. He swiped at them ineffectually. Professor Berensten looked at him with concern.

"Logan, how long were you lost in that place?"

He tried to recall the days but couldn't. "Maybe a couple of months, a month and a half. I don't know. I didn't keep count of the days, and they were so full of danger that it was all I could do just to prepare for the next attack."

She said, "This girl, Serensaa...you were close to her?"

"The elder of her tribe married us. The next day we were attacked, and I moved in time again. I haven't seen her since. I – I love her, and I want her back."

He added, "Don't you see? If I could travel in time to help Dameron, I'd be able to get her. I intend to work with Professor Wolf. Maybe he can come up with a way for me to go back."

Berensten sighed. "I see, I think... Well, until you figure it out, you'd better be concentrating on your coursework, provided you want to graduate for your grandfather."

Logan nodded.

She continued. "Here's what I've got in mind. It's too late to get credit for your dig. Dameron's gone anyway, so there's some question about how to give credit to the other students. I thought I might ask Mandi Thompson to assign grades, but she's going to therapy. She had some kind of nervous breakdown. She won't be back at school for the foreseeable future.

Now, on to your problem. You need to pick up five extra hours, in addition to a normal course load in the remaining time you have. Usually, I wouldn't allow a student to enroll in more than eighteen hours at a time, but I'm going to make an exception for you. I will serve as your instructor for independent study. We'll cover any aspect of archaeology that I feel might benefit you. You'll meet with me for one hour daily, on a floating schedule to be determined by my class and meeting load.

I want to warn you, Logan, I'll expect you to perform. I'm not going to give you credit hours for nothing. Do I have your promise that you'll work hard?"

He answered, "That's wonderful, professor. Of course, I'll give you my best. It's very important to me to graduate on schedule."

She smiled and continued discussing his schedule for the upcoming session.

Logan felt it would be challenging, but he thought he could do it. He had no urge to spend time playing games. Each day of learning potentially brought him closer to figuring out how to find Serensaa.

He said, "Would it be okay if we focused on the Clovis culture for at least part of my independent work? I mean, uh, that I've got some insights on how they lived. In Florida, at least."

"Very perceptive of you," she answered. "I thought that might be the case. If you've actually been there, as you say, your experiences and observations, even though untrained, might help in understanding their culture.

Fair warning: If you're making things up, I believe that I will notice the discrepancies. That won't be good for you, so don't try it.

One of the big mysteries is where they came from. It sounds like you could at least tell me about their physical appearance, and that might give us a clue, although I still can't get my mind around your traveling in time."

Logan started to tell her what the people he'd seen were like, but she said, "No. Let's get organized first and do this systematically. You've got all session to work with me on it. Besides, I'd like to arrange my thinking, so I don't miss anything. I believe we'll start with me asking you a series of questions. An interview, if you will. We'll do that the first week.

Oh, and by the way, the university president is adamant that any rumors about George's disappearance be suppressed. I want to warn you to avoid saying anything about your experiences or what happened. It'd be best for all of us if this was forgotten as quickly as possible."

Logan said, "Yeah. I know. I don't intend to talk about it to anyone. It's none of their business, anyway."

During the next several weeks, Logan found that he'd changed even more than he'd known. Coursework wasn't difficult any longer. His increased motivation made it easy for him to study. The courses seemed trivial, and he easily mastered the material.

He missed the physical activity of the past. In order to keep up his strength, he spent a portion of each day working out. He'd run from his apartment to the student gym, then lift weights for about an hour every morning.

On alternate days, he used the pool, gradually building up to several kilometers per swim. Time was the restrictive element here. His cardio level had increased so that he didn't become tired during the limited time he had.

He tried rejoining his Tae Kwon Do class but found it wasn't the challenge it had been. Most of the class was oriented towards getting in shape. The forms were interesting since they introduced him to new techniques, but he now realized that sparring was basically useless.

They weren't supposed to hurt each other, and no one, including his instructor, really understood the timing aspect of fighting in the way he now did. Sparring was really just a show, not an actual fight.

Things came to a head when the instructor wanted to spar with him. Logan found that the man moved as if he was semi-frozen. His own reflexes had somehow sped up, possibly due to the loss of the tangle of mental restrictions he'd previously held. Those seemed to be an inextricable part of being civilized. Now that he'd fought to the death several times, he found that he went all-out when sparring.

The instructor was disgruntled and wouldn't spar with him again. Logan quit going to the class and located an MMA gym across town.

The fighters there were far more serious about fighting, and even though they restricted themselves unnecessarily, Logan felt that he could learn more with them.

He gradually became a force in the local MMA community, but he refused actual fights. He got a reputation for being a pacifist that was undeserved.

Actually, he was afraid that he'd hurt someone seriously, and that fear kept him away from tournaments and matches.

—◆—

Throughout all of this, he moved in an emotional fog. He missed Serensaa terribly. He found that he couldn't even consider looking at other girls.

This was apparently taken as a challenge by most of the women on campus. Something about his new attitude, perhaps his mature, serious demeanor, seemed to attract women like flowers attract bees. They buzzed around him to the point that he took to hiding in the library or simply studying at home. The increased study time gave him an advantage and helped him pass his courses.

Once a week, he spent time with Professor Wolf. They worked through Logan's experiences a little at a time, and he grew to like the older physicist.

Logan became quite interested in the process and did his best to follow the professor's explanations of quantum mechanics and the supposed structure of the universe.

His math wasn't good enough to understand the mathematical aspects of the professor's work, though. That led him to begin studying advanced math in his limited spare time.

—◆—

His interest in the Clovis culture led him to co-author a paper with Professor Berensten that was accepted by a journal and published. This added to his reputation, but he discounted the experience.

If he graduated and got control of the trust, he'd never have to work for a living unless he wanted to. He studied archaeology because it made him feel closer to Serensaa, not because he hoped to find employment in the field.

Physics was of interest because it had the potential to explain what had happened when he'd traveled through time.

Professor Wolf tried to get him to consider grad school. Logan could get a fellowship in the physics department if he applied. The professor recognized his ability and obviously hoped he'd enroll. Logan wasn't sure about that. It all hinged on whether he felt he could figure out how to return to his lost love.

The year fled by. In retrospect, he saw it as a continuous blur of activity. He'd mastered his classes, earned good grades, and it was almost a letdown when he found himself graduating after the spring session.

Professor Berensten was on the podium to award him with a special certificate from the archaeology department.

He accepted it gracefully, all the while thinking of Serensaa. She seemed closer now, somehow. Perhaps the money could be used to fund studies in time-travel. He could use it to get more help for Professor Wolf.

Serensaa constantly called to him across the years. Nights were the worst. She lived in his dreams. He often found himself waking up, either in a cold sweat or with tears on his cheeks.

With his diploma in hand, Logan entered Schmitzke's office a few days after graduation. Now was the time. The man would have to abide by the terms of the trust.

He was treated the same as the last time he came in. Forced to wait until Schmitzke had time for him, despite his scheduled appointment. Logan resented the attorney's cavalier treatment. He promised himself that once he had control of the trust, he'd hire someone else. He didn't want to see Schmitzke again.

When the attorney finally ushered him into the conference room, Logan had regained control of his anger. This was the last meeting between the two, as far as he was concerned. He meant for it to be as brief as possible.

He didn't wait for any amenities. He started immediately. "Here's my diploma. I want you to assign control of the trust to me."

Schmitzke drew back, the corners of his mouth drawing down simultaneously. "It's not quite that easy, young man. For starters, I'll have to verify your transcript. That will take some time. Anyone can get a diploma printed up."

Logan tossed a sealed envelop on the table. "Here's an official copy of my transcript. I thought you might want to see it."

The attorney reached out, extracted the transcript from the envelope with two fingers, and looked it over.

After a couple of minutes, he said, "It looks like you somehow managed to pass your courses and end up with enough hours. What's this special studies course? Is that in the university catalog?"

"It was a guided research project under the direct supervision of the archaeology department head, Professor Berensten. It resulted in a published journal article. She was kind enough to allow me to take credit as lead author."

Schmitzke frowned, then replied, "Well, I don't know. The trust provides me with considerable leeway in interpreting the terms. I sincerely doubt that your grandfather had a liberal arts degree in mind. He, as you know, held quite a number of patents in the automotive field. He really only respected engineering and mathematics. Your degree is in a soft science, hardly a science at all, really. I don't think I can agree that you've met his criteria."

Logan's face turned red. With an effort, he said, "I've read the trust. The wording simply says I have to graduate in four years. I have. Besides, you've known my major field for two years. If it really wouldn't satisfy the terms, you should have told me long ago."

Schmitzke grinned mirthlessly. "It's not my job to babysit you. You were given a copy of the trust. You chose your major field. Not my concern."

Logan gritted his teeth. There was something terribly wrong. He tried another tack: "Look, Mr. Schmitzke, all you have to do is to release the control of the funds. It's simple."

"Well, Logan, it's not so easy as all that. However, I assure you I'll take it under consideration. Now I have to meet an important client at the club. I have to go now."

He quickly rose and strolled out of the room, leaving Logan to show himself out.

Outside, Logan looked around. There was a coffee shop nearby with wireless service. He went in, ordered a mocha, then pulled his laptop out of his backpack.

Once online, he ran a quick search for a different attorney. They all looked about the same. He couldn't make up his mind from the ads, and besides, he didn't want to accidentally choose one who was a friend of Schmitzke.

He finished his coffee, then reached for the computer, but stopped to answer his phone. It was Professor Wolf. He had a question that he wanted to ask.

"Logan, when you first traveled into the past, did you see a flash of light?" he asked.

Logan said, "Uh...well, I – You know that I was under the influence of psychoactive substances for two of my three trips. The third one, I was struck on the head. I'm not sure my memory would be very useful."

"Maybe, maybe not. Just tell me if there was a flash."

"I think there was." He thought for a moment and added, "Actually, both times. I saw a flash when I was hit, but I think it was due to the impact," Logan replied, trying to visualize the incidents.

He suddenly remembered his current problem. "By the way, Professor, do you know of any reliable lawyers? I've got a legal problem that involves a trust my grandfather left for me."

Thrown off stride, Professor Wolf paused a moment, then said, "My daughter is an attorney. She's quite successful. Maybe you could call her?"

"What does she specialize in?" Logan asked. He didn't want to waste time with someone who only dealt with traffic tickets or maybe divorces.

"Uh, I'm not sure," Wolf said. "I mean, she's told me, but it's not related to physics, so I...I guess I'm not sure. You know, I try to avoid attorneys as much as possible. I think...no, I'm really not sure, but maybe she does general litigation, lawsuits...that sort of thing, you know? We don't talk about it much. Would you like her number?"

Wolf was obviously thrown off by his request. Logan sighed, then said, "I'll give her a call. Would you please text her number to me? I don't have anything to write on where I am."

Wolf agreed to text the number as soon as he hung up.

Logan added, "Professor, I've been trying to recall my time trips. I'm pretty sure there was a blurring of my surroundings; it was lighter, but not a real flash if you get what I'm trying to describe. Things blurred, then grew bright, then I was there, and the environment distracted me from considering what had just happened. It was too different, and it took all of my attention."

"That may be the information I need, Logan. Thank you. I'll let you know how my calculations come out."

Wolf's phone clicked off, ending the call.

Within a minute, Logan's phone vibrated. The text had arrived. He dialed the number and scheduled the first available appointment with Wolf's daughter.

There had been a cancellation, and she could see him late that afternoon.

⸻ ❖ ⸻

Her office was in a small office park on the east side of town. Logan felt better about that. At least she wasn't right downtown in an expensive office next door to Schmitzke. There was a chance that they weren't friends.

He waited in the lobby until she came out to greet him.

"You must be Logan Walker," she said, offering her hand. "I'm Ms. Richardson. Let's go to my office. Sorry, but the conference room is a mess right now. There's evidence and depositions scattered all over in there."

Logan nodded and followed her.

She turned back and asked, "Want some coffee or a soft drink?"

He accepted a bottle of water. Then they sat in her office. It wasn't luxurious; instead, it had the aura of a working office. There were law books opened on the credenza, and several stacks of paper were arranged on her desk.

She took out a pad and a pen, scratched some notes, and asked, "Can I call you Logan?"

Without waiting for his answer, she continued, "Give me an idea of what you want with my service. It doesn't have to be complete, just enough to let me know if we are wasting time or not."

Logan leaned forward, took a breath, and began to tell the story.

"My grandfather, who died six years ago, set up a trust for me. It was supposed to be turned over to me if I could graduate from college in four years or less. I've graduated, but the trust administrator, who is an attorney, says he doesn't have to give the money to me. He's been planning on giving it to a charity. The charity thing was part of the trust document. It says that if I fail to graduate, the money should be donated to charity."

She looked up and asked, "How much money?"

Logan answered by pulling out a statement and pushing it across the desk to her. Her eyes widened as she looked at the bottom line.

"Logan, you're going to be quite wealthy. What grounds did he give for not turning the trust over to you?"

"He says that he has a lot of leeway in interpreting the trust wording and that, since my grandfather was an engineer, he knows he would have been disappointed because I didn't get an engineering or math degree. He said he'd take my request under advisement, but I know he's going to donate the money. It's the only way he can get his hands on it."

She looked at his face carefully. "That's a serious charge you've just made. What makes you think that he is trying to gain control of the money?"

He pulled out the results of his research and pushed the papers over to her.

"I'll summarize that so you won't have to go through it all. There was an archaeology professor, George Dameron, who I thought didn't like me. Now I know he was helping Schmitzke, the trust administrator. He was doing everything he could to make sure I didn't graduate."

She said, "That's the guy who disappeared, right? I heard about that. You said 'Schmitzke' is the attorney?"

He nodded.

She said, "I've never met him, but I know his reputation." She frowned, seeming to express disapproval. "Go on."

"I became suspicious. Dameron was having an affair with a student, and I thought I'd research him. Dameron was married to Schmitzke's sister, Janice. That's one connection.

Then I researched the charity that Schmitzke had mentioned. It's called the Student's Democratic Assistance Fund.

That just happens to be run by a Samuel Friedholm. His wife's brother, Jeffrey, is married to Schmitzke's other sister, Rachael.

It took me a while to find, but it's all in public records. Beyond those connections, I don't have any evidence, but it seems to me that they must have been conspiring to get the money."

He paused, then added, "Oh, I also checked on the SDAF charity. It doesn't have a very good rating. Only about five percent of donations actually go to the recipients. The rest is apparently used for administrative overhead, salaries, and fundraising."

She nodded, studying his research. Without looking up, she asked, "Do you have a copy of the trust documentation?"

That, too, was in his backpack. She scanned the forty pages, stopping at times to take notes.

"Well, I can help you, in fact, I'm anxious to help. This is the kind of situation that gives attorneys a bad name and I don't like it. Do you have any money for a retainer?"

Logan hesitated. He didn't have much. "Maybe only about a thousand dollars that I earned this summer working for my Dad."

She smiled and said, "I'll take half of that for a retainer. That will be enough for now. If we get into a real battle, I may have to charge differently, but that's for later.

What I'm going to do first is write Schmitzke a letter demanding he turn the trust over to you. I'm going to lay out the relationships between the parties and inform him that it looks to me like there's a conflict of interest. If we're lucky, that will be enough. If not, if he wants to fight about it, it could get expensive.

Knowing what I do about him, I think I'll call someone I know who is involved with the State Bar committee. Maybe I can convince him to call Schmitzke and talk to him about this situation. In fact, I may have to file a complaint with the Bar."

That didn't sound like legal work to Logan. More like some kind of strong-arm tactics. He didn't care as long as it worked.

⸻ ◆ ⸻

He rode his motorcycle back toward his apartment, stopping along the way to have a hamburger. Maybe this would work. He certainly hoped so. Meanwhile, he was now free to concentrate on his work with Professor Wolf. Finding Serensaa was uppermost in his mind.

⸻ ◆ ⸻

Ms. Richardson called him three days later. "Hi, Logan. Good news. I had to get my friend to lean on Schmitzke. Schmitzke is already facing some other complaints with the Bar. The good news is he's assigned the trust to you. I have the necessary documentation at my office. Can you stop by to sign today?"

It didn't take him more than thirty minutes to walk through her front door. The paperwork didn't take long.

When it was done, she asked, "Now that you're a wealthy man, what are you going to do with the funds?"

Logan had been thinking about it. "I'm going to leave them in the current investment vehicles for a time. I don't want to do anything too quickly. Would you be able to help me with any legal needs I have later?"

"Sure, I can help, but don't ask me to recommend investments. That's outside my area of expertise," she answered.

"How about I give you, say, ten thousand as a retainer against further work, just so we have our ongoing relationship formalized?" he asked.

She smiled. "That will do nicely. Now here's a checkbook for the primary trust account. You'll need the notarized documents you just signed to prove to the bank that you're now the administrator in addition to the trust beneficiary."

They shook hands. She said, "It's been a pleasure, Logan. Call me any time you need help or just to check-in. I'd be interested to hear how you're doing."

The motorcycle seemed to float on air as he drove away. Serensaa seemed closer than ever.

Chapter Twenty-Five

Again, The Fox

A red Mercedes SL convertible rolled up to the Crystal River dig site. It turned into a dusty parking space, idled for a moment while the top was raised, then shut off. Logan climbed out. He was dressed in new jeans and a simple tee shirt.

He locked the car and set out across the area. The university tents were gone. The dig had been shut down when Dameron disappeared. It seemed empty and lonely.

He stood in the area where the tribe's fire had been. The sea breeze made whispering noises in his ears and ruffled his hair. The wind suddenly seemed to be full of spirits, all calling to him from down the ages.

Tears came to his eyes. It wasn't the spirits so much as it was a single spirit, a clear and bright one with a streak of craziness running through her that pulled painfully at his heart. He looked at the ground, then at the distant seashore, waiting for his vision to clear.

A tingling feeling gradually came over him. He turned, not really expecting anything, but there it was. A gray fox was looking at him from a clump of palms. Logan's breath came short for a moment, and then he moved towards the animal.

It watched until he drew close, then backed into the underbrush and vanished. He pushed through the bushes, searching. The fox had disappeared. He wondered if he'd really seen it. It took several minutes to search through the clump and the brush. There was nothing there.

He returned to the center of the open area and then walked thoughtfully to his car. There must be something, some way. He felt strongly that the fox had been trying to tell him something important. It couldn't have been the same animal. That was absurd, but still...

He drove around the area for a while. There was a neighborhood nearby. He cruised the streets for lack of any concrete plan. The houses were nice but not really impressive, despite the fact that most of them fronted on a series of canals that gave access to the Gulf.

One of them, a more expensive-looking place with a barrel tile roof, was for sale. On impulse, Logan called the sales agent. The house was unoccupied, and she agreed to come right over and open it for him.

When the woman arrived, she looked calculatingly at Logan. It was apparent that she was trying to decide if he was a serious buyer. He knew he didn't look the part. Too young, dressed in jeans and a tee-shirt, but then her eyes locked on the Mercedes.

"Yours?" she asked, glancing at him from the sides of her eyes. He nodded.

She turned towards the house, walked quickly onto the porch, and opened the front door, then turned and ushered him in with a hand motion and a toothy smile.

He walked through the rooms, stepping around the furniture. The house might not be the best he could now afford, but after living in his dad's place, an apartment, and numerous trees, it looked like a palace to him. The current owners had inherited the property from a deceased uncle. They lived up north somewhere, had no plans to move to Florida, and wanted to sell quickly. They didn't want to have to maintain the place any longer than necessary.

The agent wrote the contract on the kitchen island. Logan agreed to send proof of funds and an escrow deposit the next day. He had her state in the offer that the contract would be closed as soon as the title was cleared. He didn't want to fool around with negotiating, so he offered full price with no contingencies.

The real estate agent left, practically licking her chops. She'd promised to have an answer from the sellers by morning. But, she implied, she couldn't imagine them turning down his offer.

———◆◇◆———

He moved in two weeks later. The house was still furnished. The deceased owner's family hadn't wanted to deal with the furniture, and Logan had offered them some extra cash for everything. It wasn't decorated to his taste, but it was convenient. He'd deal with changing things eventually, when and if he got around to it.

———◆◇◆———

That evening, he walked over to the dig site. It was a little over a mile away. He worked his way through the rough ground, moving between palmetto clumps and through scrub oaks and brush. Once at the dig site, he faced the sun and sat down in the middle of the old campsite.

The breeze blew softly. There was a woodpecker in a tree away off over somewhere and a squirrel chucked in the scrub oaks. The sun descended until it was nearly down. Night approached softly.

He didn't stir. He felt close to Serensaa here, and there was no reason to move at the moment. He could walk back to his house after dark, following the road rather than pushing through the brush.

The evening star made its appearance; then some other stars showed up. He was daydreaming about Serensaa. Lost in his thoughts.

Unnoticed at first, a small tingle moved over his back, gradually increasing in intensity until he noticed it. It was hard to see in the dusk, but the fox had returned. It was looking at him expectantly.

He stood and moved toward it as the small canine yapped. It was maybe about twenty yards away, near the palm trees. He seemed to float through the dusk as the trees drew closer.

He couldn't see where the fox had gone, but there was a lighter area in the stand of trees. The illumination grew gradually brighter, forming a rippling, translucent effect as if the air had become semi-solid.

Logan stopped and watched. There was something moving through the rippling air, growing gradually larger, traveling towards him from a far distance. He watched as the figure became clearer...clearer...then he saw that it was his lost Serensaa.

She halted, looking fearfully around, then seeing him, she started forward again. She stumbled over something at the edge of the rippling air and fell forward into his arms.

She drew a deep breath as he wrapped his arms around her slender body. She pushed back until she could see his face. When she saw that it was Logan, she let out an inarticulate cry of joy and grabbed his head, pulling him down for a long, passionate kiss.

They broke, and she stepped back a little after a while. She looked at him, smiled tremulously, then linked her fingers together, and softly asked, "Logan, Serensaa, here?"

He linked his fingers solidly together and answered, "Serensaa, Logan, here now."

She sighed and stepped forward into his embrace.

The End

List of Characters

- Professor Berensten - Logan's adviser and head of the archaeology department

- George Dameron – archaeology professor

- Janice Dameron – George's wife

- Cheryl and Chelle – Larry and Logan's father's girlfriends

- Samuel Friedholm – administrator of Student's Democratic Assistance Fund (SDAF) charity

- Mark Schmitzke – attorney and trust administrator

- Steve, Randy, Eddie – Logan's video game-playing roommates

- Rick, Tim, Shawn, Toby, Ralph – Logan's tent mates and team members at the archaeological dig site.

- Serensaa – Clovis girl fleeing from marauding enemy clan members.

- Mandi Thompson – Student dig supervisor, brown belt in Tae Kwon Do

- Ulfa – high ranking Clovis warrior

- Logan Walker – slacker with potential

- William Walker – Logan's father

- Ruth Watson – Assistant Dean of Students and Hearings officer

- Larry Wilson – Roofer and Logan's father's friend

- Professor Wolf – Physics professor and member of the university ethics committee

About the Author

Eric S. Martell set out to become a scientist when he was five. He has a PhD. in experimental psychology. When personal computers came along (way back in prehistory), he became adept with them and spent years in software design, working on projects that ranged from early childhood learning software to military training. He has been trained in various types of energy healing, is an expert in real estate investing and sales, and holds a black belt in Tae-Kwon-Do. He is also a pilot, scuba diver, guitar player, outdoorsman, and is addicted to both science and science fiction.

Eric's science fiction books offer both believable science and compelling characters set against realistic action. They are carefully researched, and, while his fictional science sometimes strains against the bounds of current knowledge, it is always plausible. His stories cover alien invasion in an apocalyptic setting, political structure, space travel, advanced weapons, quantum physics, hunting, war, romance, time travel, and alien worlds.

He's been published in a series of anthologies and has published many full-length science fiction novels. His writing goal is to provide his readers with stories they cannot put down and he takes readers' suggestions seriously.

Notices about new books, free short stories, opinion posts, and preview pages for many of his books can be found on his author blog at
EricMartellAuthor.com

A Request for You

Dear Reader,

I make every effort to ensure your reading experience is enjoyable. This involves multiple editing steps, interior book layout, design, and using a professional cover artist/designer. Even so, it is becoming more difficult to find readers. If you liked this book, please leave a review and tell your friends. Those small actions help a lot.

Reviews may be left on the platform of your choice or emailed directly to me through my blog.

Thank you,

Eric Martell

Venice, 2021

Also by Eric S. Martell

The Time Equation Series

Heart of Fire Time of Ice

Paradox: On the Sharp Edge of the Blade

All the Moments in Forever

Time Enough to Live

All Things in Time

The Belter Series

The Pirates of the Asteroids *

The Belter Revolution

Cyber-Magic Series

CyberWitch *

Nano-Magic

The Gaia Ascendant Trilogy

The Time of The Cat

Second Wave

Confederation

Other Books

Dustfall *

Asterats and Other Stories

*Florida Authors and Publishers President's Award Winner

9 780999 898052